WANDERER

All the Earth Round

A Nautical Poem in Six Cantos

WANDERER

All the Earth Round
A Nautical Poem in Six Cantos

ISBN/EAN: 9783337193171

Printed in Europe, USA, Canada, Australia, Japan

Cover: Foto ©Andreas Hilbeck / pixelio.de

More available books at **www.hansebooks.com**

A NAUTICAL POEM,

In Six Cantos.

BY

A WANDERER.

LONDON:

ELLIOT STOCK, 62, PATERNOSTER ROW, E.C.

1892.

CONTENTS.

CANTO I.

CANTO II.

CANTO III.

CANTO IV.

CANTO V.

CANTO VI.

INTRODUCTION.

HOLD, fleeting life ! and let my mind engage,
To trace thy footsteps at an early age,
The moments seize, that now are threat'ning fast,
To efface the thoughts and memories of the past.
  Heroic muse ! here rest awhile your wing ;
Calliope ! a mortal seeks to sing,—
Goddess reverèd since the age of man
In thoughts divine with harmony began.
  Upon him cast your all-inspiring robe,
He seeks to sing a voyage around the globe,
And craves your aid, his lengthy lay to pour,
Where Truth and reason may together soar.
  As strange is fiction, truth is stranger found,
Restrained the one, the other hath no bound,
The first created in the human brain,
The latter, birth with all creation claims.
Bright, and more bright the glorious spark has shone,
A guide divine, by which all men are known,
And though it may impair the poet's song,
Let Truth arise, and light the way along.
  My lot was cast,—as on a summer's day,
Down by the beach I strolled my lonely way,
Where stillness reigned, and naught was heard beside
The gentle breaking of the rippling tide.

With mind reflective, on the future bent,
My eyes were wand'ring o'er the calm Solent;
I lay me down upon its sandy shore,
And thoughts prospective sought me more and more.
Sunshining sparkles on its waters play,
Its green downs woo me by its side to stay;
The main invites, to join its boisterous life,
To pass my early days amidst its strife;
To leave the calm inducements of the shore,
Its treacherous wastes to wander o'er and o'er.

And as I mused, a sail came flitting past,
And why not I be moving, too? I asked;
Life's but a voyage, a troubled one I deem.
I am embarked, and now, must choose the stream
On which to float, through its allotted span,
And battle bravely as becomes a man;
Or wander forth, impotent to contend,
'Gainst warring interests, aimless to the end.
The opening future urged me to arise,
While Hope, assisting, showed the promised prize:
A prize whose value must remain untold,
Beyond the worth assigned to heaps of gold.
The prize is *knowledge;* those who wish to win,
Must quaff the bitter cup, filled to the brim;
Pass years of trial, and oft recurring woe,
Must learn to live, and live on what they know.
So that all doubt and mystery cease at last,
The future known in knowledge of the past.
Thus as I lay, revolving in my mind,
A clear solution of the task to find.
Or if to cling unto my native strand,
Or seek the future in some foreign land.
Reflection whispers, 'Seize the present time,

And be content; for that alone is thine.
The past is gone; the present fleeting by;
Obscured the future to the human eye.
Upon these moments well your hold retain;
Build on the present to the future gain;
And build with care, for in this present lies
Foundation sure of future destinies.'

Hope comes again, and then as swiftly flies,
Till hope and doubt in quick succession rise;
My native land still clings unto my heart,
And cling it will when we are far apart;
My doubts confess the leap into the dark,
But Hope, prophetic, through it sees a spark;
That spark will brighten as the years may roll,
And guide me, wiser, to a happier goal;
The world is wide, and every Briton's free,
I am resolved, and will prepare for sea.

Success attends my search to find a place,
At once adapted to my skill and taste,
Prepared, and ready, for the final start,
The launch is filled with seamen to depart.
I quit the strand, and settle in the boat,
With thoughts depressing find myself afloat.
Our destined barque rides proudly in the roads,
Ready to sail o'er ocean's dark abodes;
Her martial streamer, floating in the breeze,
Departing signs, the practised seaman sees.
The steam launch slung suspended in the air,
Swings to the deck, and safely lodges there.
And ropes are hauled, the capstan flying round,
Loud swells the song in chorus ' Outward bound.'
Hearts beating high, the seamen's gait is light,
As at command they raise the shrilly pipe.

Then hie aloft, their stations quickly find,
Let fall the sails, and stretch them to the wind.
The breezes rise, the spreaded canvas fills,
The ship, responsive, answers to their wills.
The anchor tripped, the stately craft is free,
Springs into life, and skims along the sea.
The gale grows strong, the gathering waves arise,
The ship, impelled, across the water flies.
Our native land, receding from our sight,
Sinks in the mists and darkness of the night.

ALL THE EARTH ROUND.

CANTO I.

England to Madeira.

My native land ! what thoughts spring in my breast,
As night advances and thou sink'st to rest !
Let me essay my simple voice to raise,
And at our parting sing my meed of praise.
   Though sunny climes may charm and welcome me,
My thoughts, endeared, must ever turn to thee.
Where can a land so prized by me be found,
Search where I may, the whole wide world around ?
No home to me can ever be so dear ;
My hopes in thee my drooping spirits cheer.
   When shall again this straying waif be tossed
By waters wild that lash thy chalky coast ?
When shall again these longing eyes behold
The charms thy fields, thy hills and vales unfold ?
Thy spreading oaks, thy quiet soft retreats,
Thy stately mansions, and thy rural seats,
Thy every part—thy streams, thy rocks, thy strand,
Are all alike beloved !   Adieu, my native land !
   Grand is the scene, now opening to the sight,
Of ocean's wonders ; seen in all their might,

Where Biscay's seas so restless, gathering high,
Dance o'er the tomb where many stout ships lie ;
Where labouring craft, impelled by adverse fate,
Tenacious strive to guard their costly freight,
War with the elements in unequal strife,
Through night's thick darkness and day's hazy light :
Wrestle in vain, reel to their doomèd fall,
And give the depths their store, their life, their all.
    Here many sleep by Neptune's arm laid low,
Or fierce in combat with the angry foe ;
Where Europe's navies often have appealed
To Mars' dictation, this their battle-field.
Warriors and traders share the watery tomb,
Glory and sadness meet an equal doom,
And friend and foe in death promiscuous join,
Far in the unknown depths of ocean's brine.

The billows heave in slow majestic grace,
Great in their height and ample at their base.
The gallant ship is borne up to the skies,
The dark blue waves in hills of foam arise,
A thin white spray flies from their curling crests,
And ocean rolls and heaves his angry breast ;
Then down again in deepest vales subside,
And liquid walls rise up on every side ;
High o'er the ship is seen the threatening mass,
She bounds again, and lets the danger pass ;
And storms rage on, yet safely through we go,
And brave the dangers of the blustering foe.

The scene is changed, the elements more kind,
And Biscay's seas and gales are left behind.
New life is felt, unknown since leaving shore,
From recent storms we feel the value more.

The sunny South's bright atmosphere aglow,
Tempered by winds that from the northward blow :
All canvas spread to catch the gentle gale,
Nor needs a further touch the well-trimmed sail.

The ship drives on with stretching sheets aflow,
And ploughs the waters with her forcing prow :
These boil around, and swiftly by her sides,
As torrents, rush the furious seething tides.

Blue sky aloft, and each succeeding day
The lamp of heaven pours down its golden ray.
To these bright days succeed the glitt'ring nights,
Illumed by stars and Ocean's phosphor lights,
From out whose depths the flashing gems ascend,
And far astern in glittering streams depend.

Thus merrily onward, o'er the sea we sped,
Till one bright morning brought the land ahead.
Madeira's Isle, in Sol's refulgent light,
Gilded and green, breaks fairly to the sight.
Advancing slowly does the isle appear,
Quick, and more rapid, as we draw so near.

The gentle breeze continues still to blow,
When from the boatswain's pipe the shrill notes flow :
· Hands shorten sail !' is heard by all around,
His mates re-echo to the grateful sound :
All spring to life, our spirits rise anew,
To cast the anchor, and the ship bring to,
Once more to taste the fruits so kindly given
By earth's great bounty, and the care of Heaven.

And, quick as thought, the sails are to the yard
Clewed up, braced round, and all in neatness squared.
The anchor loosed, and with its mighty grip
Our progress stops ;—it holds the stately ship.

MADEIRA.

Madeira Isle !—so named for wooded groves,
Sprang into life in Earth's prolific throes ;
'Midst molten columns, through sulphuric lakes,
And spouting fires, and fierce terrestial quakes,
With awful rumblings from the labouring Earth,
And mighty salvoes to announce its birth.
Atlanta nursed it, cooled its fevered head,
And heavenly dews around about it shed ;
Called Time to aid, to soothe and give it rest,
And clasped the treasure to her heaving breast,
Prepared its vales, ordained, in future age,
With nectar juice to warm the gay and sage ;
To crown with joy the festive board, and raise
Atlanta's fame in choice Madeira's praise.

And first, conspicuous, strikes the stranger's eye,
The flag of Lusitania, waving high.
In abrupt height Madeira seems to rise,
Upon its slope the town of Funchal lies.

The island tempts us to its pleasing shore,
Its town, its hills, and valleys to explore ;
For softening mildness, health, and beauty famed,
Atlanta's garden just and truly named ;
For generous wines and genial clime renowned,
Where invalids are idly sauntering round,
The favoured few of Europe's sick, repair,
And by the island's pure and dryer air
Postpone their fate, as each with other vies
To stretch the thread of their precarious lives.

We quit the beach and parched-up town to rove,
To search the vales, the hills to scale above,
Where pebbly pathways wind round to the tops,
On which the traveller often turns and stops

To view the scene beneath, in vast delight.
We see the flowers and fruits hang fair and bright,
The trellised foliage forms the shady bowers,
And fruits delicious bend o'er beds of flowers.

    The orange, lime, and spreading vines abound,
And clear blue waters wash the base around,
The gurgling streams rush down the rocky side,
Flashing and sparkling in the bright noon-tide.
How fresh the soil ! the scene around how fair !
What sweet sensations float upon the air !

    We roam about till day its length has run,
The hills descending with the setting sun ;
To ship again repair, to spend the night,
And slumbers sweet reward our wearying flight.

    The morn breaks clear ; aroused from heavy sleep,
To see refulgent Sol 'merge from the deep.
Across the skies he shoots his brightest ray,
And from the gates of heaven proclaims the day ;
In all his glory mounts the eastern sky,
And mists and darkness from his presence fly.
Down from on high his silver beams he throws,
Beneath his shafts the expanse of ocean glows,
And rocks beneath the placid water shows.

    Now round the ship a crowd comes from the shore,
To dive for coin or vend the luscious store.
The smallest piece is cast into the sea,
Its shining surface through the water seen
As down it goes ; but ere 'tis lost to sight
The diver sinks, and brings it up to light ;
Within his belt he deigns the prize to store,
And blandly asks to throw him something more.

    Few days are spent ; prepare again for sea ;
With anchor weighed, the ready ship is free ;
And, bounding off before the fresh'ning wind,
Soon leaves Madeira, less'ning fast behind.

Madeira to Rio de Janeiro.

The trade wind strong applies its useful force,
Direct in aim, and steady in its course ;
As o'er the sea the aerial current drives,
The ship, with added wings, across it flies.

The furrowed waters, boiling, flash and glow,
Rush in wild foam around the spurning bow ;
In snow-white spray the seething eddies fly,
Tinged with the colours of the rainbow's dye.

Sargasso Sea we then are driving through,
Whose sombre tints throw up the deepest hue
Of dark blue sea, that holds distinct and clear
The tufts of fuci floating in the mere.

Weeds, everlasting, o'er these regions reign,
Myriad mollusca people all the plain.
In dreams of fancy, lo ! before our sight
Those heather fields which yielded such delight
In bygone times, as, on a summer's day,
Across soft downs we coursed the joyous way.

So through the sea with spreaded sails we run,
Through grassy plains that led Columbus on,
Confirmed his soul in hope, inspired his mind
To persevere, the promised land to find ;
Gave him the link, much doubted by his crew,
That should connect the Old World with the New.
Its theories his ardent mind possessed,
In contemplation yield his thoughts no rest ;
His vision clears, and continents arise,
And give success to his great enterprise.

In furrows deep we plough the liquid field,
On either side the grassy waters yield,
And Cape de Verde we pass ; in towering height

The Islands rise with boldness to the sight.
 We pause not here, but, edging closely by,
Observe the mist around their bases fly ;
On their green sides we cast our longing eyes,
And mark their peaks high looming to the skies.

 Though storms may rage and sameness dull may reign,
Yet there are charms alluring in the main.
Day after day new wonders come to sight,
New heavens advancing on us night by night.
 Up near the zenith Orion meets the gaze,
His brilliance rivalled by the dog-star's blaze ;
And Betelgeuse fair Bellatrix outshines,
As Rigel on the southern slope reclines ;
New galaxies emerging from the deep,
As Northern Bears are sinking down the steep.
 The Pole-star still is flickering in the gloom,
And points the line of our receding home ;
Descending low, 'tis lost, so fast we flee,
Familiar constellations hid by sea.
 The trade wind soft yet holds with lessening force,
And moves the ship but slowly on her course ;
The laggard sails begin to flap the mast,
The failing breeze to calm is dying fast.
 Dead calm ensues, and stays the forward flight,
The glassy waters all the crew invite
To bathe their limbs, to cool the heated blood,
And sport themselves upon the saline flood.
 Then from the ship the doughty swimmers spring,
From ports and yards their naked bodies fling ;
The venturous few are stretching far and wide,
Now seen, now lost, upon the swelling tide ;
 They soon return, and close around they keep
Their floating home, that's rocking on the deep ;

Then climb her sides in day's declining light,
With sails aclew roll out the sultry night.

Bright is the morn that breaks o'er tropic's zone,
Sol, undisputed, mounts his dazzling throne.
The pitchy deck proclaims with gaping seams
The scorching heat proceeding from his beams.
    With force direct his burning shafts he plies,
Supine beneath the lolling vessel lies;
Ungoverned drifts, or dips her sweltering sides
Beneath the dark blue mass of ocean's tides.
    Wistful around, our straining eyes descry
Delusive puffs of short duration fly,
Ruffling the sea, and, passing on before,
Die off again, and then are felt no more.
    And so to drill, and practise guns anew,
With targets laid for exercise, the crew,
With cutlass, pike, and rifle are prepared,
As though a foe had suddenly appeared—
Attack, repel where closer fighting comes,
Then to bombard him with their heavy guns.
Aloft, below, from side to side they bound,
And mimic thunder wakes the silence round.
    Or now at eve athletic sports performed :
Some for wrestling, some with sticks are armed,
And some with gloves to box, aspiring hence
To learn the useful art of self-defence.
    And there a preference the *voice* obtains :
A knot is grouped to listen to its strains,
In cadence hoarse, with equal force and fire,
Familiar song that never seems to tire ;
And some to dance, and find a pleasure in
The lively notes of fife and violin ;
And some, apart, betake themselves away,

Are quite content some boyish games to play.
And one relates a story he had read ;
'Till sleep compels them to incline the head
Upon the deck, and pass away the night
Beneath a dome of blue and glittering light.

    Upon the deep a full ten days are told
About one spot ; for ten long nights we rolled,
A leaden hue upon the waste around ;
Inert and heavy, and the heat profound ;
The day's routine is lax, and lacking care,
The sports are dull for want of fresher air.

    Stern isolation ! far o'er ocean cast,
None to propound how long the calm may last ;
None to assist us with a friendly hand,
Or succour bring us from the nearest land.
With hope deferred heart sick, and were it not
For winds benign, we here might lie and rot.

    Not so decreed ; a draught the good ship hails,
With joy we hear the night-watch setting sails ;
No more we roll, but with a steady heel,
Grateful to all, its cooling presence feel.

    Bounding again across the silver sea,
With spirits raised, from irksome calms we flee ;
To catch the breeze we spread a cloud of sail,
And inward pray again it may not fail,
But pass us through as quickly as we came,
To clear these realms which sailors *doldrums* name.

    And now a shoal of nautilus we meet :
In open order comes the tiny fleet,
With pink sails set appear the fairy throng,
And tumble over as we move along ;
Caught by the surge before the driving ship,
They right again and by us nimbly slip.

Here ocean's creatures wage unceasing strife,
And, all-industrious, seek each other's life ;
With her own tactics Nature each controls,
The weak for strength she gathers into shoals ;
To smaller tribes adds wings to speed their flight.
The dolphin shoots, and bares his back to sight ;
Before his swift career they madly drive,
Spring from the sea, and on their pinions strive
To elude, outstrip him, in the mortal chase,
Skim o'er the waves and try to win the race ;
He marks their course, and knows their failings well,
That on their drying wings not long may dwell ;
From upper air full soon they must descend,
Brief is the flight on which their lives depend.

Yet in the sea still nearer seems their fate ;
The dolphin's sharp pursuit does not abate
The greedy chase, permitting no delay,
Till wearied all, they fall an easy prey.

And now the unwieldy whale is seen to fly,
Spouting the brine in his huge agony
To evade the Thrashers, who, in battle's strife,
Active and fierce assail the monster's life ;
Armed with the sword, a guard beneath him keep,
Deter the creature's diving in the deep,
Hang to their prize and wield the bony lance,
And madly all the fell assault advance.

One from the sea springs to a goodly height ;
Straight on the hapless foe with vengeful might
He full descends ; with spear his back he plies,
The wounded whale flaps his broad tail and flies.

Tremendous birds now hovering o'er the prey
Assist the closing of the furious fray ;
To glut their greed ferociously employ
Those shafts, designed by nature to destroy.

Above, below, on every side, around,
Small, great, and numerous, active foes abound,
Exulting, screaming, o'er the mammoth's death ;
His life's blood issuing with his watery breath,
Succumbs, and yields his carcass to the cost
Of general feast to all the assailing host.
   The small rejoices o'er the fallen great,
When so decided by the hand of Fate,
Whose high decrees immutable pursue,
By such details as onward lead thereto.
By force direct, or circumstances all,
Submit the weak, the strong is made to fall
Before its fiat, all resistless driven,
To die defeated or to conquer given.

   A rumour floats ; and percolating through
The quarterdeck to midshipmen and crew,
Flows round the ship in every form and guise,
Awakening fears, and dubious, dim surmise.
Into the ears of novices it runs,
The uninitiate of Neptune's sons,
   To this effect : that as we near the zone
Where Neptune sits upon his azure throne,
Or, coursing round it in his sea-green car,
Stirs or subdues the elemental war :
That as a ship is ploughing through the brine,
Cuts with her keel the equatorial line,
With voice alone her onward flight he checks,
And from the deep comes bouncing to the decks,
Commanding all, in words of thunder hoarse,
To stay awhile upon the forward course ;
To give a day—his unfledged sons produce,
With ancient rites and customs introduce
Unto him all ; and furl their lofty sail,

And hold the day a day of festival.
　All this, and more, is told with wild surmise,
Which fills the soul with awe and dire surprise.

　At dewy eve, as all their revels keep,
A voice is heard from out the misty deep ;
The sports are stopped, as to the deck they hie,
And Neptune's heard above the general cry ;
Hails loud and hoarse—the ship was driving fast—
' Ahoy !　Heave to ! with mainsail to the mast !'
And round it flies as ordered by the god,
As though some spirit moved it to his nod ;
The gallant ship fulfils the high decree,
And graceful bows obeisance to the sea,
Which o'er her prow in sprayey columns poured,
As all the train of Neptune burst aboard.
　Hitched to his car, a team of Tritons strong,
Sea-bears and dragons, fill the motley throng ;
High in its seat the god of ocean stands,
And with the trident all the scene commands.
　The sailors crowd, and on their guests attend,
All greeting Neptune as a well-known friend ;
Around his car for preference they fight,
And in the troupe evince a vast delight ;
Unhitch the Tritons from the ponderous load,
And give themselves to draw along the god.
The good ship yields beneath the mighty weight
Of ocean's god, the arbiter of fate,
　Majestic all in long procession move,
As round the ship, with care and filial love,
They draw the god to whom each often prays,
That with his aid they long may rule the waves ;
In double file in closest order pressed
Until the quarterdeck receives the guests.

And now in awe around the god they stand,
His trident raised their silence to command.
In this high presence not a word was spoke
Till Neptune's voice in full the silence broke
   Their chief among a group he then perceives,
A friend of old ; the genial god receives,
Grasps his tough hand, and gives a hearty shake :
With voice sonōrous thus the monarch spake :
   ' Long have we known thee as a faithful son ;
Our high applause thy valorous acts have won ;
In whom alike a generous ardour glows,
With ocean's trials or thy country's foes ;
   ' Whose deeds and energies have cast a name
Upon the azure field of naval fame.
And well is placed into such hands as these
The trust to bear our emblem through the seas.
Enough of this ! but know when tempests rage,
'Tis we who raise them and their power assuage.
   ' Our hardy sons we gladly greet to-night,
Engaged the morn shall find us with the rite
Sacred to us ; let all the shrine prepare
To pay the homage due with loyal care ;
Those new-fledged sons to initiate, we call
For ceremonies ; we demand from all.
Inaugurate them, and the roll maintain,
The future heroes of the glorious main.
When night has passed shall peaceful calms prevail ;
Naught shall disturb our own high festival.
   ' And now, my sons, you'll bear us to the side,
And launch the king of waters on his tide :
Across our realms we'll speed us through the night,
Our track you'll see by our phosphoric light :
Gaze on that light in glowing faith ; and then
Adieu my sons until we meet again.'

Quick all obeyed, a heavy splash denotes
That on the wave the god of ocean floats;
The ship moves on, upon her course proceeds
As fast astern a flaming light recedes.

The cynic sneers, the sceptical declare
'Tis all a myth; there is no Neptune there:
The flaming blaze we gaze on now afar
Is naught but burning pitch and blazing tar.
The faithful few watch long the fading light,
Till in the shades it disappears from sight.

A calm ensues, the old sea-dogs repair
To raise a throne, the carnival prepare;
Between the decks a spacious sail is spread
And into it the hollow hose is led,
With ocean's brine the bloated canvas filled,
And all concerted as the god had willed,
Ominous to those who know not what it means,
Save from report or shadowy fitful dreams.

The sails are clewed, and all lie down to sleep,
Except the few who watchful vigils keep,
In peaceful dreams and undisturbèd rest,
Rocked by the heave of ocean's swelling breast.
Till bright Aurora ushers in the morn,
Calls on all life its mission to perform,
And sends a glow across the vast expanse,
With ardent heat which tedious calms enhance.
Idly we roll, in expectation lie,
Watch where the ocean intercepts the sky;
When o'er the sea, beneath the rising sun,
A change is seen upon the horizon.
Is it that breeze for which we pant in vain,
Or fabled monsters coursing o'er the main?
We scan it close, a shoal curvetting near

Of rolling, rippling porpoise through the mere.
Around the sea, as far as eye can trace,
They rush and plunge, pursue the aqueous race,
And blow, and leap, beneath the surface dive,
And make the placid ocean quite alive.

More near they come, more loud the rushing sound,
Then swiftly they the lolling ship surround,
And, unperceived, old Neptune from the main
Bounds to the deck, and quits the finny train.

On all around the spouting waters flow,
The sailors hurry from their meal below,
Save those deterred ; who unprepared lie
Between the decks, beneath a watchful eye.

Supine, great Neptune in his car reclined,
Sea-bears propel him to the place assigned,
To do us honour ; and to Britons' pride
Our glorious colours line his car inside.

In bulk colossal, in demeanour bold,
He grasps the trident with the firmest hold ;
In great abundance flows his auburn hair,
And sparkling liquid gems hang glist'ning there.

From out the mass his grisly visage shown
As hard as rocks that guard his oozy throne ;
An antique crown surmounts his noble head,
And all his aspect fills the soul with dread.

The goddess queen, attendant at his side,
Upon a dolphin bright is seen to ride.
With forehead bleared, a burly giant stout,
Great Polyphemus, with his eye bored out,
And rolling back, a long and motley train
Of ill-shaped monsters, denizens of the main.

High functionaries follow in the rear,
The pompous doctor here, the barber there,

With their attendants, gravely bent on work,
The doctor's henchman, and the barber's clerk ;
Renownèd all for drinking grog and chewing,
And model artists in the line shampooing.

Beneath his arm the barber bears a roll
Of parchment, having in emblazoned scroll
The speech inscribed, by an immortal hand ;
But few the hieroglyphics understand.

For silence Neptune raised his ruling hand,
His apt attendant takes his high command,
With vast pomposity of erudition
Unfolds the scroll, and reads the short oration :
' Hail, Britons all ! we greet you here to day,
In festival to us thy homage pay ;
On thee the deities propitious smile,
Well representing here our favourite isle ;
Sprang from a race whose glorious deeds resound
Throughout our realms, the whole wide world around ;
Those deeds still emulate ; deserve our hand,
And our strong arms, that circle round thy land,
Shall be a guard, for England's foes to prove
That time nor skill shall 'vail them to remove ;
True to yourselves, with all intentions pure,
And England shall for aye remain secure.'

The speech concluded, Neptune gave the cue,
And to their posts all his attendants flew ;
The bears with joy evince their vast content,
Plunge in the sail, roll in their element,
Set up a roar, and frolicsome display
Their eagerness to pounce and hug their prey.

All stations found, all preparation made,
In hoarse resounding voice great Neptune said,
' Observe our rules—whilst each his skill employs,
Bring forth and introduce our youngest boys ;

And lest we awe, take care to bind their eyes,
And bring them singly to us to baptize.'

Bound arms and eyes, the first comes from below ;
Full in his face the spouting waters flow—
From high aloft, on every side around,
Upon him pour, until he's well-nigh drowned.
  A shifting bench, to which he's roughly led,
And Neptune's doctor asks he may be bled ;
But grave in doubt, with instruments uncouth,
More efficacious thinks to draw a tooth ;
But here again an accident arose :
The forceps slip and pinch too hard his nose,
Which makes him scream ; and whilst tormented thus,
The barber plies with skill the lathering brush,
And o'er his face the fearful razor wields ;
To all of which the subject patient yields.
  The doctor grips his wrist his pulse to feel,
In solemn tones declares he's very ill,
And questions more ; but he, perverse in doubt,
To all such questions opens not his mouth :
His motions dumb, will but his shoulders shrug,
And failing thus to give the nauseous drug,
Quick from his eyes the bandage rudely tears,
And trips him down among the howling bears ;
Who hug, denude him, wash him well about,
And, purified, he scrambles to get out.
  Then from below another patient's brought,
And Neptune's liquid powers about him wrought ;
Officials jeer, and, making ominous signs,
Declare him off—the man of modern times.
An engineer, with seamen thrown by chance,
Who when in harbour drives the steaming launch,
Annoys the sailors with his coal and smoke,

2

And vows of vengeance loud from many broke.
E'en Neptune's self turns in his car to rise,
And views this subject with suspicious eyes.
' And what is this, before our eyes so dark ?'
He asks this question of his barber's clerk.

Now this official high, of vast pretence,
Great in his office, pompous, and immense,
Of mighty consequence, appealed to thus,
Puffs himself up with ostentatious fuss,
From 'neath his arm draws the divining roll,
And reads their genealogy from off the scroll.
' Not long,' says he, 'could these have left the coast,
Nor ancient line of descent can they boast ;
The power that makes them great lay hidden long,
Itself created when the world was young.
When palms and ferns, imbibing radiant rays,
In sweltering moisture lived and passed their days :
When stately trees grew up luxuriant,
Nor fell they till their natural lives were spent,
When earth's mutations covered up the whole,
Now brought to light again in form of coal ;
Philosophers said that by mysterious ways
Great force and power lay in these hidden rays :
Touched by the magic wand of science then,
Sprang to the front these enterprising men,
Who waters brought imprisoned to the fire,
The sacred waters of thy spouse's sire !
Imprisoned brought, or quickly would they tame
The fiery ardour of the flashing flame.
' Together placed, incited to engage,
The fires will scourge, the fluid boil with rage ;
Caught in their toils, it fumes to a degree
Of awful strength, and wrestles to be free.

' Nor could they hold, with all their iron band,
Did they its powers permit its full command :
They dare not this, but gradually let it go ;
In its hot haste it takes them all in tow,
O'er lands and seas it wings its eager flight,
And these the men who prosper by its might ;
Till lands and seas with their machinery team,
And in their pride they glorify their steam.'
    Steam starts the god. ' Steam ! steam !' he cries,
With startling fury flashing in his eyes,
The trident poised, as if in act to strike,
But merely strikes spectators with affright.
' Calm all your fears,' he said, relenting. Then
Returns the sceptre to its rest again,
And slow resumes, in feigned emotions strong,
To tell a grievance he had harboured long,
Of what befell his loving goddess queen
By one of those propelled by force of steam.

    ' When first,' says he, ' the smoky brood cast loose,
And o'er our fair domains allowed to cruise ;
When it was known that one would heave in sight,
Attended by her nymphs 'rose Amphitrite.
    ' The sight amused them, yet but to beguile—'
The grisly god could scarce restrain a smile—
' They crossed her track, and viewed her round and round,
Tried to becalm her, but, amazed, they found
She still sweeps on ; and all regardless rides,
Ignores their presence, and their calm defies.
    ' Evil was there, for all the finny train
Clung close to Amphitrite, but clung in vain :
The fiery demon spouts a cloud of smoke,
As Pluto's furnace loose from Etna broke ;
And roars, and fumes, and rolls her lumbering sides,

2— 2

And breaks the stillness of our silent tides.
   'A power unknown the queen of ocean holds,
Leads where it lists, and all her will controls:
Command is lost, and she all giddy feels,
Struck sinking down by the propelling wheels.'
   And here the train of nymphs grew sympathetic,
The amorous god in tones becomes pathetic:
Bestows a kiss on Amphitrite the fair,
And covers all her face with ambient hair.
   'A ship on wheels!' he in derision roars,
And laughter hoarse with imprecations pours;
'Think not to beard us with such toys as these,
And ride triumphant o'er our boisterous seas;
Think not ye may the laws of gods withstand,
And shirk the trials of our shriving hand;
For waves shall rend, and sweeping tempests blow,
And steam shall hurl ye to the realms below.'
   And down he goes; but here disputes arise:
The dragon claims him as his special prize;
A Triton seeks to give him to the bears,
And from his claws the victim rudely tears.
   They tussle, tug, and from each other drag,
Till on his skin they do not leave a rag;
He plies his fists—alas! to what avail,
Against those rough bull hides what can prevail?
All flounder with him till he gasps for breath,
And barely saved is from the fangs of death,
As Neptune chides and stills the rising strife,
And gives the engineer his threatened life.

   The farce proceeds, and frolicsome throughout,
'Midst laughter great and hoarse hilarious shout,
As through the ordeal some are roughly cast,
Others more favoured quietly are passed.

Outside the ship a sail is stretched along,
In which aquatic sports are going on ;
Whilst at its edge, as some are dipping in,
Others shoot forth to take a wider swim.

 About the gear, upon the stretching stay,
From mast to mast, some monkey tricks display ;
Hang from the yards, their bodies dangling free,
Let go, descend, and drop into the sea ;
Seem quite at ease upon the azure tide,
Swim for the ship and clamber up her side.
So in a calm we spend upon the Line
The joyous hour, and pass away the time ;

 Till all complete, as day's declining light
Retires before the fast approach of night,
In varied tints, from faint to glowing hue,
Rise burnished hillocks on a base of blue.
Retreating Sol sinks gently down the steep,
And, close behind them, sinks into the deep.
On rising mists he casts a crimson tinge,
Adds to the darker clouds a golden fringe.
Rich, radiant streamers up to heaven he sends,
In fading colours all his glory ends.

 So ends the carnival with the dying day ;
Neptune prepares to take himself away ;
Rising majestic says : ' Before we leave,
Digest the words from us ye may receive.

 ' Our nature, changeless as yon setting sun,
Past, present, future, are to us as one ;
From day to day, from year to year, we roll
Bound the broad belt, and circle round the pole :
Thy foibles view with undisturbèd care,
Our billows promptly testing what they are.

 ' Stand by your chief, whatever he desires :
Where duty calls, there emulate your sires ;

Raise high your flag, and hand it down unfurled—
The noblest emblem yet given to the world—
A Star of Hope, whose brightly beaming rays
In unity a wondrous might displays.
Observe our laws, and find our stern decrees
Will aid Britannia still to free the seas.

' Now spread your sails ; we'll send a breeze in force,
And speed you forward on your destined course ;
Though rocks and shoals may threaten to destroy,
Use all your tact, and all your skill employ,
That, with your art and our protecting hand,
You may in safety reach your native land.'
    Thus Neptune spoke, and did our minds relieve,
By taking in a genial way his leave.
And all move off, descend the vessel's side –
The water's splash announces them in tide -
And disappear, till we can but discern
A glaring light, which rapid moves astern.
Far, far away the eye can trace the blaze,
As like a star it dances o'er the wave ;
Still farther yet, and then 'tis lost to sight :
To it, and all, we bid a long good-night.
    And off we sped, and caught the south-east trade
In gentle force, and good our progress made ;
The strengthening winds the stretching canvas fill,
As south we steer, and on toward Brazil.
    The deep-sea creatures plunge around the prow,
Of goodly size ; shoot far ahead and blow,
Curvet and dive and leap out of the sea,
And gambol at their ease though fast we flee,
As with the ship for many miles they run,
Nor e'en desert her when the night had come,
But through the dark the glowing streams are seen,

Phosphorent light in sparkling silver sheen ;
Disporting on until we near the coast,
When in the race the finny team is lost.

Now through the ship we hear the pleasing shout
Of ' Land ahead !' proceed from the look-out—
Cape Frio made, proclaimed by all aloud,
As caught half hidden by a misty cloud.

Then trim the sails, and on for it we stand,
And joyous feel to view the welcome land.
Arrived abreast—the sea breeze blowing strong,
Close with the coast, and skirt the shore along.

And now the king of harbours opens wide,
Displays its placid waters bright inside :
The scenery bold, disclosing all around
The lofty peak, the gentle rising mound.

The Sugar Loaf, conspicuous, towering high,
Marks out the passage to the mariner's eye ;
Huge granite rocks on either hand display,
With massive forts thereon, to block the way.

Outside and on the left, the beacon light
Directs the pilot through the hazy night ;
Now, like a sentinel, it guards the way
To Rio de Janeiro's spacious bay.

And as the noble harbour opes to view
Duties diverse engage the active crew,
Chains rattling loud, and ropes are ready laid,
The anchor cleared, and preparations made
To shorten sail, and up the canvas clew,
To square the yards, and bring the vessel to.

When all's prepared, the waters rushing by
The only sound, as rapid we draw nigh ;
The sailors wait at stations for the word,
And, quick as caught, the sails are to the yard ;
The anchor's cast, the flying chains resound,

To bottom dives, and takes the solid ground ;
Checks the great ship, and brings her to a rest,
And San Sebastian greets us as its guest.

RIO DE JANEIRO.

Bay of a thousand isles ! Brazilians' boast,
With caves and inlets, many leagues of coast,
With wide lagoons, where water-fowl abound,
And rocky nooks, and sandy beach around.
An inland lake, where steamboats daily ply ;
And the swift *Falua* with spreaded sails out-vie
Them in its speed, and runs the shores between,
To bear the trader home to islands green,
Or wealthy merchant, who may love retreat
And purer air within a rural seat.
Here in its midst the lonely rock is found,
Its summit high by monastery crowned,
Commanding sites monastic orders claim.
The bishop's palace, standing strong and plain,
As from an eminence is looking down
On all beneath that's clustered in the town.
Here Rio stands, within a spacious vale ;
On every side rise mountain, hill and dale,
And stately structures in the city lie,
Of palace low and churches raised on high ;
As though to stand a siege is built the pile
Of granite rock, cement, and Roman tile.

Some business comes to take us to the shore,
And with some others o'er the side we pour ;
Elated feel in touch with solid ground,

And with a friend we scour the country round.
And nags we hire, and by the Gloria lay,
And urge our steeds along an inland bay ;
Climb up a hill and through a cleft we passed,
Whose sides are crowned with heavy bastions masked ;
Obtain a view of grandeur far and wide,
Down to the edge where ocean rolls his tide.
Beneath our feet a hilly range extends,
A crescent beach with high extending ends.

    A plain of sand, as white as driven snow,
Where naught but clumps of cactus wildly grow ;
A pier-like reef runs from the silver strand,
And stretches seaward far away from land ;
Whose utter end a rural church adorns,
And adds another to the many charms.

    Then down we ride, across the drifting sands,
And reach the rock whereon the structure stands ;
Whose tinkling bell across the waters calls
Its devotees to come within its walls,
Hold festival—the banners flaunt *en fête*,
Its patron saint's great day to celebrate.

    And as we ride the worshippers among,
And wend our way the even rock along,
All presents bring : fish, fowl, and luscious fruits,
Goats, pigeons, doves, and sweet esculent roots ;
With armadillos, parrots, parrakeets,
Apes, sugar-cane, and maize, and marmosets ;
Crude articles of workmanship, and quaint,
And grunting hogs, propitiate the saint.

    The throng assembled all the church around,
The gifts arranged with care upon the ground,
An auctioneer impromptu holding forth
Their latent virtues and exalted worth,
Each separate lot falls to the highest call,

And Mother Church appropriates it all.
We took a turn around the sandy shore,
Then for the pass—the only road—we bore ;
Returned again along the inland bay,
And back to ship before the fall of day.

A great saint's day, and from the ship released,
On shore we go to see the people's feast,
The sun ablaze, the holiday in its prime ;
The bells throw out their hoarse discordant chime,
From their high domes proceed the deaf'ning sound,
From church to church they all re-echo round.
The great bell swings, and with consummate art
The skilful negro acts his dangerous part,
Whose great machine, immense in weight and power,
Hangs at the portal of the lofty tower ;
A lever plies, the bell is set arock,
Which, partly balanced by a weighty block
Of wood and iron, his monkey tricks extend
In close proximity to his noisy friend.
First then the bell, and then the block is seen,
And then the agile negro slips between,
And dances round, in gyral motions fade,
Coming and flitting like a sable shade ;
Then swings it up and there its course arrests,
And, balanced, leaves it so to take a rest.
The lever touched again, the bell is free,
And round it turns with swift velocity ;
He keeps it up, its highest speed attains,
As o'er it swings, and backward o'er again ;
Bell, block and lever, as the cord he plies,
Each on the other round the axis flies.
He springs between, all danger seems to spurn,
And pulls the lever still at every turn ;

Then eases down, and, as a grand finale,
He mounts the block and swings round with the bell.
   Report then tells, and to our ready faith,
His predecessor danced the dance of death,
For, having slipped, the monster dealt a blow
That hurled him headlong on the crowd below ;
That same report deplores that negro lost,
For blacks were then a thousand dollars' cost.
   The church pours forth its grand procession long
Amidst the clamour of the assembling throng ;
Blacks, whites, and browns in sable garments dressed,
Around the saints with pious ardour pressed.
   As these from portals wide on biers are borne
In varied postures, attitudes, and forms,
A long array of them the roadway lines,
In all the pageantry of olden times.

   Stone balconies at every window are,
To which the lady devotees repair,
Hanging from each their banners gay unfold,
Of purple velvet pile, and fringed with gold.
   The great St. George the portal's arch detains,
On snow-white steed he grasps the silver reins :
In glittering panoply is towering high
The warrior-saint, in armour cap-à-pie.
   They draw him out, and, staggering with the load,
Join the procession on its destined road,
Half hid from view his features by a mask
Of nodding plumes, o'er bright metallic casque.
   He is the attraction of this special day,
And all admire him as he's borne away,
Due homage pay, of Britain's patron proud,
And ' Santo Inglez's ' whispered by the crowd.
   The saints are many from the church enlarged,

The only mounted one, the great St. George ;
Some rich in robes, and some are plain in white,
But San Sebastian is the favourite ;
Some are exhorting, some in act of prayer ;
But Benedict the only black saint there.
And rough men too are there, with traders known,
The church's surplices o'er their shoulders thrown
Which should be white and pure ; but those are rare,
For most look soilèd and the worse for wear.

    Each acolyte a waxen candle hath,
And ambles with it as a walking staff
Of large proportions, and whose yellow blaze
Is quite eclipsed by Sol's more brilliant rays.

    Angels afoot in flesh and paper wings,
Each with a wand, on tiptoe lightly springs ;
In muslins white, and features pale and fair,
And pure white wreaths adorn their sable hair.
Of tender years, they're trained to act, and try
Their wings fantastic, and away to fly.
They're much admired, and thus their praises loud
Are echoed round by all the motley crowd.

    And here the primate and high priests proceed,
From whom all mortals reverently recede ;
State functionaries, by their emperor led,
Hold high the canopy o'er the Church's head.

    Though some assert he shows repugnance strong,
Yields with ill grace submission ; and, ere long,
'Gainst superstition, costing what it might,
He will declare for freedom and his right.
A man of science, wrapped in books and study,
He looks askance at pomp and show and folly ;
Of broader views, a man who fain would see
His people taught, industrious, and free.

To *Nosso pai* and saints all bend the knee,
Prostrate themselves ; and we, amidst a sea
Of souls devout, wedged in on either hand,
Think it unwise to singly gaze and stand,
A mark conspicuous, where the tongue is free
For sneers and jibes and native ribaldry.

We make a start to head the long procession,
Where still the people stand in ranked position ;
But like a wave rolls down the kneeling mass,
Nor gives us breathing time to let us pass.

We toil along, when some begin to grumble,
As o'er their naked legs we surge and stumble,
And are assailed by cries of *Non-de-deos*,
Pagans, heretics, infidels, and Jews !

The gauntlet run, along the narrow street,
Where odours strong our sense of smelling greet,
Arising from the shining, well-greased backs
Of ancient negresses and stalwart blacks,
Who fume and sweat, as in the mid-day heat,
The shafts of Sol down fierce upon them beat.

Yet on we press, and pant to get at large,
And pity those who wrestle with St. George,
Whose bulk colossal causes great delay,
As, shoulders high, he's borne along the way.
For to such work low slaves may not aspire
Of their own will, or from their master's hire.
So on they toiled beneath the load they bore,
As no Brazilians ever toiled before :
One weak there is who, quite exhausted, faints,
As to the square we pass with all the saints.

Praça da Constitucão, or Constitution Square,
The place is named where all assembled are ;
Amidst the clangour of the church bells' sound,

The saints proceed to make the circuit round.
We lag behind and linger in the rear
Till all are gone, and leave us in the square
To look around at leisure, bring to view
Objects of interest, or of something new.

A monument—triumph of skill and art—
For Frenchmen's hands had fashioned every part—
Rises conspicuous, standing out alone,
To the first founder of the imperial throne.

Pedro primeiro, contour fine and bold,
Holds in his hand the people's charter rolled :
In lasting bronze a stately steed bestrides,
Its graceful lines defined against the skies:
Harmonious, light, a pleasing contrast found
To all the solid, square built structures round.

Quadrangle base, fine granite rock supplies,
On which a pedestal of bronze may rise,
Around whose die in bold relief outstand
The various natives of the imperial land.

Indians, Guayazes, Amazon's warlike race,
And more, beyond our cursory view to trace,
Traditional or extinct ; now few are seen
Save negroes, reds, half-castes, and Europeans.

We loiter round, through *Campo St. Anna* rove,
A bare, large square, then on to *San Christovão*,
To where the palace, on a rising mound,
With square-built walls, high stately trees surround.

Approach we find through shaded avenues
Of graceful, light, and feathery-leafed bamboos,
Up to the palace forms the covered way,
Suppressing both the heat and light of day.

Among the trees and round the walks we roam,
Espy the imperial family driving home
In gilded carriages, in semi-state,

Returning from the high religious fête.
The emperor, empress and the fair princesses
In ostrich plumes and modern fancy dresses.
We pass them close, salute them as they go,
And in return receive the gracious bow.

We linger here, and then are wandering down
The road we came, wending towards the town,
Where still the fêtes progress till fall of night,
When all's illuminate with candle-light;
Lanterns from house and every church depend,
Bouquets of rockets from these last ascend.
All is ablaze, though no devices shown,
To universal church such are unknown ;
To her alone the offering must be given,
Who, through the saints, invokes the aid of Heaven.
Wearied afoot, and much oppressed by heat,
Cool Botafoga set ourselves to seek,
Where some hotels upon the borders lay,
Of a refreshing, quiet, lovely bay.
And as we search an aqueduct is seen,
Whose solid piers we scan and pass between ;
On double arches stands, a goodly height,
A well-built structure of the Roman type.
And here *Tajuica* rolls its waters down,
Cool, bright, and copious, supplies the town
With a free gift, as Nature free doth give
To all her creatures she creates to live.
Proceeding on through suburbs clean and broad,
Where pleasant seats are nestling on the road,
Hotel Inglez we seek is found at last,
And all our weariness is fleeting past.
Haven of rest ! we hail the inn with cheers,
As at its porch an Englishman appears.

' Oh, tell us, friend,' we said, without delay,
' Will your hotel afford a night to stay
Beneath its roof ? For food and shelter are
The things we need ; they are our present care ;
With heat and thirst and hunger sorely pressed,
For love or money, friend, afford us rest.'
　　Our host, half serious and half in fun,
For love and money says it shall be done.
' For love *and* money, friends, 'tis wisely told,
Are levers used to prise and move the world.
For love or money then, 'tis but the same :
I love my brethren, therein lies the gain ;
For love and money come with me to dwell,
For love and money shall be treated well.'

　　An urbane negro, pleasing thin and tall—
Not understanding, yet he smiles withal—
Awaits the advent of his master's look,
With running orders what to go and cook.
　　Repast discussed, a pleasant evening through,
As Boniface, relating something new,
To us at least, with many left in store,
The selfsame tales as told so oft before.
　　We lounge about, and scarce can keep awake,
All soon suggesting early to betake
Ourselves to rest, and so for bed prepare.
But, oh ! an enemy awaits us there.
　　Mosquitoes buzz ! their nightly vigils keep ;
Their siren music lures us on to sleep,
And, much fatigued, we soon begin to doze
And hope the blessing of an earned repose.
　　Oh, sweet delusion, could it long time last !
But all too soon that sweet delusion's past.
Though sound asleep, awake with sudden start,

To feel the venom of the poisoned dart.
　We rub and doze, awake to rub again,
Spring from the bed, procure a light, and then
In sharp encounter beat the curtains round ;
Then wait to listen for the plaintive sound ;
Can nothing hear, and think we've won the game,
The curtains close, and try the bed again.
But all in vain, for, lo! the swellings rise
Upon our arms and legs, our face and eyes,
The voices meekly at our ears begin,
Which tingle hotly as they buzz and sing.
　Who may contend against a foe unseen,
With subtle weapons, poisonous and keen,
Supine and prostrate, fix us in our beds,
And hold their orgies round our restless heads ?
　We cannot sleep, and long before the dawn
Lights up the way, we stroll the road along
Towards the beach, and down upon the strand
Where bathers pitch their tents upon the sand ;
Of sexes both we're stretched around the bay,
Before the morn breaks fairly into day.
　We bathe our limbs, and back return again
To where the morning meal awaits us ; then
Lay out our plans ; among them I decide
To make a tour and have a lonely ride.

　Across the bay I cast my longing eyes :
Far in the west the Organ Mountains rise,
Whose rugged peaks of granite, towering high,
Like organ tubes are pointing to the sky,
From which, 'tis said, the range obtained its name,
When to these shores the first discoverers came.
　Now from the wharf a steamboat daily plies
Across the bay where Pièdade lies,

Calling at isles that like to emeralds are
Upon the bosom of this bay so fair,
And oases of health, whose shady trees
Are daily fanned by land and ocean's breeze.

I pleasant people find upon the way,
Sombre, vivacious, talkative, and gay ;
The coloured nurses with the charge of babies,
And old men smirking to fastidious ladies.

The salutations pass with priests, civilians,
For who are more polite than these Brazilians ?
And full three hours are spent in journeying o'er
From city wharves to Pièdade's shore.

And here, refreshed, a sturdy mule I gain,
Make for the range across the sandy plain ;
And as I ride along the dusty road,
Meet ladened mules hard toiling 'neath the load
Of land produce ; in teams they're wending down
Towards the port, for shipment to the town.

Seven the team, its leader's head adorned
With bells and flags, in single file they're formed ;
March quickly on, and equidistant keep,
Though ruts and obstacles beset their feet.

And by their side the negro trips the way,
Whistles and sings a guttural roundelay ;
And hails with joy the port as seen at last,
Ending the journey and the toilsome task.

My well-trained beast keeps up a steady pace,
With ease some miles his active footsteps trace ;
On either hand the cane-brake land extends,
And groves of pines the negro slave attends ;
Hums as he toils a rustic theme to cheer
The sense of solitude that greets him here.

And then a corn-field, bearing pods of maize,
Whose silken tufts the balmy soft wind waves ;

Like scarlet plumes they're nodding o'er the fields,
And render tribute in abundant yields.

The gentle hills, with coffee blossoms crowned,
Vie with the orange rows that skirt them round ;
Deep in the vale the plantain-tree survives
Beneath whose shade the sweet banana thrives.
I gain the base, and wind the mountain's slope,
Led on by change and all-inspiring hope.
The summit gained will greet my mind's accord,
And patient toil receive its just reward.
For to succeed climb boldly up the hill,
Mount all obstruction with undaunted will ;
Let naught deter thee when thy course is right,
Repulsed again, again renew the fight.
Try all thy skill the foe to circumvent,
Though chasms yawn, and rocks are split and rent :
Though forests dense and prowling beasts you meet,
And mountain torrents fierce assail your feet ;
And though the summit be denied control,
A vantage still is gained to view the whole.
And here a snake across the roadway lay,
Stands on its coils, as to dispute the way.
But, scenting danger, on his belly glides,
And in the mountain jungle safely hides.
The first ascent is passed ; the mountain's side
Affords a road more level, smooth and wide ;
And winding round, and deep in a ravine,
I halt to look upon the opening scene :
Between the spurs a spacious vale descends,
And far below among the hills it ends.
And as I gazed upon the varied dell,
My sight arrested on a panther fell,
Sleek, young and glossy ; o'er the road I ride,

3—2

Steals swiftly on, and mounts the upper side ;
Appears again upon a fallen tree,
With glaring eyes fixed steadfastly on me.
    My mule now starts, and pricks his ears and shies,
And as we pass, the panther keenly eyes;
Admonished by the spur, the danger past,
He moves more steady, confident and fast.
And on he goes, a brisker motion keeps,
By zig-zag ways climbs up the second steeps.
Those granite peaks are reached as he ascends,
Close by their base the crooked road extends ;
Those granite peaks high pointing to the skies,
On passing by I try to moralize.

    ' How long,' said I, ' high towering in the air,
Washed by the dews of heaven, have you stood there ?
Yes ! ope your rocky mouths and tell, I pray :'
Though mute they stand, there's something seems to say,
' Take Nature's book, peruse its pages well :
Whatever others, this the truth will tell.
Reflection used upon her secret plan,
Will tell thee, long before thy race began ;
When fires terrestrial cast us to this mould,
Withdrew their heat and left us in the cold.'
    ' 'Tis true,' I said, ' and more I plainly see
The word " Eternal " writ on thee and me :
For know, the atoms that compose this frame
Were once mixed with thee in terrestrial flame ;
In fusion held, with scoria long alloyed,
Vast time consuming, yet were not destroyed.
    ' Through countless years this globe has had to run,
With fire within, without the tempering sun,
With other spheres observing its true place,
Turn on its axis, run through boundless space ;

To one thing tending since the whole began,
To fashion this—this thinking thing—this man.
A mite withal, but with a mind of might
To see its author through so grand a light.'

The rocky pass is neared, the land-breeze through,
Rolls o'er the brow and down, as evening drew
On us apace ; but soon to change its course,
When from the sea it veers in greater force
Towards the sun, and follows in the west,
Until the morn sets in and gives it rest.
The brow is reached for landscape beauty famed,
Picturesque, sublime, and Boa Vista named.
Vista Boa ! where all in grandeur lies,
But modestly this wondrous scene implies.
A natural pass, with lofty wooded sides,
Through which a balmy sylvan zephyr glides,
Invigorates the traveller and obtains
His ardent praises as he thus exclaims :
'Oh ye, who dwell within the city's walls
Or at full ease in close polluted halls,
From ennui sighing for a new sensation,
From study pining for a relaxation,
From plodding daily in the mart or fair,
Awake to blessings of the mountain air !'

And here I halt to scan the scene around ;
My mule, impatient, paws the rocky ground.
'How now,' say I ; 'come, stay thy eager flight,
Why so much haste to quit this gorgeous sight ?
'Tis true a chasm yawns 'twixt you and I,
Your thoughts are in the earth, mine soar on high :
From acts divine the tree of knowledge sprang,
And with its seed imbued the soul of man ;

From this fair earth to heaven it turned his face,
And gave dominion to the favoured race.'
   The panting beast the fresh green grass espies,
Then takes the rein, and to the bank he hies ;
And as I yield it, glad to take a rest,
Transported felt, and thus my thoughts expressed :
   ' Feed on, my nag, and browse without control,
As I alight and feed a rapturous soul ;
Commune alone, while here no voice intrudes,
Save Nature's, breathing through her solitudes.'
   Ah ! what a heavenly sight is here around !
The forest trees, all gay, with blossoms crowned,
Blue, yellow, purple, mixed by Nature's care,
Their balmy fragrance floating through the air.
   From out a deep ravine, and bursting bright,
A large cascade rolls down the steepy height ;
O'er rock, through gorge, the sparkling waters take,
Join other streams, and wander to the lake,
Upon whose plain the numerous craft appear,
Their white sails mirrored on the surface clear.
Outside of all, as far as eyes can reach,
Great ocean's waters roll, and wash the beach :
A scene sublime, and in degree the last
Of mighty grandeur, not to be surpassed.
   As o'er the slope my ravished eyes are led,
Bright humming-birds are hovering near my head ;
Around a bush they pause upon the wing,
Then sparkle, dart away, and, buzzing, sing ;
And as I dream of future realms of bliss,
My ideal should be such a scene as this.
From Heaven's high throne, with eyes celestial see
Great Nature in her vast entirety,
A heaven of joy, inspired by mutual love,
No thoughts conflicting in the vault above ;

Where all as one, one essence through the whole,
And truth triumphant flows from soul to soul.

But Sol declines behind the western hills,
And all my mind with thoughts of danger fills ;
To pass the lonely road ere night entraps,
And with its mantle all the scene enwraps.
And sudden bounding from my reverie,
Turn to my mule, and hasten to be free.
Say, ' Run, my nag, outstrip the night and wind,
For darkling clouds are gathering up behind,
Huge, black, and threat'ning, spread from pole to pole,
And thunders loud are bellowing through the whole,
Driven from the sea, and rolling o'er the plain ;
They may be with us ere our speed can gain
The friendly roofs that bear Tereza's name.'
So on we ride, until a spark of light
Breaks through the gloom of fast-approaching night ;
Large drops of rain are falling thick around,
Transmitting odours from the dusty ground.
Slack not our speed or even stop to rest,
Till Teresopolis greets us as its guest.
   Rough greeting this : the place is new and bare,
But the elements will drive us anywhere,
To any place to shelter from the storm,
Which threatens high and rages with alarm :
Loud thunder rattles with tremendous roar,
And tropic's naiads down a deluge pour ;
Full copious streams rush from the wooded hills,
And every gully spouts with new-made rills.
   The lightnings blaze with vivid flash and fork,
An instant cease, and all is pitchy dark,
As on I ride towards the nearest door,
Bound from the saddle to the earthen floor,

Unceremonious, uninvited stand,
With streams of water flowing from each hand,
Amongst a group of shelter-seeking strays,
Caught in the storm upon their different ways,
I find carousing, laughing, singing, smoking,
And, to my mind, they are in humour joking
At my expense, to see me so alight,
Hurried, obtrusive, and in such a plight.
　　But, lo ! a voice above the general din
Is hailing loud from out a room within—
In Anglo-Saxon fast and sparkling runs,
In tones peculiar to Columbia's sons !

　　' I say, stranger, make your way inside ;
I reckon, friend, you've had a dampish ride.
Give way, ye churls, and hold your jargon, too,
And let a spark of civilization through.'
With this he drives and elbows through the crowd,
With voice authoritative, sharp and loud,
Reached where I stood, and, grasping both my hands,
Was pleased to talk to one who understands
His native tongue, invites me as his guest
With ' Come in, friend, and try to get a rest,
And join me in a ready meal to sup ;
Peg down, peel off, drain boots, and liquor up.'
About he stirs the embers on the hearth.
' Of brands,' says he, ' my friend, there is no dearth,
Had for the cutting, as you may suppose,
And useful now, at least, to dry your clothes.
Now say, my friend, what liquor you prefer,
Though small the choice to be procurèd here,
A mixture black they call *Vinho do Porto*,
A spirit white they name *Casacha forte*,
Neither of which could any one pretend

With any decency to recommend.
But here's a flask my private wants supplies,
Of old rye whisky from the States,' he cries ;
' Take a stiff draught, 'twill aid you in your sleep,
And hold the damp from penetrating deep.
Now let us sup ; small choice is here, I guess,
The people poor, with lands like these to bless,
A Christian country, where—though queer it seems—
These everlasting idiots live on beans.
Here's salted hog, I would have better planned
Had I but known you were so close at hand ;
Farinha coarse which deal with if you can,
For taken dry it well-nigh chokes a man ;
And twists of bread as solid rock as hard—
Our host will tell you fit for any lord—
That fed on this the mountaineer is blessed,
And hungry men can eat it e'en with zest.'
We tried it all, with little more was pleased,
Till satisfied and hunger stood appeased.

In stirring tones my friend is ever poring
O'er all he'd seen away out west exploring,
To where a line of rails was soon to go,
Along the vale of Rio San Francisco.

' Magnificent !' he cries, 'and all surrounding,
Along its banks luxuriant lands abounding ;
A thousand miles the stream is broad and free,
But falls and shallows block the way to sea.
A splendid stream, as yet of little use,
Until the cars shall roll with its produce
Towards the coast, where lie in every port
The world's argosies, ready to transport
The staples rich, abundant there at hand
To feed and clothe the folk of every land.

'And now,' says he, 'I guess I'm going back;
To-morrow's dawn shall find me making track
'Cross country where I shall put up a space;
Petropolis, a far more favoured place.

'A good day's ride, through forests dark and drear,
With weather bright some prospects fine appear;
So cheer up, friend—there's sunshine left,' he cried;
'The skies will clear.' And to him I replied:
'Oh, generous friend, I pledge you all good speed,
A friend in season is a friend indeed;
A friend unsought, and yet when needed most
Is there to succour and to act the host;
A friend unasked, with every thought of good,
Holds right divine in nature's brotherhood.
The best of all, whatever we may say,
Of brotherhoods conceived and made to pay.'

My friend replied, 'The circumstances such,
I reckon, boss, you do not owe me much;
The gain is mine; I could afford a walk
Of some few miles, my friend, to hear you talk.
To list once more to a full English voice
Wakes all my soul and makes my heart rejoice;
For six long months my tongue has naught availed,
With Portuguese alone my ears assailed,
So I'm the winner, friend—well paid, you'll see,
By the lucky storm that drove you here to me.'

But, oh! the rain my mind with boding fills;
The thunder rolls, and rattles through the hills,
Outside afloat with new-made running streams,
And pitchy black except when lightning gleams;
Annoying, too, is heard the saying cast,
The rainy season set: it long may last.

'Oh, friend of mine! now tell me if you might

Where I may rest my wearied limbs this night :
Some sheltering roof before the hours I waste,
That's more congenial to a Christian's taste.'
   ' Small choice you'll find, I guess,' my friend replies,
A spark of humour beaming in his eyes.
' If out for change and comfort is your aim,
I reckon, friend, your search will be in vain ;
Though small the *rancho*, rough the daily fare,
You may do worse than settle where you are.'
   With some concern I turn my eyes to trace
The room around—my new-found dwelling-place,
Where for a floor I find the solid earth ;
From forest trees the walls derive their birth :
The spreading palm its lathwood had supplied,
To different uses different trees applied ;
The builder's craft but little art employing,
His rough material close around him lying.
   With kneaded clay the lattice work he sticks,
For all Brazil is innocent of bricks ;
The young bamboo he takes unto his aid,
Plaits to a mat, and for a ceiling laid :
To roof it in the cedar soft must fall
Rived into shingles made to cover all.
   Devoid of glass, nor tight in any form,
Our mountaineers such trifles hold to scorn ;
They're Nature's children, hard in Nature's care,
Her trainings suffer and her trials dare.
   And in a corner of the place I found,
On upright stakes, sunk firmly in the ground,
A rough-hewn bench, on which is stretched and dried,
To form a bed, a rough and tough bull-hide.
And anxious thoughts upon me sorely pressed,
As words like these unto my friend addressed :
   ' 'Twas from my ship, now lying in the bay,

I wandered forth, and took this lonely way ;
On for Constancia I had set design ;
But, fate adverse, I must that thought resign.
  ' A long-lost friend has there made his abode,
Some few miles out, I learn, upon this road ;
This night forbids, I on the morn depend
To hail Constancia and my long-lost friend.'

  ' If that is so,' my friend replies, ' I guess
I may relate some news that I possess.
Early this morn towards that place I pressed,
My mule to feed, myself to take a rest ;
But with intention there to make a stay,
And with your friend and mine to spend the day.
  ' I had not seen him for a year or more,
And thought to dine with him as heretofore ;
Enjoy his voice, with thoughtful topics ripe,
The friendly liquor and the soothing pipe ;
With minds consonant pass the sunny day,
And for a space to dream the hours away
In social converse, lolling at our ease,
Inhaling fragrance from the blossoming trees.
  ' These were my thoughts ; alas ! it was decreed
Such dreams of happiness should not succeed ;
For as I neared the place, all things looked queer,
Hedgerows neglected, overgrown and drear.
" Heigho !" said I, " there's certain something wrong,
My British coadjutor's dead or gone ;
Whiche'er it be, there's no one left behind
So true and free, hospitable and kind."
  ' A negro slave was quickly at my side,
Whom I at once with anxious questions plied ;
Before he spoke my mind was full of dread :
His only answer was, " My master's dead

Some few months since, and I am left alone,
To mourn the loss of that good spirit gone."

'I questioned more ; he, answering me, replied,
" 'Twas said by his own hand my master died,
But that's not true ; mysterious death had come,
But not by him the fatal deed was done."

'And more I gathered from this negro kind :
Some creole children had been left behind,
Who now the owners were of the estate,
Thrown both together to degenerate.

'An untrustworthy, cold, effeminate race,
For whom stern Nature does not find a place,
Who soon die out, the blood too much alloyed,
The propagation falling null and void,
Had left him, with a few, to guard the home—
Gone far away, none knew where they had gone.

'That black was gentle, and of talents rare ;
He kept the house with all domestic care,
And was a favourite of my friend, I knew,
Whose long connection to affection grew.

'He English spoke as he had always done:
My friend had taught him as he would a son.
He mourns him now for all the love he bore,
Our friend to all is lost for evermore.'

' Be sure, my friend,' said I, ' 'tis news indeed,
And well withal I did not there proceed ;
Of those behind are strangers all to me,
My presence there may not so welcome be.

'And of my friend, I little knew when young,
And many years have rolled their course along
Since he left home, and all that held him dear,
Among Brazilians came to settle here.

'Since death's oblivion covers up my friend,

And brings my search to an untimely end,
Arrests my progress in a sad defeat,
And turns my mind to contemplate retreat ;
Yet two full days or more I have to spare,
Before the hours allotted finished are,
Ere I return to crew and ship again,
To speed with them across the open main.'

  ' Well, now, I reckon, boss,' my friend replied,
' You may with me in this *rancho* abide
Until the morn. Your time will serve you well
To come along, through forest, hill, and dale,
On to Petropolis, where I reckon, friend,
You may as ready to your ship descend ;
And where I promise you, the night to dwell,
A full appointed, cosy, clean hotel,
Whose genial *chef,* sound, rubicund, and full
Of jovial quips, a thoroughbred John Bull,
Who knows your notions, will attend to you,
And all your British tastes for comfort too.'
' Well pleased,' said I, ' to go as you suggest ;
So now, my friend,' I said, 'arrange to rest,
And as the hour of night is growing late,
Call in our host and him interrogate
As to what means he has at his command,
What bedding, clothing, well-aired sheets at hand ;
For as the night I deem is growing cold,
Sound sleep may find me warm in blankets rolled.'

  Our rough-cast host, a shaggy mountaineer—
Who on a lonely road one well might fear,
Of mixèd race, though current in his veins,
Some lusty blood of Portugal retains,
From Lusitania his ancestors came,
Knows naught of Portugal except the name,

Nor aught about the crossing of the Douro,
Of Torres Vedras or Ciudad Rodrigo—
His worldly knowledge not so far extending,
His geography at the city ending ;
Bronzed by exposure and the tropic sun,
By varied means a livelihood had won ;
Feels independent—though with anxious cares,
Provides a *poncho* and the couch prepares ;
' Fit for a prince !' exclaims, with leer suspicious ;
To differ with him would be injudicious,
And so I yield to all conditions hard,
As he, obsequious, styles me thus, 'milord' :
With final salutations then departs.
Then from his couch my friend, amused, remarks :
　' You are not taken with our host's attentions,
Yet give him credit for some good intentions ;
His usual patrons are not much inclined
To study taste or anything refined.
His condescension, too, I reckon, friend,
He strives his best to make you comprehend.
Driven by storm, well, worse we might have had,
Though rough without, within he's not so bad.'
　Fatigued I felt, for rest in peace I sued ;
Soft chary Sleep a length of hours I wooed,
Alternate turning on my back and side,
But wooed in vain upon my bed of hide ;
Alone to those the generous boon is given
Who lie contented at the will of Heaven.
So sleeps my friend, sonorous sounds revealing
Oblivion sweet upon his senses stealing.
In contrast to my fickle fretfulness,
Soft Somnus holds him in forgetfulness,
As, when the pilgrimage of life is done.
And good or ill marks out the course we've run,

The wearied soul, awaiting life to cease,
Yearns for the goal of everlasting peace,
His sister Lethe's found with balm to steep
All ills and blessings in eternal sleep.

Next morn at dawn a gleam of hope appears :
Aurora blushing through a crevice peers,
And bids us rise, a hasty meal partake,
And mount to greet the vestal morning break.
And off we start the highway course along,
With mules refreshed are dashing swiftly on
Through flooded grounds and jungles dark and drear.
Round slippery spurs, I follow in the rear,
And track my leader in the narrow way :
O'er ruts and rocks the crooked pathway lay.
With no conception what my eyes may bless,
Relieved from this umbrageous wilderness.
Here in a nook, the hill and road between,
A rough-hewn cross beneath the mist is seen ;
A weighty balk is raised to brave the storms,
And creeping plants spring up about its arms :
Ominous and weird, left here to indicate
The spot whereon some traveller met his fate :
A lonely place, uncanny, and we fear
Some tragic scene has been enacted here.
Low murmuring sounds awake the silent wood,
As distant thunder rolls the sylvan flood.
More near, more loud, we catch the rushing sound,
Till in a roar the vales re-echo round.
Down o'er the rocks the swollen waters run
Across the path we wish to pass upon :
My leader but a moment hesitates,
Spurs on his beast, and first the water takes.
'Cross must,' says he, 'there lies no other way

But to proceed or where we are to stay.'
So on we urge to ford the rocky bed ;
Our nags with care the treacherous bottom tread,
But ere Columbia's had the rapid passed,
His footing slips and down his rider's cast ;
But quick regains.   Breast high the waters stand :
He seeks his mule, and makes towards the land,
Remonstrates with it for its want of care ;
Together spring and landed safely are.
We halt awhile, an open recess found,
Shake out our clothes and spread them on the ground ;
A dry rock find whereon to make a spread
Of *Mina* cheese and hard-baked, home-made bread.
Two pocket flasks a generous wine supply,
But scant the meal on which we both rely.
The sun shines brightly on our resting-place,
Deep in the mount, from falls, the waters race,
Leap in their course, impelled down from the height,
Rush o'er the rocks, impetuous in their flight.
Along their bed towards the brink they pour,
Fall o'er the ledge, and in the abysses roar.
Above the rock whereon the travellers lie,
A fuchsia spreads its graceful tendrils high,
Springs up aloft, and runs amongst the trees,
And waves its branches in the gentle breeze.
Across the stream tall trunks their limbs entwine,
Knawed at their roots, their heavy crowns incline ;
Grown old, made gay by parasitic charms,
They clasp each other with outstretching arms—
Dependence mutual with declining days,
Be-arched with wreaths and veneration's bays.
Their rounded limbs the cardinal adorns ;
Creeping festoons hang from the archway forms,
Beneath whose shade the dancing waters flow,

A lovely valley stretching far below,
Whose sylvan slopes for many miles around
With blossoming trees like beds of flowers abound,
Down to their base where lies in glittering sheen,
Meandering through the vale, the silver stream.

　　And now, refreshed, our journey we renew,
With spirits raised the devious way pursue.
In file we ride, in van my leader leads,
He knows the road and onward swift proceeds ;
And to converse he turns himself around,
As the strong mules press quickly o'er the ground.
I in my friend a good companion find,
A pleasant fellow with a generous mind,
A Yankee born, and yet, with pride he claims,
The noble blood of Britain in his veins.
Reads Burns and Byron just as well as I,
And holds his claim to Shakespeare equally ;
Of his great country wondrous tales relates,
With England nowhere to the United States.

　　' Then what induced you, friend, from it to roam ?'
' Guess I'd rather feed on beans at home,'
Was his reply.　' Although my business here
Will take some years to finish yet, I fear !
Down farther south, a road of rails to make ;
But if the rain pours down at this great rate,
Some time must yet elapse ere we can start
To pierce the mountain through its granite heart ;
Roads broken up, no transport can be had,
The highways flooded and the byways bad.'

　　And now emerging from the moistened wood,
Clear in the mere again with joy we stood,
High on a rock, exposed and bared to light
Of shining Sol, that breaks upon it bright.
Here, basking in the sun, a huge snake lies,

Quick on its coils it meets the sharp surprise,
Disputes the way with jaws distended near,
Then to the jungle glides away with fear ;
And as he moves he bends the younger trees,
And marks his track among the rustling leaves.
   The prospect fearful, we alight again,
Our beasts with care we lead on by the rein ;
Caution observe, the better part we think,
The treacherous rock slants steep towards the brink.
Across we move most carefully and slow,
Then stop to gaze in wonderment below :
A charming view for many miles around,
Large tracts of forest hills with blossoms crowned ;
And where we stand to view the glorious scene,
A natural garden round about is seen.
Upon the rock, in every crevice, grow
Rare bulbs and roots that make a lovely show.
We linger long, unwilling to depart,
Then mount again to make another start :
Downwards proceed, descending to the rills,
Then mounting high again the forest hills,
Into ravines where strong effluvia rise,
Where undergrowth in sweltering masses lies,
Tall ferns and palms and tropic's flowering plants,
In graceful forms and wild luxuriance.
   And winding round the narrow pathway long,
My friend from sight all suddenly is gone.
I think him lost ; but as I reached the rise
Quite whole and safe he greets my anxious eyes.
Full five yards down, upon a jutting rock,
Which had received them with a sudden shock,
There sits my guide, astride, with eyes upturned,
And, statue-like, unmoved and unconcerned.
   Upon my friend below I, sitting, gazed

4—2

For moments long, in wonderment amazed.
At length I said, 'Is this the second act?
If so, excuse me, for I must turn back.'
'Turn back,' I said, but to turn back, indeed,
Seemed less in reason here than to proceed.

  'Simple,' says he, 'come, show your courage strong :
Follow my lead and you will not go wrong :
You keep your mule, your mule will keep his feet,
And both are landed decently and neat.
Withal, my friend, 'tis well that rock was there,
Or I and mule an equal fate might share ;
Too close the edge along unheeding tripped,
The ground proved rotten, and away we slipped.

  'My trusty nag is young, and strong, and brisk ;
I hope to save him, but I think the risk
By hand to aid might well endanger all,
And drag us down together in his fall.
So first, my friend, we will his trappings save,
Leave to himself how next he might behave ;
Thus unencumbered, he the task to try,
Climb up the slant, or in the bottom die.'

  He then dismounts, and strips his mule quite bare,
Saddle and trappings safe recovered are ;
He scrambles up, assisted by the reins,
By scrub and rift the narrow pathway gains.
His faithful mule, who, to his master's call,
Dares to ascend or in the bottom fall,
The danger sees, and, planting firm his feet,
As if a goat, attempts the dangerous steep.
Close to the bank with stiffened limbs he clings,
Makes for the path, and upward sudden springs ;
Retains his hold, and shakes his shivering sides :
My friend remounts, and onward swiftly rides.
Emerge again upon a summit high,

With naught above us but a clouded sky ;
A scene divine is then revealed to us,
Grandeur sublime, awful in loneliness :
Mediæval forests hundreds of miles broad,
Where none but creeping creatures ever trod,
Beneath our feet and running far away,
Whose rugged steeps and gentle vales display
Magnificence ; hills piled on hills recall
Our insignificance compared to all.
As still as death, and yet there's life within,
And everywhere about its runs are seen ;
Serpents slip past, and all the feline race,
Onças and cats find here a lurking place.
The lizard tribe, of every size, abound,
On foot and wing small game infest the ground ;
And through the wood at intervals outrang
The loud hoarse note of large-billed plumed toucan ;
And groups of apes are gambolling in the trees.
A very paradise on earth to these ;
The living trees share in the general lot,
To rise and flourish, propagate and rot.

My guide rides on and leads, devoid of care,
Our mules prick up their ears and sniff the air ;
A moaning sound is heard within the wood,
At which he stopped and undecided stood,
But quick explained we must the straight way dare,
Though near at hand may be the panther's lair.
We urge our beasts, and in a dark defile
I hail my friend to tarry here awhile.
Addressing him, I said, ' Come, tell to me,
For lost am I as in an unknown sea
With reckoning gone, to every quarter blown,
The ground delusive, unstable, unknown ;

Among these hills in jungles dense immured,
The guiding star of day from sight obscured,
No friendly mark my place on earth to find,
With compass varying, barometer unkind.
Oh ! tell me, friend, how distant lies the land
Of fair Petropolis for which we stand ?'
   He thus replies : ' Now, trust yourself to me,
A pilot true I'll prove myself to thee ;
Straight as the crow across the landscape flies
So straight and true the path of honour lies.
Though aberrations seem beyond control,
The constant needle trembles to the pole,
And though the sun obscured with mists remains,
With indications of the coming rains,
And though the distance may to you seem far,
Still reckon me your friend, your guiding star.'

   Then on we ride, from danger never free,
Now from a slip, and now a fallen tree,
Now in the mire, and now in stiffened clay,
Across palm-stalks laid down to mend the way,
And then a brook that's running swift and deep,
The unknown bottom and the slippery steep,
Until emerging into light of day,
Out from the wood upon the broad highway,
Where ladened mules jostle, swerve and dash,
On every side the softened clay they splash ;
Encountering others, with a crash and thud
Flounder, collide, bespattering each with mud ;
With rough bull-hides lashed down across their backs
To keep the produce dry within their packs,
Most difficult we find to clear the rush,
The flying mud the colliding mules crush.
As now abreast, the miry way we ply,

On either side again plantations lie,
A pounding mill, quaint, primitive, and weird,
Beside the road, and by a stream is reared ;
Quite unattended, slowly lifts its head,
And pounds the coffee in a mortar laid.
The ponderous beam strikes with a blow of might,
And thuds and creaks throughout the lonely night.

   My guide rides on, and never seems to tire,
Perceives me labouring through a sea of mire ;
' Come on,' says he, 'and bear up bravely, friend ;
The journey long is drawing to an end.
I guess you'd rather now be under sail,
And, snugly reefed, be driving through a gale ;
Blow high or low, there's none throughout the fleet
To envy thee thy rough uneasy seat.'
   ' That taunt,' I said, ' I must confess to you,
More galling is to me that it is true ;
Prefer I could the foaming flashing main,
A flowing sheet to be my courser's rein.'
Then, spurring on, I give my beast the reins
Up to his side ; my friend, amused, exclaims,
' The iron horse for me, hot-breathing steam,
The rush and rumble of the flying team ;
The spinning wheels, the fiery meteor trail,
The fleeting train upon the slippery rail ;
To read, to smoke, to loll the time away,
And ride at ease along the iron way.'

   And now a roadside *venda* comes to sight,
At which we halt, and from our beasts alight,
On benches sit, and from a butt in draught
A pint of rosy Lisbon wine is brought ;
Refreshment take, await a passing shower,
To feed our nags and pass away an hour ;

To rest disposed, a brace of pipes produced,
And flakes of fine Virginia introduced ;
Converse at ease, from off the miry road,
And friendship found us in that happy mood,
Where mind to mind, and thought in common ran.
Ah ! what is man without his brother man
To plan, to plot, to think, to feel, commune,
And conquer all things by their high presume ?

My friend interprets all our wants and needs,
In English words my talk with him proceeds.
' Now, tell me, friend, if you will be so good,
How first you made yourself be understood ;
For, left alone, whatever I may seek
Seems quite impossible for me to speak.'

' Well, yes, I reckon, friend, it would you please
To see how I got through with Portuguese.
Begin, I guess, as meek as missionary
When I confront them with my dictionary.
They rattle on, and work both head and hand,
Gesticulate to make me understand.
To "slower speak " I'm always pleading, praying,
That I may catch distinct what they are saying.
Try then my book, but ne'er a word can find
That I have caught and settled in my mind ;
Then force a smile, hob-nob with patience good,
As though I had their meaning understood.

Again my book to find a word to say,
Speak slow and clear, so that my listener may
Full comprehend, but, oh ! they are so dumb
I don't believe they know their mother-tongue,
So get impatient, slap my book, and skittish—
End by blaming them in thorough British.'

We mount again, although continued rains
In showers assail us ; and my friend exclaims,

' Petropolis ! we'll on and halt no more,
Though darkness covers, and the heavens pour ;
Though muddy roads beset our mules' feet,
And most uneasy's found the saddle's seat ;
We will not stop until we're well in sight,
The cheering blaze of civilization's light.'

We then push on, the woodland's silence broke
By the loud barking of the tree-frogs' croak ;
The rain blown past, the stars light up the skies,
Like meteoric atoms flash the flies ;
Swarm on a tree to settle for the night,
And fire the bush with incandescent light ;
As sparkling gems the sprayey branches hung,
Across the road a glowing flame was flung.
Too quickly past, for now in shadows deep,
We trust implicitly to our mule's feet,
Hang to his sides, and let him travel on,
To pick the way as best he may along ;
Till fair Petropolis my mind relieves,
And the bright hotel two tired souls receives.
A genial host, of English extract he,
Complaisant, generous, bountiful, and free,
With hands extended, at the open door
Welcomes my guide, a well-known friend of yore.
' How are ye, Jake ? companion, too, I see ;
A friend to you must be a friend with me.'
Then calls aloud to all his sable band
Of woolly negroes, and on either hand
Consigns our beasts to one's peculiar care,
Directs another to a meal prepare,
A third the bath with water warm to feed,
With change of raiment as his friends may need ;
Enjoins them all to study our behests,

And treat us kindly as his special guests.
    Assembled here, a knot of English find,
A few Brazilians seemingly inclined
To know their ways, their language learn to speak,
And find amusement in the eve's retreat.
    Here bagatelle and billiard balls are rolling ;
Piano grand, a tenor voice carolling.
And some at chess, upon a move dilating ;
And some on trade and politics debating,
Their coffee sip, their cigarettes enjoy,
Whilst draughts and dominoes their minds employ.
    We dress and dine, the long saloon regain,
Where good companionship and prudence reign,
And where our *chef* with genial words attends
To all suggestions from his guests and friends.
    A leading spirit of the assembled throng,
To watch decorum, or to sing a song,
Or play a game ; for he can teach them all
To mate a king or place a billiard ball.
    Still in his heart the love of England hung ;
He sings the songs his youth had often sung,
Of glorious deeds performed by sea and land,
Of Neptune's heroes fighting hand to hand.
With songs domestic and of rural life,
Gives 'Tam o' Shanter' with the patient wife,
Of life's carousings, and its many ills,
And 'Auld Lang Syne' awakes Brazilian hills.
    The evening spent, with light a negro led
Us to our rooms, and to a wholesome bed.
Contented slept throughout the night, and sound,
Till Sol in strength was drying up the ground ;
When up we start, for time had gained apace
When I should rise to look around the place.
    Our host encounter, with his usual smile ;

Is pleased to show me through his domicile,
And round his grounds, which he with skill and art
And patient toil laid out in every part.
  And here is culture of his own creation,
The tropic fruits with northern vegetation ;
Banana fronds luxuriant spreading fair,
And orange-trees whose blossoms fill the air
With fragrance sweet, and form the shady groves
And avenues along the well-kept roads.
  Then on we wander through the wooded dell,
Where lovely palms and spreading fern-trees dwell,
As o'er the vale the Turkey buzzard soars,
A naiad there its crystal liquid pours.
High from a rock the silver stream depends,
Pure, cool and bright on rocks beneath descends ;
Loud o'er their bed the gurgling waters run ;
Bound high and bright and glitter in the sun ;
And rushing on through clefts along the dale,
Is lost to view in an umbrageous vale.
  Then back to dine, the goodly dame we found,
With daughters three, full occupied around,
Against the rule, yet all industrious these,
Much for their health, and more their sire to please.

  And sons have they ; whilst some at school engage,
Others in Rio learn a useful trade ;
Devoted all to each, and pure and free,
In conscience strong, and firm in unity.
All prejudice of foreign lands survive,
They show Brazilians how to work and thrive.
  The meal discussed, I rise to give adieux
To honest folk, and off my way pursue ;
Columbia's hand I grasped, the friend I'd made—
With hearty shaking, thus to him I said :

' Adieu, my friend ! we ne'er may meet again ;
Remembrance long my memory will retain
Of all your kindness, and the journey through
The wilds of nature seldom brought to view.

' And hence in life, my friend, my pledge shall be
With Anglo-Saxons peace and unity ;
Distinct as nations, rivals in the chase
For liberty to all the human race ;
March side by side, and wise enough to see
The nobleness of blood fraternity.'

' Adieu,' he cries, ' regards to old John Bull :
I trust that long we may together pull ;
The truce may last, friend, for a generation,
But rivalries don't end at liberation.

' His boast is great that he should rule the sea,
And trying to his nerves that boast must be :
America, I reckon, must be ours,
In spite of all his boast and all the powers ;
From north to south acknowledge our control,
New York the hub, I guess, round which they roll.

' Then he is welcome, friend, to guard the seas
From plundering hordes and dastard piracies ;
And hold his own around his sea-girt fold,
And all his progeny throughout the world !'

With this I start, the mount descend again,
The road well kept, zigzagging to the plain,
Through verdant vales, towards the lake I draw
Across the flat, and to the port Maùa ;
Then take the boat and steam across the bay,
Arrive at town before the fall of day,
And joyful feel that fate had set me free,
To see so much of such a fine country.

CANTO II.

RIO DE JANEIRO TO CAPE OF GOOD HOPE.

AGAIN we seek great Neptune's rough abode,
And from this point to circle round the globe,
Eastwards away our lengthy course we shape,
To make the land of Good Hope's boisterous cape.
    The breezes rise, propitious urge the way,
The flying ship submits to no delay ;
We aid her flight, and give her press of sail :
She feels its weight, and scuds before the gale.
    But soon it veers, the south-east trade we take ;
Close hauled and steady, progress good we make.
The nights are bright, the moon lights up the main,
The weather warm and all is snug again ;
I look around on all that eyes may see,
The boundless sky, the glittering silver sea ;
In compass small about I idly stray,
Then on the deck at ease supinely lay ;
So silent all, with nothing to commune,
Except the stars above and brilliant moon.
Peer up the mast, and note the pointed spar
In gyral motions round a far-off star ;
Through space immense, impinging on my eyes,
Invites my thoughts to contemplate the skies.
    Ah ! what a field of romance is there here !
A common bond connecting sphere with sphere ;

In one great whole harmonious nature binds,
And just equivalents for each she finds :
Moving ever; granting animation
To look through eyes into immense creation,
To see with awe her vast and minute forms,
Sublime in grandeur and divine in charms.

Soft-shining moon ! ordained to cast the light
Of glorious Sol upon us through the night,
To guide the wanderer and his way to cheer,
Inspiring confidence, dispelling fear ;
Thou bright attendant of thy mother earth,
Since from her glowing side she gave thee birth !
Down from on high thy silvery beams are thrown,
Around me here and on my far-off home :
What eyes upon thee at this moment fall,
And at thy apex are converging all !
Maybe those eyes that watched my childhood's days,
My rising boyhood and its wayward ways ;
May be those eyes of love that volumes spoke,
With sigh on sigh re-echoing sighs awoke,
When I set sail, to wander o'er the deep,
And left those eyes to gaze on thee and weep.

So clear the night, so pleasant every day,
Games, cares and sports beguile the time away,
As on we sweep across the waters bright,
Till land again comes greeting to the sight.

Two rocks are marked, just at the surface rise,
The ocean's wave across them restless flies ;
Upon them both perpetual labour reigns,
Bellows and Anvil their appropriate names.

We near the shore, and cast a longing eye,
Though no great beauty canwe here descry ;
In Simon's Bay we house our bleaching sails,
For sand-hills noted, and for boisterous gales.

Upon the left, some twenty miles away,
The rising tableland and Table Bay;
Ensconced between the rocky mountain's sides,
The sheltered colony of Cape Town lies;
Snugly secluded, and on either hand
The Lion Mount, and towering tableland.
A snow-white cloud is laid upon the range,
A sure prognostic of the weather's change.

SIMON'S BAY.

By houses neat this sandy bay is faced,
Whose whitened walls proclaim the Dutchman's taste;
Who still plods on a competence to gain,
But ill contents him with the British reign;
But trade he must, and so the drover plies
His useful trade, and to the town he drives
Oxen, proverbial for their length of horn;
A stately pair the head of each adorn.
And meagre flocks of fleecy sheep we find,
With heavy tails, on tumbrils drawn behind;
These in the uplands tended, fed and cared,
Where meads in plenty bound them everywhere.
Driven by fate to quit their pasture lands,
To reach the town through barren drifting sands,
Betake themselves to market and to death,
Panting with thirst, fatigue, and want of breath.
Here as the winds are sweeping o'er the hills,
The fine sand drives, and every crevice fills,
Makes white the decks, invades our eyes and teeth,
Permeates our food and everything we eat.

And now refreshed, refitted, put in shape
To prosecute the voyage around the Cape ;
Preparing all for rough and wintry winds,
Which off this coast the practised seaman finds.

CAPE OF GOOD HOPE TO SINGAPORE.

The anchor weighed, the ready ship is free,
Accepts the breeze and glides away to sea ;
Pursues a course between the south and east,
Of Neptune's gifts anticipates a feast.
   The ocean heaves with long and steady roll,
And Æolus reigns supreme around the Pole,
In volume full directs his winds with force,
And sends us flying on the destined course.
   The mighty ocean throws phosphorent light,
Illumes the waters through the gloom of night,
Which boil and foam and rush on every side,
And flash and sparkle in the rolling tide ;
For miles around the curling waves aglow,
Bound to the ship and frequent flashes throw
Upon her sails, her hull from stem to stern,
As through a sea of shining light she's borne.
   Upon the way a group of islands rise,
And up their sides the bounding billow flies ;
Prince Edward's these upon the chart are shown,
And by their place upon the globe are known.
Volcanic force had placed them where they lie,
To guide the mariner shoot their peaks on high ;
His place distinctly on the earth they tell,
Confirm his care, and bid him long farewell.

Here albatross—sea-birds gigantic—dwell,
Around the isles their thickening numbers swell,
And thousands swoop about the moving ship,
And skim the waves ; their pointed pinions dip
Into the sea, then soaring swiftly high,
Spread out their wings and darken all the sky.

In circle great the navigator plies,
To catch the gales that from the south arise,
And as we trace the waste of waters o'er,
The winds in strength their blustering forces pour.

Heroic Muse ! come, tell in easy strain
Of incidents and dangers of the main;
What acts of valour, individual deeds,
And feats of prowess, emulation breeds.
Say what transpired on that boisterous eve,
As far away the islands fast recede,
When sudden through the ship the startling sound
' Man overboard !' awakes the crew around.
Quick shorten sail, the helm put hard a lee,
Ship broaches to, and meets a fearful sea ;
Huge, towering high, it leaps above the rest,
Its great bulk swelling ; and its curling crest
The bowsprit springs, and dashes o'er the prow,
And sweeps the deck with its abundant flow.

The life-buoy loosed, a boat is lowered fast,
From out of which an officer is cast
By accident—too anxious of delay
To save the life of him that floats away.
The cutter manned, and loosened from the ship,
Is labouring hard upon her toilsome trip ;
The last in danger first assistance lend,
As albatrosses thick on him descend :
With hardened bills they round about him hover,
And strike their victim with tremendous power,

Who barely saved is from a punctured head,
As with their oars they strike the monsters dead.
  The billows heave, and cause a great delay,
The man is neared, and then is thrown away
Just but to seize him.   He, exhausted quite,
Throws up his arms and disappears from sight ;
When from the boat a seaman, plunging, springs,
Fast clutches him and to the surface brings ;
Exulting all, their strong exertions raise,
Their shipmate cheering in loud voice of praise.
  And struggle on, amidst the moaning dirge,
And nearing close are gaining on the surge,
They seize the man who wrestles with the waves,
And drags with him the officer he saves.
  They labour still, although 'tis growing late,
To find the first, or something of his fate ;
The life-buoy see, away some distance from,
Unoccupied, and tossing idly on.
They near the spot, but nothing can they find,
No trace of him they seek is left behind ;
Give up the search ; once more the ship regain,
And leave their comrade buried 'neath the main.

  Meantime, on board, the bowsprit claims our care,
Though sprung severely, keeps its place, and there
It is secured, with spars and fishes long,
With chains and cordage all set taut and strong ;
Auxiliary aids their purpose answer well,
To save the masts and hold the straining sail.
But ere 'tis done more casualties appear,
For all are zealous in the work to share.
One more conspicuously is hurled amain
Into the deep and then washed back again.
  Tremendous seas ! the ship terrific rolls,

And lying to the canvas ill controls.
To hoist the boat and grapple with her crew,
The men attentive to their stations drew.
Some active start, and, bounding o'er the side,
A wave bursts up and hurls them in the tide ;
The raging seas no breathing time afford,
And some are grasped, and some are hurled aboard.
And ropes are thrown, and some their bodies lash ;
Into the sea, to save their comrades, dash,
Regardless, each in daring bravery vies,
And cast their own to save each other's lives.

When all is done, the ship, brought under sail,
Again drives on, and steady through the gale
The roll is called to know who missing are,
Evading still their efforts and their care.
One answers not, nor will he e'er again,
The cause of all no further cares will claim.
The ship runs free, and stronger gales arise,
With easy plunge across the sea she flies,
Nor reef a sail, nor lessen any speed,
Although each spar is bending like a reed.
The cordage proves unequal to the strain,
The braces fly, the mainyard snaps in twain.
Still on she bounds, and onward lively springs,
The yard in danger hanging by the slings.

A sabbath morn.   At once unbend the sail,
So shall we profit by the favouring gale.
Hand down the spar, the broken pieces bind
With small spare booms about the deck they find.
Fish round the whole, convert the tapering yard,
And on the mast the bulky mass is reared,
Clumsy appears, in strength it does not fail
To stretch the canvas to the powerful gale.

Then on we bound, pursue the watery course,
The wind still fair, nor lessened in its force.
High at the topmast's head the sailors stand,
To scan the sea around and search for land
Or passing sail, to keep a watchful eye
For anything except the sea and sky.
 A week is passed, when from beneath a cloud
Land is perceived, the look-outs hail aloud
From topmast high, and from the prow below,
' Land ho ! away upon the starboard bow !'
Here in mid-ocean bold the islands stand,
The landmark's sighted named Kerguelen's Land,
Or desolation, handed down to fame
From barren soil left by the crater's flame.
Close by the rocks we sail and swiftly sweep,
As the stout ship ploughs up the briny deep,
And by them fly and urge the way along,
The wind continuous, steady, fair and strong.
North-eastward stand, as on a circle sail,
To catch the strong south gales which seldom fail ;
Though long the route, the powerful winds are ki nd,
The goal desired shall we the quicker find.
Prefer we do to bear with Neptune's waves,
Than farther north to be becalmed for days,
Maybe for weeks, within the tropic zone,
The sport of Sol and breathless waves alone.

 The seas are long and high, the wind is hoarse,
As the good ship is borne upon her course.
On every side she spurns the flashing spray,
Through night's dark shadows and bright sparkling day ;
And on she bounds, the watery way she cleaves,
Runs with the wind and with the waves she flees.
As to a nymph she flaunts her flowing robes,

About her breast the spray of ocean throws ;
Sports with the sea, and tries a lead to gain,
Drives through the waste, and swoops along the main.
We near the land, although far out of sight,
Of great Australia, bearing on the right ;
To northward keep, and find that every day
Brings brighter skies and Sol's benignant ray.
Into the zone of Tropics' soft expanse,
The southern gales force on the quick advance,
With ardour less, still strong and steady blow,
And seem to follow us where'er we go.
    Onward ever, till the joyous shout
Of ' Land ahead !' is passed from mouth to mouth.
Great Java's head breaks clear and towering high,
Bold, black and frowning intercepts the sky.
Close by its base, on which the wild waves break,
We clear the point and enter Sunda's Strait ;
Between the land a kindlier welcome find,
As ocean's wild domain is left behind.
On green-clad hills we rest the eager eye,
From off the wastes of naught but sea and sky.

    Soft blows the wind, the waters smooth and bright ;
The islands green bask in a sea of light,
And perfumed air that gentle Zephyr breathes
From lands of spice across the silvery seas—
Those Eastern seas, whose balmy glories long
Have waked the echoes of their praise in song ;
Have borne the planter to the fruitful strand
To tame a race, and yoke it to the land ;
Have lured the trader to its teaming fonts,
And nursed the pirates in their sheltered haunts.
    Sail gently on, the islands thread between,
The glittering waves dance in a rippling sheen ;

Our long sea voyage drawing to an end,
A few more days our destination send;
The main in sight, we near the wished-for shore,
And cast our anchor safe at Singapore.
To rest awhile, away from southern gales,
Re-fit the ship, and mend the riven sails.

Appear a wreck, the clumsy looking spars,
Proclaim the boisterous gales—the watery wars.
The slackened shrouds and weather-beaten hull,
All tell the story true, complete and full.

SINGAPORE.

Here on his way the mariner stops to rest,
A place convenient 'twixt the east and west,
As on the great highway the island stands,
A central point of vast producing lands;
An oasis upon his way is thrown,
Salubrious, warm, and all that's needed grown.

And now the crew begin to work amain,
Replenish ship and set her right again.
The broken spars for models sent ashore,
And search is made the island round for more,
Nor ready found; the place does not afford
A trunk sufficient for the broken yard.
Small trees there are, and tough and strong and sound,
Together worked, with bands of iron bound,
Complete the yard.   The rest are all prepared
And finished quick, and in their places reared,
With studious care efface the many faults,
And painting cancels Neptune's rough assaults.

Whilst thus engaged, I seek again the shore,

Eager to see new places held in store,
With heart elate am rowed towards the strand,
And feel the charm of setting foot on land.
A charm that's felt alone by those who stray
Far o'er the ocean's lonely watery way.
    And just as Sol had dried away the dew,
And from the earth its quivering vapours drew,
We reach the shore, for fresh provisions seek;
Abundance find, with fruits and roots replete.
Mixed population, English and Chinese,
And some Malays, though very few of these.
The round of stores and Chinese shops is made,
Chinese and English doing all the trade.
Coolies robust—unclothed their sable skin—
Around a mortar large the pestle fling;
Half filled with rice, they pound from morn to eve,
Prepare the grain for winnowing with the sieve,
Then piled in sacks, and ready to be sold,
The staple food of all the Eastern world.
And dext'rously their task of work fulfil,
Stir with the foot while all are pounding still,
With measured stroke they strike in turn around
The steady strokes produce the measured sound
As to machines their work in order tell,
And like machines perform their labour well.

And here we find the busy trading mart,
Of which Chinese absorb the greatest part ;
Whose spacious stores, with wharves project from land,
And on them all the ample products stand,
To be exchanged for dollars current free,
With annas, mace, and pice, and the rupee.
    Through Chinese town we pass, Malay town too,
Whose exhalations on our senses drew ;

To grovelling trade shall health itself be sold,
Accumulating filth as well as gold ?
    Filth here and lucre are together thrown,
And trade will haunt the meanest places known—
The barren rock, the low miasmatic land,
The valley dank, the parched-up desert sand,
The musty room, where cobwebs crowd the wall,
The plainest structure raised into a hall.
Its capital wherein its votaries meet,
And cast the gauntlet at each other's feet,
Wits are their weapons, secret hid to strike
Against the purse-strings of the unwary wight
Who, uninitiated, dares invade
The sacred precincts of unsparing trade.
    Here rendezvous the fleets of nations all,
And numerous are the keels both huge and small.
From earth's extremes it welcomes as to home,
And heeds not what they are or whence they come.
    Imperious trade demands the passage free
For all its ships that cover every sea.
Its key of gold will open every port,
Or hurl its thunders at the opposing fort ;
By one or other must they all give way
Before its conquering, all-absorbing sway.
    But I diverge.   Now let us to the theme,
To scour the land, and see what's to be seen.
Consorting with a friend, the streets we trace,
Into hotels, bazaars, and every place
We roam around, a targe for Phœbus' shafts,
Bright, needle-pointed, hot, and falling fast ;
The bleaching ground reflects the scorching ray,
Vapours arise, in wavy quiverings play.
    We ponies hire, and in the broiling sun
Make for the open road and take a run,

As strangers reckless in the mid-day heat,
That drives the natives into shades and sleep.
  Time is their own, but, passing wanderers, we
Have far to go, and all the world to see,
So let us ride along the road alone ;
The present moment only is our own;
The past is gone, to hope the future given,
And all the rest is kindly locked in Heaven.
  We gain the road, the nutmeg groves among,
On either hand they skirt the way along ;
The verdant fields we scan, and onward go
By villa neat and shaded bungalow.
  Still further yet, more beautiful retreats
Of merchant princes, with their country seats ;
Those Europeans choose the higher land,
Away from jungles low and parching sand,
Where tropic insects swarm, mosquitoes bite,
And keep the body heated through the night.
For here 'tis cool, and shaded round with trees,
Whose branches wave, moved by the woodland breeze ;
Between the breaks of foliage peer the halls,
The stately mansions, with their whitened walls.
  Then back return before the failing light
Shall leave us on the road to darkling night ;
For though a colony of English here,
For friendly roof at night we've much to fear.
  Caste holds its own, to recognise opposed,
To wandering Englishmen its doors are closed ;
Should night o'ertake, from these must keep aloof,
And seek the humble stranger's friendly roof.
With pleasure he will share his meat and drink,
Nor care what all the world may say or think.

STRAITS SETTLEMENTS.

To ship again.   Down through the straits she moves
Among the settlements for health to cruise ;
And for a day we at Malacca stayed,
Supplied with fruits, and curries ready made.

Then weigh again, across the waters stand,
And quickly bring to view Sumatra's land ;
And lay along its coasts, then back away
Across the strait towards the high Malay.

As zephyrs breathing from the spice-grown shore,
Down through the strait a flood of odours pour ;
And far to sea the sylvan breezes stand,
And cast a scented halo round the land.

On ocean's lap green isles recline at ease,
Whose charm's discovered by the softest breeze
Fanning its breast, and as it placid lies,
Stealing blue tints from off the calmest skies ;
In varying colours, decked with spangles o'er,
Sparkling it breaks, and fringes all the shore
By which we steer, and roam the coast around,
Till at Penang our anchor takes the ground.

A pleasing spot, where once an active trade
The place to fame of some importance made ;
The eye the proof of fallen traffic greets
In tufts of grass that grow throughout the streets.

Neglected wharves, no m re the Chinese fleet
Of trading junks fills up the void complete ;
They find the port where trade had shifted o'er,
The greater centre, growing Singapore.

I wander round to seek and see the whole,
And through Malay Town onward take a stroll,
Where high on poles its habitations stand

To elude the noxious vapours of the land ;
Whose walls are dry, and not devoid of art,
In which the stout bamboo affords its part ;
Against the wind the Indian matting proof,
The leafy palm supplies the coolest roof.
   Health-giving baths in every street abound
From open wells, all walled secure around ;
The air smells sweet, a mellowing warmth that glows,
And from the fruitful earth a moisture flows :
A sense of softness permeates the whole,
And tropic's languor rests upon the soul.
   Still walking on among the suburbs rove,
And wander through the nutmeg's pleasing grove :
The bursting fruit as peaches hanging high,
Its scarlet mace disclosing to the eye.
And passing through, emerging in the road,
Where still remains the merchant's neat abode,
With avenues laid out in curving lines,
On either side is edged by ripening pines.
   Along the road and by the grassy fields,
Where growing rice its great abundance yields,
Where lime and orange trees and mango high,
And spice of all kinds, in luxuriance lie.
   Tall sugarcanes in swampy flats abound,
The plantain's foliage casts its shade around ;
At intervals descend the genial showers,
And wash the leaves of Nature's fairest bowers.
   A brook I cross, and all along its side
The natives lave their garments in its tide ;
Whilst at their feet the gurgling waters run,
Suspended in their hands, before the sun,
Their flimsy cloths to dry and bleach retain,
And half denuded wait to dress again.
   Then night, advancing, terminates my stay :

Again the ship for sea is under way,
Cruising the isles around the waters o'er,
And back once more return to Singapore.

Here long we lie fast bleaching in the sun !
Most ardent pray that orders soon may come
To anchor weigh, once more to set us free
Upon the wide, refreshing, silver sea.
Then from the main there comes a tale of woe,
Which stirs our ire and makes the blood to glow :
Two half-starved creatures from a tiny boat,
For four long weeks in it they'd been afloat,
Exposed to all the dangers of the sea,
From Borneo's coast and from its pirates flee.
They now arrived in such an abject state,
Laboriously their doleful tale relate ;
But when restored, and free from every foe
They told their long and tedious tale of woe.

PIRATES OF BORNEO.

' From West Australia, bound to Chinese seas
With general cargo in exchange for teas,
Becalmed upon the Bornean coast we lay,
An hour before the sun proclaimed the day ;
When, peering through the haze, perceiv'd a *prahu*
Towards us draw, and cautiously to row ;
Advancing near, disclosed a numerous band
Snake-like were stealing from the nearest land.
' At once we guessed their errand boded ill,
And dire alarms began each breast to fill ;
A boat was cleared that at the davits hung,

And into it a bag of biscuit flung.
  'We snatch a compass, and some clothing too,
A keg of water with spare bedding threw :
Which barely done : The pirates rapid glide
Towards the ship, and clamber up her side.
  'A fight ensued in which our captain led,
And with a cutlass struck the foremost dead,
About him laid—the pirates fought so well,
That at his feet the greatest number fell ;
With handspikes fought against such odds in vain,
For by their spears and kriss were many slain ;
Thrown from the ship and cast into the tide,
Contending hot, the gallant fellows died.
  'I and my mate, though wounded, sought the boat,
And from the mêlée cast ourselves afloat ;
In dire presage we pulled away with might
And found our safety in a speedy flight.
  'No thought we gave of how or where to steer,
The pirates seemed the only cause for fear,
And welcome night had drawn its sable veil
Ere we, to rest our limbs, of it avail.
  'Next morn, as dawn brought forth its hazy light
We saw the pirate-land was still in sight ;
Towards its coast we dare not ply the oar,
But stretch to sea and shun the fatal shore.
  'Nor whither knew ; but sober thought and rest
Had told the main lay somewhere in the west ;
For it we steer our course, in hope to find
Some passing sail or stroke of fortune kind
To snatch us from the pitiless, frowning sea,
Our thoughts relieve and set us once more free.
  'Long days we passed upon the glassy deep,
With ocean's waters calmed and hushed to sleep ;
A scanty share of bread and water use,

This chance of life too soon we fear to lose.
With utmost strength we toiled from day to day,
The scorching sun poured down his brightest ray,
So fierce his shafts upon us blazed and beat
That face and hands were blistered with the heat.
For nine long days we struggled with the oar,
Though far we knew must lie the distant shore.

   ' The tenth bright dawn, as Sol rose from the sea,
More red than usual he seemed to be ;
By this we augured, from his crimson light,
A breeze may find us ere the coming night.

   ' The sign proved true, for soon we sniff the air :
Draw o'er the leaden waste crisp, fresh, and fair :
But, passing on, it leaves us once again
Hoping 'gainst hope, and striving but in vain.

   ' Still not despair, another may not fail,
And fortune in the boat had placed a sail ;
That shred of canvas all our hopes inspire,
May yet suffice to grant our great desire,
May waft us o'er the dark and threatening sea
Towards the coast, though far away it be.

   ' Again there comes a whisper from the deep,
And breezes steal around and by us sweep ;
With stronger voices they begin to hail,
To step the mast and spread the hopeful sail ;
The mandate catch, with joy we raise the mast,
Our dark forebodings all receding fast ;
We skim the sea, the breeze we run before,
With great relief we rest the tedious oar ;
Then calculate our speed, and, something more,
Reckon most closely on our scanty store ;
Then drop it short, all reckoning we scout,
So little is the chance its lasting out.

Demure we sat and gazed the boundless deep,
In turn we watched, in turn we fell asleep ;
High rose the seas, the breezes stronger blew,
Poised on the wave the wingèd dinghy flew.
Though hardly pressed, and billows threat the bow,
The sail we touch not nor a reef allow.
For four long days and nights these perils last,
And death seemed borne on every surge that passed.
Still strove we much to grasp the steering oar,
Our sinews tried till we could stand no more ;
Exhausted fell, from toil and raging thirst,
Our swollen veins with fever well-nigh burst ;
And all seemed lost ; we seize the living draught,
And with it all our hopes of life were quaffed.
But we were saved : the gale attains its height,
And gradually subsides towards the night ;
And clouds had gathered fast and promised more
That heavenly rains should down upon us pour.
We blessed the rain for which we panted long,
Which copious fell, continuous and strong ;
Prepare to catch the streams before they fail,
And spread across the boat the saving sail.
New life receive, our hopes again are raised,
Feel grateful for the boon, and Heaven is praised.

'And soon 'twas past, with all its bounties spent
Had well supplied the needed element.
Half filled the boat, too dangerous all to hoard,
Reluctantly we threw some overboard ;
Retained enough to last a length of course,
And calm our fears from such a dreaded source.
'Fortune still smiled ; the morning's sun we hail,
And in the west we think we see a sail ;
Something there was, but what could not descry :

Our fears still hang towards the enemy.
Or friend or foe, we steer towards it straight
To solve the mystery and our course to make.
For hours we pulled ere we could well maintain
'Twas pointed rocks upshooting from the main.
With straining eyes we gaze upon the rocks,
Perceive the sea-birds hovering round in flocks,
With stronger strokes direct towards them stand,
Eager to learn if on them we might land ;
And, craving, think of something there to eat,
Our hunger quench, and all its ravings cheat.
No place for landing could we yet descry,
And round we pulled, and every nook we try,
And judge it hopeless, when with joy is seen
A small unruffled surface in between
The rocks, whose chasms had an opening left
Of space enough to pass us through the cleft.
We watched the chance when heaving swells were spent
To ply the oar, pull swift, so in we went.
We breathe more free, and to our great delight
Fish in abundance greets our hungry sight ;
We climb the rocks, which tear our hands and feet,
To grasp at anything we find to eat.
  ' Birds on their nests at the intrusion stare ;
We seize them quick and hurl them in the air,
And beat them off, most eagerly devour
The eggs which they defend with all their power—
A grateful boon, received in hunger's cause,
Which keeps us from the doom of Nature's laws.
  The sail employ, fulfilling every wish,
And as a net is used to take the fish.
So tempting these, that just as soon as caught,
To eat them raw engaged our foremost thought.
  ' Another course we take to meet desire—

For until now we had no thought of fire :
A glass to catch the burning rays of light—
In better times found useful for the pipe—
Was traced, concealed about our well-soaked clothes,
Which knew no change since first began our woes.

'We search the rocks for fuel, and not a shrub
Could be obtained, but in abundance scrub
Of drift and dried guano thick abound,
Which fills the fissures everywhere around.

' We make a fire, and watch the curling smoke,
Its cheering blaze our grateful senses woke ;
Then cook the fish and eat them, cook again
Till naught of all we had with us remain.

' We clear the boat, land all our scanty stock,
And spread our bedding on the sun-dried rock :
In waters pure our moistening garments lave,
Then catch more fish, undress ourselves, and bathe.
Of comforts think once more in great detail,
And for an awning spread the useful sail ;
In sweet repose we bury all our woes,
Secure from bursting seas and wild internal foes.

' And well we slept, nor did we ope our eyes
Until the sun in force had bid us rise.
Around the place a lonely search we make,
And in the centre find a silvery lake,
A perfect basin, formed on every side,
Some spaces which let in and out the tide ;
And fish in shoals beneath its surface swim.
Across its plain the sea-birds graceful skim,
And heed us not ; but sailing closely near,
Suspect no violence and no danger fear,
But walk around and stay to watch awhile,
And gaze upon the invaders of their isle.
And more we searched the rocky place around,

6

But not a drop of water fresh we found ;
And as we think of this we guard the more
The precious liquid stock we had in store ;
And close we watched, in hope we may descry
Some friendly sail that, near us passing by,
We may attract by signals of distress ;
But how or whence might come we cannot guess.

   ' And as the wind was springing from the west,
Once more we think to dare the watery waste,
Get all to boat, a stock of fish and fowl,
And dried-up scrub to make the bailer boil,
Which in the boat as if by chance was thrown,
To cook what food we may alight upon ;
With loads of eggs, for which we had to fight
Those brave sea-birds, which tried their puny might
Against our strength with such persistent will,
That from defence we sometimes had to kill.

   ' Complete for sea, and with an ample store,
Cast loose the boat, and leave the rocky shore.
Safe from the rocks, with gentle breezes flee,
As our good craft skims gaily o'er the sea ;
To make the main, or, what would please us most,
To catch the trader plying round the coast.

   ' But all too soon again the breezes fail ;
With anxious thoughts we watch the flapping sail,
Then take it in when it assists no more,
And ply with strength again the labouring oar.

   ' Long were the days we rowed upon the deep,
And every night partook of grateful sleep ;
No watch we keep, the glassy ocean, smooth,
Could not affect our course or make us move.

   ' And every morning, with the rising sun,
With care we scanned the misty horizon ;
The needle told us we were steering west,

And the rising sun confirmed us in the test.
But where we were, how far the land away,
A secret deep enwrapped in mystery.
    'And as our stock again is getting low,
We ardent pray the promised breeze to blow,
Slight puffs and whiffs of short duration fly,
Scarce fill the sail, and pass us softly by.
  'We thought we saw the land, the vision flew,
And darkening night, approaching, closed the view,
And morning breaking, anxious still we sought,
But not a speck upon the waters caught ;
Whilst clouds perplexing fall upon the sight,
Delusive fly before our eyes.   And like
The mariner unskilled, with reckoning lost,
In hope and fear upon the ocean tossed,
A sail espies, which may direct his course,
Is wafted off again by adverse force,
The promised land goes melting from our sight,
And buries all our hopes in misty night.

  'We urge our way, and ere an hour had sped
We something saw again bear right ahead ;
With joy we greet the sign, and inward pray
That from our eyes it may not melt away.
    'We watch it close, and there it stands secure,
Its high green sides do all our senses lure ;
With bending oars we make towards the land,
In eagerness to touch its welcome strand.
    'A rocky isle, round which the surges roar,
Forbidding here to land upon its shore ;
But round we row, a better beach to find,
Or where the swell, embayed, will prove more kind.
    'We find it out, and take the shallow sand,
Leap out and drag the boat towards the land :

Exhausted quite, we reach the higher ground,
But not till night had thrown its shades around.

'And here we slept till Sol was shining bright,
And sand-flies rigorously began to bite ;
Then started up to search again for food,
And dive into the thickness of the wood.

'And as we wandered round, delighted, see
A sparkling streamlet running towards the sea ;
Ourselves prostrate upon the rocky bank,
And of its limpid waters deeply drank.

'And down we scrambled over rock and bush,
Now wending careful, then with headlong rush,
Then with a bound once more we safely land
Upon the beach, and stroll along the strand.

'Discouraged more towards the boat we tend,
Still hoping on that fortune soon may send
Some passing sail, or something good to eat,
Or fish, or fowl, or any kind of meat--
To stay the direful need in which we stand,
And satisfy stern Nature's fierce demand.

'Together roam disconsolate around,
When sudden, roused up by a startling sound,
A turtle rushes close by where we stand,
And well-nigh blinds us as it throws the sand.

'Upon its fins pursues its hasty flight,
Ere we can turn to see what gave the fright,
We seize the creature, though much strength we lack,
And struggle hard to turn it on its back.

'Secure we have it, and, with time for thought,
Begin to think what fortune kind had brought ;
A sense of thankfulness at such a find—
Fish, flesh, and fowl together here combined.

And as we view it with our craving eyes,

The starving spectre from our vision flies;
Then back we turn the creatures' eggs to seek,
Embedded in the sand a goodly heap.

   ' We quit the hoard, and run to fetch the boat,
Which quickly launch, and get again afloat :
For now the tide was high, had higher flowed,
And covered all the sand o'er which we rowed ;
Towards the place where our great bounty lay,
Its strong fins flapping loud to get away.

   ' We near the spot, with joy leap to the land,
And haul the boat upon the bleaching sand ;
To make a fire about for drift we look,
To boil the water and the eggs to cook.

   ' Our great good-fortune all our woes atone,
And single-handed had not come alone ;
For while we sat and ate to hearts' content,
Our eyes glanced wistful o'er the element.

   ' A speck we think we see, but it may prove
A myth, for to our eyes it does not move ;
Then look again, with vision clearer see
The speck grows larger, as it seemed to be ;
Then both can see it, and at once decide
It must be something floating in the tide.

   ' And back towards our finny friend repair,
Which still industrious flaps the empty air ;
Then calculate to get it in the boat,
And how much deeper might it make her float.

   ' Again our eyes direct towards the waste,
Our anxious thoughts to satisfy in haste ;
" It is a sail !" we both exclaim at once ;
Our hearts spring joyful as the news announce.

   ' Quick to the boat we drag our heavy prize,
As on its back the helpless creature lies,
And pull away to get within the hail,

And not allow to pass the friendly sail.
  'A huge black *prahu* a trader proves to be,
As close she neared and skimmed along the sea ;
A press of sail had kept us from their view,
And by us o'er the sea she swiftly flew.

  ' We gave a shout so strong that all on board
Turned sharply round towards the sound they heard ;
And talking loud, with great relief, we find
Them luffing up and shooting to the wind,
Her spread of sail all fluttering in the breeze ;
When up we pull, the offered chance to seize ;
With care approach her with our loaded boat,
When from her side they cast the friendly rope.

  ' We lay along in eager haste to know
If we may be admitted to the *prahu :*
A consultation 'rose, in which 'twould seem
Our prize the turtle was the absorbing theme.

  ' By signs we tried to make them understand
That all we wished for was to make the land :
One word we caught from them, and nothing more,
On which we seized and hung—'twas Singapore.

  ' Significant, their motions then declare
The turtle was to be the price of fare ;
We contemplate our prize, admire and pause,
So little dreamed 'twould serve in such a cause.

  ' Then take their offer to assistance lend,
And barter off our great unwieldy friend :
With ropes secured, they hand it o'er the side,
And we were rescued from the boundless tide.

  ' Next day, with great relief, we made the land,
"Twas Singapore were given to understand ;
They brought us close until the harbour find,
Our little boat still towing on behind ;
Then let us go, to seek as best we may

The open roadstead that before us lay.
Upon her way the friendly craft proceeds,
We give her hearty cheers as she recedes;
Then raise the sail, a light wind blowing fair,
We make the harbour straight, and here we are.'

   The story told, the news vehement ran ;
The word goes forth ' For sea !' the work began ;
The tanks are filled, the sails are eager bent,
The barge away for ammunition sent.
   Boats laden deep arrive, provisions stored,
The anchor weighed to hunt the pirate horde,
And active all with spirits bounding high,
' For Borneo !' ' For Borneo !' the cry.
   And as the ship is wafted on the way
Towards their haunts, impatient of delay,
The busy crew, whose wrath had risen high,
Look to their arms, expectant service nigh.
Each cutlass whet, to carbines give inspection,
To deal the buccaneers a sharp reception.
   The land we make, and close in with the shore,
Send off the boats, the rugged coast explore ;
All dangers dare pertaining to the sea,
The rocks, the shoals, the neighbouring isles alee.
   And find the ship beneath the higher land,
A blackened wreck upon the sandy strand ;
Destroying flames had set the pirates' mark,
And left with charred-up ribs the plundered barque,
A prey to waves to work their will with speed,
To efface the stain, and blot the dastard deed.
   Then quit the wreck to search around the land,
Exploring creeks, and traversing the strand ;
Then scour the plains, in jungles deep deployed,
But not a fragment of the ship destroyed

Could there be found, or any creature plying
To tell us where the pirate gang were lying.
　We sail the coast along, on shore renew
The search, in vain, to find the dastards who,
With plunder gorged, had sneaked without delay
Up winding streams, and hid themselves away,
To share the booty with their chiefs renowned
For deeds of violence all the coasts around.
　Those buccaneers, who all the seaboard hold,
Have grown in power, are insolent and bold;
All rights usurp, all freedom they suppress,
With strongholds raised they every tribe oppress;
And deem they rob, with safe immunity,
The world at large with high impunity.
　But there's a power of which they little dream,
A power unheeded as it is unseen—
A power, though far away, and all unknown,
Shall stretch its arms, and strike the pirates' home:
A power that will demand a strict account,
And judge them right to pay the full amount.
　A nucleus formed there is, within their isle,
Round which its summoned forces shall defile;
Shall watch them well, and weave its web around,
And catch the pirates on their hunting-ground.
For here is one who quits the scenes of home,
In his own yacht, unaided and alone,
Who seeks the pirates' haunt, and settles there,
And shows what man can do if he will dare.
　A man of honour, gentle, kind and brave,
Foregoes his ease a hardy race to save;
Wild seems the thought, and reckless mad the plan,
Conceived and carried by a single man.
But so it is, with high intentions pure,
The début gained, the end he might secure:

No fears can daunt, no dire obstruction baulk.
Here down he settles on the Sarawâk ;
By acts persuasive, enterprises bold,
He beards the pirates in their strongest hold,
Adopts their tongue and tells them what he means,
And peaceful tribes draw to him in his schemes.
He builds a fort, assisted by the few
Who outward sailed with him, composed the crew
Of the trim yacht, now anchored on the tide
Of waters smooth that by her gently glide.
Combines her force to an attack resent,
Protects the post with her light armament.
He then instructs to trade with neighbouring isles,
The lawless keeps in check by force or wiles.
The friendly tribe applaud his gentle sway,
Rajah proclaim him, and his laws obey.

He feels secure, and tracks the pirate hosts,
Directs the British force around the coasts ;
The inland tribes in gratitude are bound,
And ' Rajah Brooke !' make everywhere resound—
The foreign man who saved them from the yoke
Of pirate rule, and all its powers broke.

Here, as we cruise discouraged round the land,
A steamship spy directly towards us stand :
And as she neared an Indian warship proved,
In company came, and close beside us moved.
Civilities pass between the national ships,
As Neptune's sons can feel in ardent grips ;
No selfish thought with these a place can find,
A mutual cause inspires the generous mind.
Was here to watch, in concert to assist,
Last from Penang, her name the *Nemesis ;*
Had come to find us, and to bring the news

A pirate fleet was mustering all its crews,
With chiefs renowned preparing hostile host,
To put to sea to rove around the coast.
The time of calms had taken at the flow,
With dire intent on ships becalmed to go.
Its aim was clear and placed beyond a doubt.
That day the news from Sarawâk was brought.
We catch the tale inspired, and canvas make,
Our course towards the stream Cerberus take,
To watch the hell-dog at its foaming mouth,
To learn how soon the horde may be about :
Nor waited long, for plying close we saw
The schooner yacht come down, towards us draw :
And gave the word, the fleet was fully manned,
And shortly would descend towards the strand.
All are alert, persistent calm ensues ;
The boats prepared with their respective crews,
All fully manned, and night and day prowl round,
To pounce upon their prey whenever found.
The steam-launch hies, and goes well up the stream,
To give the signal out as soon as seen ;
Discerns them first, and quick the news she brought,
The pirate fleet for sea was standing out.

A broad continuous line approaching fast,
Black as the slime that venomous creatures cast,
The running stream ebbs on towards the coast,
And bears it down, and disembogues the host.

Long snake-like *prahus* that swiftly glide along
To tom-tom strains, and short discordant song,
Of warlike deeds, by pirates sung before,
The song which these are doomed to sing no more.

The next shall be a yell of wild despair,
When retribution seeks to strike them there ;
That retribution lurks behind the land,

Shall soon be seen in conflict hand to hand ;
Shall crush the noxious spawn ere it hath birth,
And clear the evil gang from off the earth.

The boats are off, and out to sea away,
To head the fleet and bring it there to bay.
It onward sweeps, devoid of line or rank,
Or thought of spite that hangs upon its flank ;
High in their minds the joys of plunder rise :
Delusive dream of life, how swift it flies !
Clear of the land, *Nemesis* steams away
To cut them off, across their rear to lay :
She and the launch assigned positions take,
To hem them round, and all the mass to rake.
The pirates soon our dire design had caught,
And all the fleet was hushed as quick as thought.
A moment more, and then they do descry
Their only chance is now to fight or die.
Their voices raise, and with a general shout
Turn round at bay, elect to fight it out ;
Defiant yell, which o'er the water floats
Their jingalls firing at the approaching boats.
The last they sent, for by this signal given
The pirate host is in confusion driven
Headlong, pell-mell ; against each other drive,
Leap with a scream, and roll into the tide.
For from the boats the ball and grape shot rain,
And meteor rockets whisk their tales of flame ;
Full in their front the flying weapon hies,
And in their midst the bursting fragment flies.
The fiery serpent hisses in their ears,
Annihilates, or strikes them dumb with fears ;
Encircles round as with a wall of fire,
Through which they cannot break, nor dare retire.

Our sailors dash, too eager for the fray,
Towards the mass with hardy strokes give way,
Drive in their midst, and laying their oars in,
They hand to hand with cutlasses begin.

Some poise the shot with force inspired to throw,
And send it crashing through the yielding *prahu*,
Which quickly fills ; and still the demons fight ;
On every side debarred from hasty flight,
Unto our boats they cling in wild despair,
But havoc is the word, and none to spare.

From out the host, in desperation's rage,
A few there are who dare the foe engage,
As like a cat the agile Dyak springs,
And 'mongst the crew his tawny body flings.

With kris in hand, up with a sudden bound,
Selects his man, and plants an ugly wound ;
Clings to his foe, and hacks his manly breast
Before he can be rescued by the rest.

The fight is close and short, the spouting gore
Exhausts their strength, and smears their bodies o'er ;
Fierce is their grip, they tumble o'er the side,
And, locked together, roll into the tide.

Nor time to watch them where their bodies float,
For by this act they threat to board the boat ;
But off she backs, and ere they've time to spring
Full in their eyes our men a rocket fling ;
The flaming meteor checks the wild design,
And to their fate compels them to resign.

The steaming launch aloof at distance lay,
Ready to pounce and track the straggling prey,
When some, more bold, from out the mêlée drew,
As swift as arrows from her prowess flew ;
She with a shot o'ertakes them in the chase,
The sinking craft at once resigns the race

When fairly sunk, then off she goes again,
And in the hunt pursues the flying game ;
Now singly fights, and now again she runs
Within the range of *Nemesis'* active guns.

As like a hound which guards his master's sheep,
With watchful eye upon the flock to keep,
Runs round the whole, and if one chance to stray,
He quick pursues, and tracks it on the way ;
Yelps, barks, and bites, and makes the straggler leap
Towards the whole, and herds them in a heap ;
So with the launch, the pirate host to guard,
Keeps well aloof, and circles round the horde,
To centre drives where *Nemesis* in their midst
Is using them as would a mill its grist.

Arm of science ! let me now declare
What retributive feats fell to thy share ;
How steam subdued had lent its active aid
To *Nemesis*—who casts her dreadful shade
On all around—whose sputtering iron and flame
From out her sides in streams continuous came.

Some of the host hang to the shattered wreck,
And some in desperation seek the deck
Of the fatal ship which meets with fire and sword
The active few who vainly try to board,
Who up her sides with kris uplifted dare,
Where pike and bayonet hurl them in the air.

Though beaten down, in numbers still they cling,
As bees cling to the victim of their sting ;
Fill up her spokes, and, crouching on her flukes,
She gives a turn, and grinds the swarthy brutes.
And goes ahead, and back again she steals,
And slaps them under with her crushing wheels.
In streams infernal pours her fire and flame,

In all the fury of her vengeful name.
　Above the dim of war, goes up the sound
Of mingled yells and groans from all around ;
What woe, what curses deep, that hour gave birth,
How sternly judged their doom of hell on earth !

　The strife goes on until there's not a boat
Whole on the surface left, or seen to float,
Of pirates who had gaily sung the song
Of plundering conquests as they pulled along.
　That little cloud that lurked within the bay
Had cast its shadow, and had closed the day ;
Eternal sleep succeeds life's transient breath,
And all is hushed in everlasting death.
　Of all their numbers very few escape
To reach the land, and there their tale relate
To chiefs renowned, the dreadful truth to tell,
Where lies their fleet and what to it befell.
　Complete the work, and *Nemesis* takes the van,
And back we steer towards fair Labuan ;
Where coal abundant on the surface lies,
And forest trees luxuriant from it rise ;
Which, as it should, yields up its bounties stored,
To those who know the use of such a hoard.
　These rovers quit the wealth-abounding field,
For what few things a plundered ship might yield ;
And little dream or care the labour lost,
The severed ties their dastard acts have cost ;
Take what their ignorance suggests the best,
And to destroying flames consign the rest.

　Here halt awhile, then cruise around the land,
To show our force, and awe the pirate band ;
For Bruni make, run up as close as may,

And threat the town, and bring the chiefs to bay.
　Then back again, for Sarawâk we steer,
And watch with interest the mainland near ;
Make for the stream, the jungles get among,
The crooked course meandering along ;
Arrive at Quop, and to an anchor come,
And Rajah Brooke salute with twenty-one.
　Dense jungle woods surround on every side,
And dip their verdure in the shaded tide ;
The booming guns re-echo through the shore,
With voice more loud than ever heard before ;
Raise high the crouching natives' anxious fears,
As mimic thunder rattles in their ears.
　Few days are spent upon the sylvan flood,
The strange game-hunting through the tangled wood,
Or from the bank to cast the barbèd hook,
Or round the native village take a look.
Half-naked men, and naked children quite,
With swarthy women in their costumes light,
Where houses mean and scattered huts are found,
On poles, above the bank, high from the ground,
And view the site where, on a future day,
Beneath their Rajah's vigorous, even sway,
The town shall swell, and trade, with rapid strides,
Shall raise its pillars to their wondering eyes.
　The stream that now runs idly clear and free
Shall bear its laden navies to the sea ;
With kindred channels take its destined place,
To feed and clothe the growing human race.
Here, far inland the noble warship lies,
Washed by the waters of the meeting tides ;
The banks surrounding bind her close within,
And leave but little space for her to swim.
She bold appears, and bears her banner high,

Which over all superior seems to fly ;
Dictatress stern, that violent deeds should cease
A guarantee secure of future peace ;
The pioneer to welcome useful trade,
The harbinger of freedom to the slave ;
All-powerful, to petty tyrants awe,
And teach them truths of even-handed law.

 Then down we sail, along the coast-line ran,
And soon descry again fair Labûan.
Close by its strand we let our anchor drop,
And for a week we at the island stop.

 This settlement, new-made, but spreading fast,
To many pioneers has proved their last.
Miasmatic fevers lay their bodies low,
And numbers quit it and the unseen foe—
Till human skill the moistened land shall drain,
And, health assured, they may return again.
 From Labûan we ply the coast along,
Pass pleasing isles, and anchor at Ambong,
And weigh again, still close to land we lay,
And, cruising on, touch at Maluda Bay ;
Then quit the coast, and out to sea we ran,
And make the isles of soft Balambanqan ;
There stay awhile, then work away from land
Eastward, on for Cagayan Sooloo stand ;
To visit chiefs, and let the pirates see
The power of England floating o'er the sea.
 Within the reefs their haunts protected lie,
But we determined to an entrance try ;
Steer for the isle, undaunted lead the way,
Where rocks unknown across the passage lay ;
Grope with the lead, and feel the shallows round,
Yet fail withal to pass the treacherous ground,

For now a sandbank holds the good ship fast,
The ebbing tide is running swiftly past.
To get her clear prove all our efforts vain,
Until the tide in flood returns again.
Meantime prepare—the boats drop from the side,
And from the deck are launched into the tide.
With guns and shot are loaded fast and deep,
To light the ship the flowing tide to meet.
The weather fine, a gentle breeze prevails,
Sufficient in its force to fill the sails,
The rising moon illuminates the night,
And finds us working by its silvery light.
With anchor laid, and hawser ready taut,
Await the rising tide to heave her off.
Around it swells, and soon attains its height,
And sets the ship on even keel upright.
The order goes, the boatswain trills his pipe,
Loud stamp the sailors to the lively fife.
Give something must, the anchor, hawse, or ship,
The first holds steady with a mighty grip,
The capstan whirls, the men apply their strength,
The trembling ship begins to start at length.
Quick and more quick the quivering deck they beat
Until success attends their lively feet ;
The keel is free. the ship afloat, and then
Unload the boats, hoist in, and off again.
      The dawn of morn thus finds us working clear,
And close toward the pleasant low land near.
The ship, with flying colours, boldly runs
Beneath the pirate monarch's threat'ning guns.
Laid broadside on, and ere an hour had flown,
Our chief his orders and his mind makes known :
Two cutters, well equipped and fully manned,
An officer appointed to command,

7

With an interpreter, placed in the boat.
The zealous crews, already lie afloat,
With arms at hand, their oars erect arise,
They dare all risks, or doubtful enterprise.
  ' Be firm !' he cries.   ' Tell that yon haughty lord
Dire retribution waits, with fire and sword ;
Lynx-eyed, is watching all around the shores,
And in full justice ample vengeance pours :
Go, bear this message to his royal ear.
Make him digest it, and our power to fear :
That if another craft in peaceful trade,
By his marauding *prahus* be waylaid,
To strict account we hold the one who reigns,
And will return to wrap his town in flames.
Yes, tell him plain, and tell him truly too,
Short work we'll make of him and all his crew.'

  The boats move off, and landing well succeed,
To carry out the plan their chief conceived,
With arms equipped the sailors spring to land,
And range themselves in line along the strand.
In martial order march up through the town,
Though sentinels block the way and portals frown :
On either side these weak obstructions fling,
And force themselves an audience of the king.
No points of ceremony bar their course,
They go by given leave. or go by force,
To where his majesty in state is found,
His guards and councillors assembled round :
Nor wait for etiquette, or more command,
But in they rush, and to attention stand.

  Their leader then : ' Now, say, we've sought him here
To tell him truths which he must learn to fear,
That he at once from freebooting desist,

Or be prepared to England's power resist :
That if he once allows another fleet
To be despatched our trading ships to meet,
Our orders are, to tell him plain and true,
Short work we'll make of him and all his crew.'

The pirates wince beneath the threat'ning words,
And in their rage clutch at their half-hid swords ;
Short wavy weapons, 'neath their garments' fold,
Whose hilts are studded o'er with shining gold.
And there stop short, for in an instant then
Our sailors' leader calls, 'Attention, men !'
And at the word, at once to all around
Their rattling arms send forth an ominous sound.

That foreign word they may not understand,
But like a charm it acted in command ;
The king grew pale, his voice in accents weak,
Calms his retainers, and essays to speak.
Begins a rambling wild excuse to plead,
And lowly bends to all they had decreed.
Fame trumpet-tongued had spread the news around
And far forestalled us with its echoing sound :
He would not think of piracies, in view,
Of all he heard of us, and all he knew.

' We know enough of Englishmen,' he cries,
' Their deeds of warfare hear without surprise :
Oft have we met them on the watery waste,
And once—almost alone—escaped in haste :
Not many leagues from this our native shore
We felt their prowess then and want no more.
When unprepared, they fight like warriors well —
As some amongst our fellows here could tell—
What they may be when full equipped for fight
We have no mind to know, or try their might.
And since ye will thy countrymen to spare,

The English race shall be our special care.
But there are some now roaming o'er the sea
Whom to destroy becomes our destiny.
Unwholesome craft, obscure and wandering far,
Are proper forage for our dogs of war :
With these in future we will be content
To fight and conquer on our element.'

Our leader joins : ' Let him be undeceived ;
The great highway of nations must be freed.
Tell him that retribution, stern and dire,
Lynx-eyed, is watching with its sword and fire ;
Our country's ships are not our care alone,
But to all nations shall their blood atone.
Leave them no doubt, no compromising pleas,
We'll seek them out and sweep them from the seas.'
The interpreter the knotty words translates,
And sets the pirate council to debates,
When hushed again, the king essays to rise
And in a voice subdued, he low replies.
' We know we are denounced both near and far—
You call it plundering, and we call it war—
If stay we must, the noble part is played.
And must we then descend to grovelling trade,
Explore the mine, or turn the stubborn soil
In personal contact with the sons of toil.
To war with nature, touch her harden'd breast,
Upon a par with those who, by her blessed
With docile souls, and patience to endure
Their daily tasks in spirit meek and pure ?
So let it be ! Ye may be in the right,
But come what will, we must decline to fight ;
Rich fruits we have, with wild luxurious beeves,
Rice, ginger, nutmegs, anything you please,

All which we render to the warlike race
To compensate their wrath and win their grace.'
   Our leader here rose equal to the task,
'Tell him,' he cries, 'this warning is the last :
By no such parlance can we be deceived,
The goaded Lion is not thus appeased :
No presents he can offer will atone,
His fate on future conduct rests alone :
His beeves we take not, save to us they're sold ;
For them we'll pay in cloths or solid gold ;
But if he dares again desert his post,
Or sends his pirate yawls to prowl the coast,
Or on the ocean seeks unlawful loot,
We'll seize his island and himself to boot.'
   Then round he turns, with stern and lofty mien,
Awaits the interpreter to close the scene :
Marshals his men upon the open plain,
Back to their boats in order leads again.
Short time they spend to argue out the theme,
They leave the pirates to digest the scheme.

CANTO III.

BORNEO TO HONG-KONG.

WE sail away, and cruise the island round,
Send boats ashore, and, fresh provisions found,
Lay in a stock of beasts with grass to feed:
The anchor haul and on again proceed.
The clear blue waters glitter in the light,
We thread the maze of islands green and bright,
And coral reefs as to a network run,
Fringed with the spray that sparkles in the sun.

   The ship moves gaily, with her canvas spread,
Though oft we hear the cry of reefs ahead;
And shelving rocks beneath her bottom lie,
Seen through the azure by the watchful eye.
And there with care the seaman in the chains
Calls out the depths in slow monotonous strains,
Hangs o'er the side, suspended from the shroud ;
' By the mark six !' he boldly calls aloud.

   Silence prevails to catch the fathoms deep,
As o'er the rocks below we swiftly sweep.
' And a half five !' again he hoarsely cries,
So close beneath the keel the bottom lies.
Then hauls the lead, and takes another cast,
And still the shelving rock is shallowing fast :
Surrounds on every side, and to recede
As great a danger waits as to proceed.

And, anxious all, we listen to the sound
Of leadsman's voice, and pass the word around ;
Mute patience reigns, await expectant shocks
Of the great ship against the submerged rocks.
But she, unmindful, runs before the wind ;
Repeated casts again no bottom find :
The reef is cleared, and swift she onward rolls,
And in the distance leaves the threat'ning shoals.
  All danger flown, we greet the rising breeze,
To duties turn, and feel our minds at ease.
And running on we scan the doubtful chart,
And islands find where none are on it marked.
At one of these we anchor in a bay,
And all the crew on shore spend Christmas Day.

  Abandoned huts and marks of fire we find,
The only traces left of human kind.
And grave suspicions rise within each breast
That pirate hordes had used the place for rest.
Perhaps to watch the unsuspecting prize,
Which slowly passing or becalmèd lies.
Wolf like, to wait the early dawn of day,
To pounce aboard and sudden seize their prey.
I wandering through the bushes thick among,
Pursue with care the intricate track along,
And bring before my eyes the sunny strand
Where savage corsairs filled with plunder land ;
In spots unfrequented carousings hold,
Unknown, uncontemplated by the world ;
Which slumbering on will leave to barbarous bands
The desecration of the fairest lands.
  The sailors roam the unknown island through,
But on the fleeting hours so swiftly flew,
Approaching night proclaims the pastime o'er,

And drives them to their boats hauled to the shore.
With ardour raised, we quit the silvery strand,
And 'Christmas Island' name the new-found land.
North east about we ply the sunny way,
And for the group of Philippine Islands lay :
Across the gentle sea Mindora stretch,
Until the town of Zamboanga reach.
But first heave to, our high respects to pay
The Spanish flag, that tracks us on the way.
A tiny war-boat bears it o'er the tide,
The Spanish don mounts up our vessel's side :
In mien punctilious, common to his class,
Grants his consent to let the good ship pass ;
And struts the deck, as though the lives of all
Within the ship were at his mercy's call :
And condescends to give the nearest route,
And even deigns to point the passage out.

As by our side the gun-boat makes delay,
The vessels hug each other while we stay :
As in acknowledgment they seem to be
And bow their heads responsive to the sea.
As a war-horse when sudden called to halt,
Approaches to his side a new-foaled colt,
Heedless of all, the fleeting moments spare
To sniff the stranger o'er, in loving care ;
Tossing his head, impatient of the curb,
That would his high solicitude disturb ;
Nor stays his fondling till his rider's power
Awakes him to the business of the hour :
So with the craft upon the watery way,
As the *Capitan de Puerto* revokes his stay.
They separate, we through the channel reach,
And cast our anchor near the sandy beach.

Next day, alone, I wander to the shore,
And Sol's bright beams full down upon me pour
At Sabbath noon, when tropic's people rest
From worldly cares, as by the heat oppressed ;
In quiet nooks their soft siesta keep,
And all the town is silent set in sleep.
I stroll along the island's level roads,
Passing the country people's neat abodes ;
To grandeur these have no pretensions sought,
Pure independence is their only thought.

Here, lolling idly, find the cavalier
To light guitar breathes forth a plaintive air ;
In liquid notes exalts his loved one's charms,
With soft appeals to fold her in his arms.

Back turn again to town, which now is gay,
As Phœbus shoots across his slanting ray ;
Where flageolet resounds to loud tambour,
And songs domestic dulcet voices pour.
Where sun-burnt lads and dark-eyed lasses seen,
Fandango tripping on the open green,
In sober merriment the hours employ,
Each radiant feature beaming high with joy.
And by I pass, although I fain would stay
And join the frolics of the holiday ;
Much could enjoy the spirit of the song,
But on this day I hold their revels wrong
For me, in kindred feeling to delight,
And pass away the hours till coming night.

Again aboard, and northward steer away,
Up through the pleasing sea Mindora lay ;
With breezes light along the good ship rolls,
Passing the maze of islands, rocks, and shoals.
And oft escapes, and often takes the ground,
Though boats are out, before, the reefs to sound.

Useless the chart, the coral sea unknown,
And islands rise where none at all are shown.
Though reefs among, and rocks do rudely chafe,
Our ship holds tight, and bears us onward safe.
Though like a lake the studded water lies,
Its bright tints borrowing from the ambient skies,
Yet oftentimes in unison it bounds
To the inharmonious typhoon's roaring sounds ;
When o'er the reefs the foaming billows seethe,
And far too close the threat'ning rocks beneath,
A vessel's caught, and driven o'er the plain
Amidst the furious howling hurricane.
Close to the wind we point our slanting sail
To catch the monsoon's steady north east gale.
Encompassed round with islands, through we ran
The passage by the northern Palawan.
And clear them all, and leave them on the lee,
And shape our way across the Chinese sea.
Naught now descry, to sight all land is lost,
Till in full view we trace the Chinese coast ;
And near the shore, and track the land along,
Run through the pass, and anchor at Hong Kong.

HONG-KONG.

A barren land, close to the Chinese main,
Whose rocky sides a goodly height attain,
And at whose feet the town Victoria lies,
And by the sea huge blocks of stores arise.
    Around the ship the boats in numbers flowed,
The better class by Chinese lasses rowed.

Light are their craft, and neat and clean and plain,
A canopy to guard from sun and rain.
With single oars upright old men propel
The open *sampan* and the number swell.
Rough clumsy craft, devoid the gentle care,
Content their owners with the humbler fare.
   With patience great around the ship they lay,
Await the sign the strangers to convey
To any part within the harbour's bound,
Or any place the rugged shores around.
And as I note, the deep clear water's hue
Which well retains the ocean's purest blue ;
The ship unmoved upon its bosom lies,
And lands adjacent greet my anxious eyes.
High towering hills, though barren to the sight,
For change of scene my longing thoughts invite.
Companions aid, my willing mind invoke,
As ardent youth prefers the better boat.
The signal give, the oars now splash the tide,
And lightly shoots the galley to the side,
With two young damsels ready to obey,
To waft us gaily to the shores away.
Their modest mien and pleasing features fair,
Their neat attire and trimly braided hair
Excite our minds to praise, remark, and jest,
But all such jokes fall blunted on each breast.
Their floating house is sacred to their charge,
The pretty nymphs the theme will not enlarge,
But shyly turn and swiftly row to shore,
Of our attentions wanting not the bore.
Their honest hearts 'gainst every vice preserved,
Their thoughts of love are otherwise referred :
Some darling care or youthful lover kind,
Protects their person, and directs their mind.

With modest grace they smile, receive the fare,
And leave on us an impress of the pair.
　　We land, and through the town Victoria roam,
Where English merchants, proud and wealthy grown,
Have raised their stores, and hold an active mart,
Distinct in place, at distance set apart
From Chinese town, which huddled in a mass
Upon the hill's steep side, is growing fast ;
A difference marked between the two we trace,
A strong effluvium rising from this place,
Peculiar to the towns where Chinese dwell ;
Where burning joss-sticks, acting as a spell
Outside the habitations of the poor,
To drive the evil spirit from the door.
　　We wander round the place and back again,
Cross Lymoon Pass, and make the Chinese main,
Where, more distinct from British intercourse,
The natives all their customs hold in force.
Along by-paths and paddy-fields we stray,
Following a pair domestic on their way
To some pursuit industrious, poor but neat,
Our eyes attracted to the woman's feet ;
Deformed for life, whate'er the tyrant cause,
Or bigotry, or custom's doubtful laws ;
Before him on the road the husband sends
In hobbling gait, with staff her way she wends.
　　Contrasting here the ladies of our own,
Doubt not they are the loveliest creatures known—
Where custom dwells in almost every act
Yet kindly spares them all their limbs intact.
And that although a handsome form's inviting,
A pretty ankle's thought the most enticing.
These Orientals, held to slavish forms,
To cheat the god of Love, despoil his charms ;

His strength they fear, and hence the mutilation,
That none may flee the great celestial nation ;
Or if they stray away to foreign shore,
That none but Chinamen may love them more.

Here in the cosy harbour long we lay,
With balls and parties to divert our stay.
'Till, roused to action, all the boats are manned
To chase the corsair junks, about to land
To plunder stores that are at West Point lying,
With daring boldness their exertions trying,
In open day, to land and make a rush,
And suddenly to all protection crush,
And ere alarm and aid could given be,
To seize their booty and put off to sea.
But ere our boats appeared upon the scene,
The vile design had all frustrated been :
The slight obstruction, calculated meeting.
Had proved effectual to their aims defeating.
And, closely pressed, back to their junks they ran,
When by the boats a stirring chase began :
With oars and sails they swiftly ply the course,
Use all their skill and put forth all their force,
And neared the lagging craft - the larger one—
Which by the other two was far outrun.
She sails before the wind, and tries to gain
A small inlet upon the Chinese main.
Perceiving which our boats make for the spot,
When from the junk there comes a well-aimed shot :
The water struck, and o'er the barge it sings,
Ricochetting upon its iron wings ;
And in their teeth it throws the flying spray,
And serves to urge the crews to swift give way.

Cut from the shore, the junk shoots to the wind,

Luffs up, and throws another shot behind,
Far wide the mark it whistles on its path,
To stir the deep alone it mischief hath.
Approaching near up runs the flying barge,
And from her bow lets off the sharp discharge,
But dropping short it misses aim in turn,
And harmless falls close by the junk's high stern.
The pirates veer, again another shot,
More true in aim, between our boats let drop ;
Which throws a sheet of water flying on,
And takes the gunwale of the farthest one.
The pirates lose, by wavering in their track
To work their guns and craft much skill they lack.
Again the barge another shot lets fly,
And sends their rudder into splinters high.

At once the junk comes to, no longer flees :
Her coarse sails flutter useless in the breeze.
Her crew in consternation throng her deck,
Struck dumb with terror by this sudden check.
Yet to surrender scorn to yield compliance
And with their weapons flourish a defiance.
Up shoot our boats, a sudden volley poured,
And with a shout the hardy pirate board ;
A sharp encounter on her deck began,
Which soon was cleared of every Chinaman.
From such impetuousness they haste to flee ;
Some leap below, and some into the sea ;
Some lying maimed, and some had breathed their last,
The dead and dying o'er the side were cast.
The rest secured, and back is made the trip,
The prize at anchor lies beside the ship.
A large, unwieldy, cumbrous-looking craft,
Low at the bow, and high raised up abaft :
Her armament a pair of thirty-twos,

Lashed to the deck, and difficult to use.
Her men about the mast are seated round,
With arms behind, and legs securely bound :
Demurely look, and savage at their fate,
A fiendish mixture of low scorn and hate.
In rags, unkempt, as beasts ferocious are,
Outlawed and shunned, devoid of every care,
The wonder 's not that all should wish to rid,
But why on earth such creatures wish to live—
Fit objects are to either hang or shoot ;
The lawyers claim them as their legal loot,
Go through the form of trying pirates known,
Who for defence no friends or money own ;
As though a wig and gown could better send
Into perdition those who, pre-condemned,
Await impatient to yield up their breath,
And suffer all the time a living death.
By process strange, to which there's no reply,
Are told in plain Chinese they have to die ;
Back to the scene of their exploits are led,
From which they had precipitately fled.
And through the town produce but slight commotion,
As bound and guarded, march to execution.
Are handed to the minions of the law,
Charged by the Fates the thread of life to draw ;
To Eternity their fellow-men to cast,
And clumsily perform the sacred task ;
By cumbrous means the rovers' necks disjoint,
And leave their bodies dangling at West Point.

Hong-Kong to Macao.

The ship moves off, now gaily sailing on
Towards the stream of world-wide fame, Canton.
Whose near approach is clearly indicated,
By yellow wash with which 'tis impregnated.
　　The monsoon's change had brought the vernal showers,
To gladden earth, and spread its plains with flowers ;
Had sent its waters down with such a force,
As caused the ship to deviate her course,
Veer with the stream, and westward point her bow,
To stay a day at Portuguese Macao.
　　And here our Transatlantic cousins meet,
In two war-ships that comprehend their fleet ;
With stars and stripes the British flag display,
In honour of Victoria's natal day.
　　The common stock their friendship high reveal,
In mutual sports and generous goodwill,
And join conclusions to their prowess test,
To strive from each the proffered prize to wrest,
Of silver dollars liberally bestowed.
To crown the victors in the races rowed.

　　But first, our chief, alert to duty leal,
And ever studious of the public weal,
Is rowed to shore, and there constrained to hear
A sad complaint that fell upon his ear ;
Told by our consul, who had strove in vain
To aid a captive, and his freedom gain.
　　Says he : ''There's one whom late I saw,
For some offence against religious law
Was seized, ill-treated, by the rabble mobbed,
Most roughly used, and by fanatics robbed

Of that respect which Britons justly claim,
As the reward due to their country's fame.
Lies well secured within the dungeon's wall,
From which we hear the voice of Justice call,
Appealing to the honour of our land,
To lend its aid, and with protecting hand
Release the captive, strike oppression down,
And claim the dignity of the British crown.'

Our chief replies—his features with a frown —
'Conduct us to the Governor of the town.
Released he will be without hesitation,
When so requested by solicitation.'

But here his generous spirit sadly erred ;
The Gov'nor listened to the suit preferrèd,
Then brusquely turned, unhesitating said,
' Released he may be when the fine is paid.'
With mien disdainful, moved himself away,
Nor listened more to what he had to say,
Contemptuous left amidst the railing sport,
Of jeering priests, and tricksters of the court,
High indignation fills his lofty soul,
His rising wrath but ill kept in control.

' No fines we'll pay !' was then his quick reply,
' We on our arms and on our cause rely.
An hour from hence, we can no more afford,
The man I ask for must be safe aboard.'

' Enough !' they cried, and tauntingly exclaimed,
' 'Twixt you and us we want no more explained,
Our laws sustained, shall take their even course ;
Withhold the fine and try your puny force.
Away at once, betake yourself to boat,
And find your safety in your ship afloat.'

' 'Tis well,' he said, ' we take your terms and scorn,

8

And soon will meet you in another form,
And never yield to these unjust demands,
With England's honour trusted to our hands.'
　　Then off to ship, and ere an hour had flown
His plans he lays, and thus his mind makes known—
' Before the games we enter on this morn,
Our country's duty calls aloud to arm.
Let this suffice, we know our mission well,
There lies an Englishman in bigot's cell.
We failed as suitors, now we'll try our force,
Right for our guide, we lead in honour's course.
Prepare you quickly, for the shore depart,
And law we'll give them, simple, sure, and short.
To them unknown, derived from such a source
As justice wields, against usurping force.
Boats' crews, away ! myself will take command,
Buckle your arms, and follow where I land.
We'll seize the chance when unprepared caught,
Prevent all mischief in a quick assault.'
　　He strides the deck with an impatient pace,
With all the warrior glowing in his face :
The sailors spring to do his high behest,
Imbibe the ardour of his swelling breast.
His orders take, and soon the boats are lowered,
With rifles charged, quick o'er the side they poured,
Undaunted fly to serve a righteous cause,
And strike the fetters of oppression's laws.
Himself the last, and to his first command
He orders thus :—' As we proceed to land
The anchor slip, and whilst with jibs she runs,
Get in and load and double shot the guns.
See all is clear and take her closely down,
And warp her broadside to the embattled town ;
Await the sign that all is going fair,

Or otherwise for action quick prepare.'
  With this they are off, and ply the bending oar,
With steady strokes, they sweep towards the shore.
'Tis justice hails ! and waves her flaming brand,
They catch the mandate of her high command.
She must succeed though strong the forces brought,
Though close and dire the daily fight is fought,
Though victims through the strife fall thick and fast,
Right over wrong must still be found at last.

  They gain the shore, and rank along the strand.
In martial order, stands the daring band.
Their chief, solicitous of life to spare,
Admonishes to use their utmost care.
Should aught obstruct to baulk their free retire,
To curb their ardour and retain their fire,
Assaulting none save in their self-defence,
Nor break their rank save under good pretence.
  The boats lay off, assigned positions take,
With howitzers the crowded street to rake,
Should such assistance be required of them,
To give their aid to the retreating men.
Up through the town a steady march is made,
No more concerned than marching to parade,
Towards the prison where the victim lies ;
And, close behind, a crowd collecting rise.
In open day they dare the city's might,
For Queen and country, God defend the right !
  True to his post the sentinel guards the way,
When from his hands his arms are snatched away,
Is sternly told to hold his gibbering tongue,
And not attempt to bar the way along.
He takes the hint, and just as quickly saw
Resistance useless was to such *sang-froid.*

No interruption mars the well-laid plan,
The word was given and the work began.
While here are some to force the gates allowed,
Others are there to check the rising crowd.
Up to the gaol swift retribution flows.
The portals trembling with its steady blows ;
The massive bolts their rapid progress stop,
With powder blasts they shake the stubborn lock ;
Then seize a ram, whose heavy strokes they ply,
And barred-up gates must quick asunder fly ;
Pour in the breach and down the doorway fell
That held the prisoner in the loathsome cell,
Before their will all vile obstructions flee.
The aim is gained, the victim snatched and free ;
The crowd behold them with astonished eyes,
Nor dare molest or touch their well-earned prize.
Then march him out, and through the shattered gate
Marshal again, in compact order wait,
Form'd in a square, they dare the threat'ning mob
To break their rank, their lawful prize to rob.
Back through the street in silent triumph led,
The flag of England fluttering o'er his head ;
With steady stride they march towards the beach,
With doubtful chance if it in safety reach.
For as they guard their charge on every side
Commotion starts and spreads out far and wide ;
Rolls o'er the town, re-echoes from afar,
To clamour wakes the slumbering notes of war.
Their bugles sound, their drums proclaim alarms,
And to their call the soldiers rush to arms ;
Along the rampart lines the panic runs,
And in hot haste they rush to load the guns.
Some partial power, its favourite sons to save,
Confounds the cowards and protects the brave ;

Void of command to lead the rightful way,
Confusion dire asserts its lawful sway.
In thoughts conflicting all their minds are tossed
In hesitation, all their chance is lost.
The band makes good its rapid safe retreat,
And by the crowd is followed through the street.
Who, close, gesticulate, molest would try,
When down! to the charge, and off again they fly.
    Our gallant chief undaunted leads the way,
Cries, ' Forward, men, make no undue delay,
The signal raise, call all the boats to land,
And range yourselves in line along the strand.
Divide the men for each respective boat,
Defy them will we when we get afloat ;
And shall have read a lesson to them then
Of how to treat again our countrymen.'
And down they march, and through the lines defile,
The ramparts thick with scowling men the while.
Beneath whose guns they cross the bridge and moats,
Regain the beach and slip into their boats.
Each leads the way, for sure protection runs
Beneath their frigate's heavy covering guns ;
No more the foe their cares of safety taxed,
The end is gained, their efforts are relaxed,
Their object's care is safely put on board,
The guns unloaded, and the ship unmoored.

    Now when the crews had snatched a partial rest,
And with the noontide meal had been refreshed,
Just as the day-star in the zenith flames,
They haste to celebrate the promised games :
And here Columbia with Britannia vies,
Adorned as each her gayest colour flies :
Both guided by the same celestial light,

Rivals in war, in arts of peace they fight.
Exhort their sons to win by force of will,
And in their honour try their strength and skill.
As when at war so in their peaceful games,
Befitting heroes of such glorious dames.
And off they start, and brush the seething tide,
'Midst cheers and clamour echoing far and wide,
When in the front the race Britannia led,
And then Columbia shoots her flag ahead.
Again abreast, and round the point they sweep,
And in the tug awake the silent deep ;
Their active oars the sullen ocean lash,
And from their prows the foaming waters splash.
Britannia leads, and then again recedes,
The goal is nigh, she holds and yet precedes ;
Excitement rises with the pending fray,
And by a length she bears the prize away.

Diverse the sports, and close the stakes divide,
And close must be where two such rivals strive.
Long may they strive in peaceful acts to gain
The world's applause and everlasting fame ;
In their pursuits the prize of science chase,
To raise the blessings of the human race.

Next morn we weigh and spread our sails amidst
A heavy rain with gusts of wind and mists ;
With quickening force it drives the ship along,
And rapid sends us flying to Hong Kong.
And as we lie, resuming guard again
Between the island and the Chinese main,
Diversified relations soon began,
With the Mongol our friend John Chinaman,
Who laves our clothes, provides us with fresh mea
And acts as purveyor in all we eat.

CHINESE SEAS.

Now I'll diverge : and treat of trade and barter,
Of Jack with John upon the silvery water
Beside the ship, where John his stock hath laid,
To out of Jack's hard earnings drive a trade.

For keen-eyed John in trade with Jack the free,
Can beat him soundly in his native sea ;
Though Jack may drive the hardest bargain home,
Still finds John's patience greater than his own.

And holds, in decimals, a good invention
To assist him to compete in trade contention,
That these were given to his foreign brother,
Because, poor mortal, he could learn no other.

Nor could he make his brother understand,
Had he not digits ready on each hand,
Endowed by Nature true, with supple joints,
For universal use with just ten points.

' How muchee, John !' and here Jack holds a pine,
His fingers too, to his own price define ;
With these he calculates, and plies them well
With interjections—to divert the spell.

For John is mild, with no impatient care,
As one who lives and breathes celestial air ;
Whose almond eye is soft, and calmly blinks,
As undisturbed the Mongol sits and thinks.

Then opes his lips, and gravely turns his head,
As though he had not heard what Jack had said,
And slowly points his tapering fingers through,
And holds the number up he wants to view.
The softest smile then lights the blandest face,
Which more than aggravates our Jack-tar's haste.

Yet deal they must, and so again renew,

Jack's wants are many and his dollars few.
Another finger as he feign would try
To make John think he's careless if he buy;
'Till patience dwindles far below its proof,
Throws down his coin, and carries off the fruit.

And as we sail the rugged coast along,
We're followed by the trader of Hong Kong;
Who tracks our course, doth all his skill employ,
To keep in sight and join us at Amoy.

Now it is known that in the same degree,
Traders alike could never yet agree;
And soon 'tis found he in collision meets,
A citizen direct from Amoy streets.

Amoy's indignant, casts a scornful frown,
And calls him pirate, outcast from the town;
And works himself to a high pitch contrary,
Infringing on our sailor's vocabulary;
For strange it is that at this distance small,
A common language is unknown to all.

A wordy strife in which a jargon rages,
As would defy the savants of the ages,
From out of it a language to distinguish,
Mixed as it is with Kong, Amoy, and English.

Some doggrel catch from out the fume and fuss
Of simple sentences proceeding thus:
'I Kum su Kow! I John Chinaman,
I Amoy—you twice-eye man; you God—m.'

Rare sport for Jack, who feels a keen delight,
In hopes to see a genuine Chinese fight;
And pats his man, and in succession jeers;
And cowards calls them, with sharp jibes and sneers;
As with disgust he soon begins to see
They have no mind to fight upon the sea.

The boats afford no ample space to spare,
To show the prowess of the sporting pair,
Who fight with teeth, and head, and legs, and arms,
With guttural hissings, and loud fierce alarms.

Then on we sail, with favouring winds we ran,
Until we sight the island of Chusan ;
Make for the land, and run the coast line down,
And cast our anchor close in with the town.

Assembled here, and well inside the bay,
Large junks of war and merchants numerous lay,
Pennons and streamers all their mast-heads crowd,
With gongs and tom-toms sounding long and loud.

A landing make up through the plank-laid street,
Where shops on either side and traders meet ;
Fancy bazaars, with every useful trade,
On piles above the sea are level laid.

And here more pure the Chinee find again,
Who prides himself a cultured citizen.
More clean his home, his wife with little feet,
His children robed in fancy dresses neat.

Signs o'er their shops that tell a close relation
With Englishmen, who hold in occupation
Their island round, and custom dues, until
The war indemnity is paid in full.

And strange appears where, higher up the town
A sentinel is pacing up and down ;
Joss-house before which has been quite vacated,
To allow marines therein to be located.

A fine broadway with shops on either side,
Through which no wheeled vehicles ever drive.
Ladies are prim, and little children neat.
Itinerant barbers, shaving in the street,
A close shave give, they do but leave the crown

From which suspended hangs the long tail down.
    We wandered on as curious minds dictated,
To other temples not so desecrated,
Where gilded Joss, upon a chair of state—
Handmaids, on either side, upon him wait—
Half dozing seems, celestial and obese,
Recumbent lies in supernatural ease.

    More idols find, good specimens of art,
Quite natural, and finished every part ;
The place itself is neat and clean withal,
An air of sacredness pervading all.

    Near to the porch, a railed in iron cage.
So chastely wrought, our serious minds engage.
An altar placed within the centre found,
With various kinds of gifts all spread around,
Where devotees their proffered treasures lay,
Which Joss is said to duly take away.

    Outside the town we scan the pleasant hill,
Whose green clad sides with admiration fill
Our natural tastes for landscapes fresh and fair,
And sweet perfumes that impregnate the air.

    Whose budding plants are shaping into crops,
On terraces from base to utter tops :
On level ground and stretching far below
The tea bush flourishes in equal row.

    Then back again to where the joss-sticks burn,
Where John stands ready to a dollar turn ;
Though enemies, and hard ones too, are found,
The active dollar makes us friends all round.

    Here o'er his stall some borrowed English find,
That all his friends may read who feel inclined,
Attracted by the sign may come to hail
His subtle calling, or his wares for sale.

And some we note peculiar, quaint and rare,
As though some wag had lent a finger there ;
One running thus : ' I Sam Slick watchmaker.'
Another : ' Here lives John the biscuit baker.'
Again : ' I John Chinaman first class chop.'
And then : ' Lookee Jack ! I curio shop.'
And more alike, we could not well define,
And if we could, could not be made to rhyme.

Behind a screen there two celestials sit,
Unsweetened tea from tiny cups had sipped,
One 'rouses up, as from a dream reviving ;
And one dreams on, from opium smoke imbibing.
Some fleeting moments in a world of bliss,
From cares terrestrial, far away from this,
Which must be paid for—as all bliss must be---
In corresponding hours of misery.
Too soon he 'wakes to find his nerves unstrung,
To face the world again he fain would shun.

And so we're off, and leaving fair Chusan,
To northward steer, for great Yangtse-Kiang.
And sailing by the eastern coast we hung,
And cast our anchor at the stream Woosung.
When from the Tchin-san isles around the coasts,
Swarm to the ships innumerable boats
Of every kind, but most the long *sampan*,
Some trifle bringing to the foreign man,
To be exchanged, as fortune kind may throw,
Haphazard trading with the stranger crew.

A rough class these, half-naked and untamed,
By Chinese citizens ' barbarians ' named ;
Outcasts, untaxed, untutored and unknown,
Classed quite distinct and unacknowledged grown
Who live on fish, and what they chance to know
Of roots and fruits of little care to grow.

With these Jack has to deal, in trade to join,
Who have no knowledge of the use of coin —
Poor clamorous creatures, curious all to see,
They lack the caution of the real Chinee.

Now Jack will boast- and 'tis with force averred,
That his profession broad is never learned.
Variety in all in which he delves,
More changeful than the elements themselves ;
But true or false as this assertion made,
A cosmopolitan should be in trade.
For here he is, beside the ship, divining
Intrinsic worths ; in sundry goods defining,
'Twixt sweet potatoes, yams, and luscious fruits,
'Gainst bottles, ribbons, beads, and iron hoops,
Such calculation keen as would defy
The practised experts of all time to try.

Nor needs he now want for a sumptuous dish,
Where buttons made of brass secure a fish ;
An empty bottle may a chicken buy,
A rusty hoop a sucking-pig supply.

He singles out a chicken, with some yams,
With many reck'nings up, and many d—ns ;
And haggle must —'tis part of Nature's plan
To get from all as much as e'er we can.
And hard must be that deal in calculation,
That has no coin to lay for its foundation.

Suspicion haunts—they fail to understand,
If the supply is balanced by demand ;
Jack's duties call him, can no longer stop,
So with a stroke he cuts the gordian knot,
Worked to a point, impatient of delay,
Each seize the other's goods, and rush away ;
Abruptly closed, examine at their leisure,
The pros and cons of each acquired treasure.

Traders are all !—the meanest the inception,
For civilization brings trade to perfection ;
Or saint or sinner, surely man was made
To find his occupation most in trade :
Some trade in food, some even in starvation,
Upon our fears, the safety of the nation,
Some on our sins, and others on our passions,
Upon our weaknesses for dress and fashions.

Of our necessities many sow the seed,
And with the produce trade upon the need :
Some trade in loss, and others trade in gain,
On the inventions of another's brain.
And some on truth, but mixed with lies forsooth,
For few indeed will trade in simple truth—
Some on their greatness o'er the weak and small,
And some on force, most potent of them all.

Refined are those, who o'er this orb terrestrial,
Who trade on faith, and flowery lands celestial.
But most refined of those are found to be
The technical traders in philanthropy.

Time may be wasted, patience much expended,
The list be lengthened, catalogue extended,
But to what end, except in trade to find
The peace of nations, blessing of mankind ?

Here now must cease all further speculations,
A sudden breach is made in trade relations,
Not from a petty jealous underhanding,
But from an empty vague misunderstanding.

Some fifteen miles away there stands Shanghai,
Within whose walls a mandarin doth lie ;
As etiquette with civilization runs,
Should be saluted by our booming guns.

Jack waves his arms, doth in plain English say,

And they're not off, he'll blow them all away.
Points to the guns, and shouts with might and main,
They stare with open mouths, but still remain.

The swarm is great, and pressed in as a wedge,
That none can move save from the outer edge,
They heed him not, and maybe cannot hear,
The distance far, and for the hubbub near.

The occasion for it cannot be disputed,
The Governor of Shanghai must be saluted.
And what if one a gun-wad should resist,
From such a horde he could not well be missed !
Much less by those who wear extended tails,
Celestial eyebrows, and long tapering nails ;
Whose wives go hobbling through the well-swept street,
With little maidens crippled in both feet.

So Jack let loose ! your thunder in their ears,
Its hoarser call will heighten all their fears,
Its signal voice will give the word to start,
Nor will they hesitate to quick depart.

The gun goes off, and with its rolling roar,
A high commotion sets towards the shore,
With rush and tumble sweeps the long *sampan*,
Ram-jam collide to get away who can.
A babel raise, they clamour in the race,
The guns in rear are bellowing in the chase :
Nor do they halt, or any effort stay,
'Till in their isles they hide themselves away.

Next morn at noon is borne upon the tide
A gala junk, that comes the ship beside ;
With silken streamers, rowers neat and trim,
And bearing in her stern the Mandarin.

Marines are ranked, and form in honour's guard,
As robed in silk the Viceroy steps aboard.

Silent the voice, in courteous form received,
In motions dumb around the ship proceed.
Descend the deck, and down upon the main,
Extensive are the attendants in the train ;
In rank they follow one another round,
Embroidered silks are all their vestments found.
From cords and tassels—passing in procession—
Hang down the emblems of each one's profession.
His chancellor the seals of office wears,
An attendant high the polished chop-sticks bears.
The doctor, barber, cook, must be presented,
Seamster and scribe, in person represented ;
And many others whom we could not name,
That follow in the long meandering train.

They then depart, but now the booming gun
Has no effect on these to make them run.
Lay on their oars, and make a courteous stay,
Then doff their colours and pull right away.

Then off we sail, and southward point the way,
Against the strong monsoon, close-hauled we lay,
Stretch far away and make the passage long,
Until again we run in for Hong-Kong.

HONG-KONG TO SINGAPORE.

Replenish stores, again for sea we veer,
And for the Philippines direct we steer,
And find the islands green, and calm reposing
In slumbers deep, a silent awe imposing.
Between them steal as gentle breezes blow,
Across our path the isles their shadows throw,

With many small ones dotted here and there,
Which by refraction seem to float in air.
Strict watch is kept, for in these beauteous seas,
The shallow reef unknown too oft deceives ;
As 'neath the keel unseen is sudden springing,
When all save watchmen are asleep and dreaming.

    Safe through the pass till Luçon comes in sight,
And off Manilla lay to for the night.
The town at distance seen, and pleasing looks,
Renowned for fibrous grass, and fine cheroots,
Volcanoes grand, typhoons, and quakes terrestrial,
Delicious fruits, calm seas, and skies celestial.
And then we stretch along within the bay,
And by a stream of small dimensions lay.
Protects the town, and has across it thrown
An ancient bridge of architectural stone ;
With well-built wharves and muddy waters deep,
Which hold, and shield, the numerous merchant fleet.
And here I stroll the pleasing country round,
Beyond the town, on elevated ground,
And stop to listen to the martial band,
Which sends its notes across the quiet land.
Its strains and echoes through the pure air seem,
To awake the soul to contemplate the scene.

    There far inland the green-clad mountains rise,
And here below the well-kept city lies ;
Lit by the sun the sparkling ocean glows,
On all around a sense of grandeur throws.
The smaller islets, green within the bay,
Upon their bed of burnished silver lay;
The palms are spreading out their fan-like leaves,
And wave them gently in the moving breeze.
Fringing the shores with many shadows deep,
Whilst at their feet the ocean seems to sleep.

Around the suburbs, strolling up and down,
I turn to scan the centre of the town ;
Where churches high. with Roman steeples stand,
And monasteries of the priestly land ;
With houses built to stand the earthquake's shock,
With solid bases of hard granite rock.
Here too I visit, on my lonely course,
A factory large and active, in full force
Of native girls, which seems to me despotic,
To bind them to roll up the weed narcotic
Into cheroots, whose fragrance fills the air,
But uncongenial should be to the fair.
I did say fair ! but that 1 must revoke
—With such a group it may be thought a joke—
Where no variety of colour lack
From pale-faced white through tawny unto black ;
Still all seem equal, so they justly are,
And with their tribe each must be thought as fair.

Still on I wend my way up through the town
And meet the grandiosas driving down ;
Sombre Spaniards, with signoras gay.
Roll through the streets in line at fall of day.
Vivacious ladies, with an ease profound,
Whose dark eyes flash on every one around.
A careless independence marks their mien,
Although they come to see, and to be seen.
From out the town, across the bridge they flow,
And somewhat ape our pompous Rotten Row.
Then back to ship, and here the time we wore
In mutual compliments 'twixt ship and shore.
The stately Spanish, ready with propriety
To spend their evenings in gay society.
Then off we sail, and ere a day had sped,

9

A floating forest was descried ahead.
In grotesque forms some trees are slanting found,
But more upright as if in solid ground,
As though an island with a rocky bed,
To realms below all suddenly had fled :
Some gloomy force had snatched it from the day,
Had left its trees and scrub to float away.
Whate'er the cause, as far as eye can trace,
The floating debris fills the vacant space.
   We hold our way, and sail the forest through,
To quarters beat to exercise the crew,
And pound the floating islands as they pass,
And smash the trees, and flying send the grass :
Manœuvre round, engage on either side,
And lay them shattered on the heaving tide.
Amongst them all the active frigate flew,
And gave a broadside as a last adieu.
Day after day we scarce lose sight of land,
Which now on this and now on other hand ;
And reefs perpetual blocked the wished-for way,
As some we shun, and some across we lay.
In waters deep, where there upon the chart
An island stands, and is distinctly marked,
Where should be reefs, there none at all are shown,
The sea unstable, unsurveyed, unknown.
   'Twixt Borneo and Palawan we run,
And follow slowly with the setting sun,
And as we think for open sea to keep,
We find ourselves encircled by a reef.
And loud command, with ' Hard a starboard ' hails,
The watch starts up to quickly trim the sails ;
The yards fly round, she shoots towards the wind,
And vainly strives to leave the rocks behind.
But barely round, the good ship springs and jumps,

And takes the ground with heavy surging thumps :
Along the keel is heard the rumbling sound,
Which quickly ceases with a fearful bound :
Stops short the progress of the stately ship,
And Scylla holds her with a mighty grip.
Our fears are raised, it happens at that time
When Sol and Luna draw direct in line,
And swell the wave that bounds from pole to pole
And hides away each reef and shallow shoal.
It lures the mariner with its open seas,
High bears him on the rocks and then recedes
And leaves him stranded, far from friendly land,
Or quick assistance from a helping hand :
By Neptune's forces often overpowered,
A prey to Scylla's dogs to be devoured.
The sea is smooth, for here the Nereids dwell,
Long intervals soft winds and calms prevail,
We sound the well, and to our pleased surprise,
The water in it does but slightly rise.
  The good stout ship sustained the fearful shocks
As to a ball : she bounded o'er the rocks,
With cordage straining, oaken timbers creaking,
And still withal so very little leaking.
The sails are furled, and launched the larger boats,
Quick by her side the fleet assisting floats,
In deepest water out our anchor lay,
And o'er the stern the stoutest hawser pay.
Some short time have for yet the tide to rise
The practised seaman all his art applies,
The capstan whirls, obedient to the word,
The hawser snaps, and swiftly flies aboard.
The ship lies fast ; too late again to try,
For now the swelling waters, gathering high,
Recede again, and rapidly in ebb,

Leaves her more firm upon the rocky bed,
And, heeling over, tells the chance is small,
That from the danger she may float at all.

Full on her side she lies as 'twere a lee,
The guns are loosed and cast into the sea,
First by the breaching each is duly slung,
And from its end the floating trunnion hung,
To mark the spot the iron monster lay,
To rest in peace until another day,
When toils succeed, and favouring fortunes smile,
To float again, and all the rocks beguile.
Will then return, disturb their oozy sleep,
And snatch them from the all-engulphing deep.

The leeward guns are cast into the tide,
The others hang suspended from the side,
Await the flow, their places they retain,
To assist the gallant ship to right again.

The winds are flown, the waters cease to beat,
And o'er the rocks they run in swift retreat ;
Through channels rush, and o'er the shallows slip,
And bare the coral reef around the ship.

And o'er she lies, like to a stranded wreck,
Affords no footing on her slanting deck :
We quit her side and roam about the reef
Firm in our faith, and in our strong belief,
The rising flood great ocean will decree,
To loose us from the rocks, and set us free.

And round we stroll, from rock to rock we leap,
Explore the wonders of the silent deep ;
Where peering from its cell the insect lies,
Anemones of varying forms and dyes.

We many shells of shape peculiar find,
Zoophytic branches, curiously entwined,

And contemplate the polyp, bared to light,
Which builds its palaces of purest white,
That it may live to practise Nature's art,
And in her realms to take an active part.

Though solid rock their strong foundations are,
There's yet a power far beyond their care,
Which raises up the lofty mountain steep,
And buries islands far beneath the deep.

Certain but slow, the transformation yields
From seas of green, to greener tints of fields :
Then back again, from fields and leafy trees
To bounding billows, and wide open seas.

Far out at sea on lonely rocks we stand,
And trace the horizon in search of land.
No friendly shore, or higher reef, altho'
We lie within the archipelago.

For save the ship we scan around in vain,
She rears her bulky side above the main :
Leviathan huge appears, as stranded high,
Heaved by some mighty power, and left to die.

Impotent all its strength to circumvent,
The sallies of its natural element,
With which it used to fight and bravely dare,
The united forces of the sea and air.

Diverted thus the rapid moments flew,
We scan our home from every point of view,
The goodly ship perceive in such a trim,
And wonder whether she will right and swim
From such a bed of rocks, whereon she lies,
Her guns erect and pointing to the skies,
Her yards obliquely crossing up and down,
And masts that seem to shoot the horizon.

The tide begins to cover all the plain,

And drives us to the stranded ship again,
We climb her sides, and scramble down below,
Most anxious wait the rising waters' flow.

And from a beam suspend the plummet line,
For slightest lift or movement to define ;
Too near the ports, the tide is rising high
And every kind of scheme we think to try.

Of every mind most anxious thoughts partake,
For not a movement does she seem to make ;
The waters swell and trickle in the ports,
When loud a voice is heard, 'She starts ! she starts !'

From out the silence breaks the welcome sound,
'She lifts ! she lifts !' re echoes all around
When with a roll, up sudden from the tide,
She finds her balance on the other side.
All catch at beams, or swing off by a rope,
Or with things loose, rush rapid down the slope ;
The waters foam to make their level good
Dash in and cover all things with the flood ;
She dips her heavy side beneath the main
Then rolls, with partial balance, back again.

Up start the men, with feelings of relief,
To light the ship, and haul her off the reef :
Get out more stores, the guns remaining last,
Then to the sea the whole of them are cast.
Then heave her off, unload the boats, begin
To find the guns, and hoist them singly in,
And labour on for hours, with some mishaps,
But duty calls and every mind enwraps.
And whilst with these they work with might and main,
A rope gives way and lets one fall again,
A seaman springs from out the launch's crew,
To bottom dives, and reeves another through.

All are dragged up, none from the task abstaining,
Till with three cheers we hail the last remaining.
    Then set the sails, and grope the doubtful way,
As for the coast of Borneo we lay :
And find the land, close with the shore we ran,
And cast our anchor at fair Labuan.
Stay but a day, to coal and water ship,
And back to Singapore we make the trip.
    Here in the roads awhile we rest : anon,
Our chief decrees, to view the site whereon,
At no far distant day, docks shall appear,
And factories their smoky chimneys rear.
    Away we start to sail the island round,
And few the hours—the place, New Harbour, found ;
Run in the cove between surrounding hills,
Which Nature claims, and fresh with verdure fills.
Mosquitoes, too, which will be put to rout
When civilization comes to smoke them out.
Dilating cease, on all such trivial things,
And search the place and find what fortune brings.
A central refuge on the great highway,
Where mariners' disabled ships may lay ;
Repair their hulls, provide their stores, and then,
With all complete, put off to sea again.
    Good harbour-room is found for any fleet,
On one side gentle rise, the other steep,
With space sufficient to construct the docks,
Whilst land on every side the harbour locks.
Deep water found, and clear pure air to breathe,
No pestilential swamp to sickness breed ;
With sandy bottom, and convenient dip,
To rear up wharves to lay the largest ship.

    Then off we are, to sail the circuit round,

Pass through the strait where rocks and shoals abound :
Between the land appears an open joint,
And where Malaya forms its southern point,
A narrow way; to wind the passage through,
Where shallows numerous, active keep the crew ;
To trim the sails, emerge in open tide,
And keep the island on the weather side :
Complete the round, and stand in for the shore.
And furl our sails again at Singapore.

SINGAPORE TO JAVA.

Replenish stores, few were the days we spent,
When out we stand upon the element,
And southward steer : whilst on the pleasing way,
Stars light our course by night and Sol by day.
And short the time before the land we gain
And touch at Anger, on the Java main,
Then coast along the island's green-clad shore,
Where streams and rivulets their waters pour.
A glimpse we catch of nestling white abodes,
As on we steer towards Batavia roads ;
Espy the town between the islands low,
And at Batavia let our anchor go.
A pleasant place, though subtle danger lurks.
And Fate untimely oft its sway asserts.
Its history some strong inducements urge
To change of scene.   I from the ship emerge,
And with a friend descend upon the strand
To seek the pleasures of the smiling land :
Invigorating sniff the mountain air,

Which softly steals across the woodland fair.
And feel the joys, as through the town we lead,
When from our ship and floating prison freed,
Are felt by those who long have been debarred,
From such as fields and trees and fruits afford.
  We haste to view this ' Empress of the East,'
Who from the ship had comely looked at least,
Who to enjoy had many a hero bled,
And trumpet-tongued, had fame her praises spread.
Are undeceived we each to other own,
As round the town and through the streets we roam :
Quite disappointed feel to find the place
So much neglected by a thrifty race.

  If ever beauty graced her ancient halls,
Or art sublime adorned her lofty walls,
These are effaced ; the queen has grown more sage,
And tropic beauties quickly change with age.
  Still glories past before our eyes are shown,
In mouldering ruin, slow decaying stone ;
And thoughts of bygone years on us obtrude,
And fill our minds with contemplation's mood.
  Oh ! could these stones the barbarous tale unfold,
Of high oppressions in the chase of gold,
They then could say they saw the strangers, come
From far off lands, invade their peaceful home.
How then their skill had hewn them from the rock,
And raised them to the structure block by block ;
They then could say, they saw the victims broke
To subject freedom to their tyrant yoke,
What years of rapine stained the fairest soil,
And drew the hearts' blood from the sons of toil.
  How opulence indulged its love of gain,
And heaps of wealth had crowned its sordid aim ;

What banquets held within their well-built walls,
What revelry re-echoed through their halls,
When in the heyday of their princely power.
Regardless of the crime, and evil hour
When tyrants all must feel the pending blow,
And, with their halls, be all alike laid low.

We quit the town, and stroll the suburbs round,
Through pleasant roads by many a villa crowned ;
Stop to admire one chosen from the rest
Which shows conspicuously the Dutchman's taste.

With spacious hall, well paved, and clean, and white,
Enclosed by garden foliage green and bright.
Harmonious borders skirting paths along.
And smiling children sporting on the lawn.

All speaking comfort, affluence, ease and health,
The proper functions of acquirèd wealth ;
Where gentle care, with mirth unfettered runs,
With joyous prattle from the little ones.

Along the road we walk and reach the turf,
Where pleasant games combine with social mirth
To render Europe's sons the joys of change,
And give their minds a wider field of range.
Divert the hour from opulency's chase.
To join with Nimrod in the lively race.

Beside the course the Dutch and English are,
And most of these with open chaise and pair,
Domestic ladies, affable and free ;
Daughters of these, aspiring each to be
The future wives of rising thrifty sons,
Who now are busy to promote the runs.
Grave modesty in every mien expressed,
And honest hearts in all appear confessed.

No gaudy colours flaunt to mar the scene,
Neat white and black the most conspicuous seen ;
In greetings meet the Dutch and English dames,
And, anxious all, await the coming games.

And then they are off, and England leads the van,
And yet may win because she thinks she can,
As firm of foot she plies a steady force,
Straight in her aim, unwavering in her course.

But now the praises of the Dutchman rise,
And now the English colour forward flies ;
In ecstasies, they shout, 'They come ! they come !'
English ahead—no--neck and neck they run ;
Abreast they lead, and passing closely by,
The soft green turf from their swift fetlocks fly ;
Together spring, and acclamations rise
As, by a neck, the Dutchman wins the prize.

And now in earnest all the sports begin,
Competing numbers try each prize to win,
Those swift of foot pedestrian matches make,
Their chosen chief decides, and holds the stake.
Light supple boys with sable skins contend,
And all their vigour to the task they lend.

Whilst marshalled these, the sod engaged to trip,
Arms bound behind, are some prepared to dip
Their heads into a tub, with water brimming,
Where on its surface are the prizes swimming ;
Unbounded merriment each feature fills
And shouts of laughter echo through the hills.

See on its end a pole well greased arise,
And at its top there hangs the tempting prize ;
Few dare attempt the slippery staff to climb,
Though sleek Malays are fain the prize to win.

Turn from the pole, and try in sacks to jump,
And on the sward they fall with heavy thump,

Whilst mirth hilarious doth each soul possess,
And fair hands clap with joy at each success.

The sports are finished, as the races end,
Vehicles move, and, moving, homewards tend ;
The friends together join the gathering throng,
And merry faces fill the way along.
The human stream of life, fast ebbing down,
Soon empts the course, and fills the sheltering town,
Where balls and parties are assembling gay :
Prolong the night, and close the happy day.

Here pleasing pastimes 'guile the time away,
And all seem willing to prolong the stay.
An oasis in the ocean, as to fare,
The Dutchman's garden is his special care.
Naught troubles him where he may lay his head,
As he will thrive where others fear to tread ;
Takes to a swamp, and toils to clear it out,
To raise his cabbage and to make his *krout*.
Abundant fruits his cultivation yields,
And rising crops of all kinds 'dorn his fields ;
Milk bearing kine off his rich pastures feed,
The woolly flock he multiplies by breed.
All these combine the system to attune,
And to seafarers are a grateful boon.
Alas ! the swamps, which drained appear so fair,
With their miasmatic vapours taint the air.
Upon the crew the pestilence alights.
The unseen scourge with virulence affrights.
Day after day in threes and fours they fall.
Death indiscriminate hovering over all,
We set our sail the noxious land to flee,
To find a purer atmosphere at sea.

JAVA TO AUSTRALIA.

Soft moans the sluggish wind, with fitful force,
And slowly leads the ship upon its course ;
The baneful land still holding in the sight,
It seems to lower upon us through the night ;
As round the decks in groups the sailors lie,
Ask of each other which is next to die ?
In fear and trembling every night we sleep,
And wake to bury victims in the deep.
Assailing more, the fever holds amain
And high delirium rages in each brain ;
In agonies of death they writhe and toss,
And mutual friendship mourns at every loss.

And night by night, and every day by day,
Some more are seized the heavy debt to pay ;
In lucid moments knowing as they lie,
That naught can save them but that they must die.
And though the scene is lovely to the view,
The dreadful fever decimates the crew.
And day by day is launched into the deep,
Some kind companion in eternal sleep.
For three long weeks the scourge our constant guest,
Though all known means are tried to stay the pest.
On Java's coast how many victims laid
For fleeting life was death untimely paid.
Here I acknowledge something 'kin to fear,
The scourge afflicting is unpleasing near.
My serious thoughts in meditation run
In silent contemplation of the Sun.
Languid indulging, in the mid-day light,
Daydreams as fanciful as those of night,

Which dwell upon the scene that death is bringing,
And in my breast such thoughts as these are springing.
   O glorious orb! which darts thy cheering ray
Far through the unknown illimitable way,
Thou greatest wonder of created things,
On all alike around thy radiance flings,
And warms the insect as the mightiest kings.
Thou parent sphere! whose brightness lights the way
Of smaller orbs, that sweep within thy sway;
Whilst these obedient to thy power and will,
The smallest detail of thy laws fulfil.
Whilst at thy bid the winter's blast doth flee,
And blossoms spring to life upon the tree;
To thee the birds their songs of praise prepare,
To thee the savage kneels in fervent prayer.
All things to thee an adoration prove,
Great source of light and life and joy and love!
Whilst quick'ning myriads into active life,
In dreary swamps engendering poisons rife,
Thy subtle shafts propitiate the birth
Of noxious gases from the labouring earth.
Thou bidst the breeze to blow, and, lightly fair,
Upon its wings the seeds of death to bear;
Appointing place whereon the bane shall rest,
Dropping it broadcast on the lives thou gav'st.
Afflicting strangers with thy scourging wand,
And leaving whole the natives of the land.
Shall such as I against thee impious rave?
Or meekly ask the sacrifice to save?
No, let me praise thee for thy bounties given,
And rest assured that all is right from heaven.
Still there he shines and useless him to pray,
As well ask Nature on her path to stay;
Whose ways are just, unswerving in her laws,

And life and death but details in her cause.
For such as us shall Nature be retarded?
No! such presumption's rightly disregarded.
Then mourn it not, but use the means bestowed
Upon the race benignantly endowed
With gifts of reason. Fly the baneful shore,
Seek Neptune's plains which soon shall health restore,
Whose cure is rough, yet true to Nature's laws,
And will remove the deleterious cause.

Then Eastwards on we hold a steady course,
The light winds bearing us with gentle force;
Far out at sea by Java's shores we lay,
No beacon fire to guide us on the way,
Save Nature's own; great Sol pours down his light,
And Luna helps us by the coast at night.
Again we near and pass the tranquil strand,
Where houses white are seen beneath the land;
With hillsides green, and many a lofty peak,
Which throw their shadows o'er the silent deep.
    We sail along, pass through Madura's strait,
And Baly island on the right we make;
By Lombock's tow'ring peak we closely draw,
And sight Tumbora mount in Sumbawa.
And close by this a smoking mountain see
Which by the chart is named Gooning Apee;
From its high point dense clouds of smoke ascending
And debris hurled as from the sky descending.
We steer close by, and with the coming night,
The burning island yields a wondrous sight.
Great Pluto fierce is stirring up the fire,
As if some wrong had moved the god to ire.
Or Phlegethon, when charged with fiery tears,
Swells his broad banks, a raging fountain rears,

Chokes the vast gulf his molten streamlets made,
And, spouting high, roars in a fierce cascade;
In rivers broad, rolls down the mountain's side,
With hiss tremendous rushes to the tide.

Indignant Neptune curbs the fiery font,
And furious rages round the burning mount.
Upon their confines he and Pluto meet,
The mighty brothers fierce each other greet.
In vain great Neptune throws around his waves,
And foams and boils and steams and wars and raves;
Still hotly burns great Pluto's fiery blood,
But Neptune cools it with his mighty flood.
Whilst not a foot can each the other trench,
Or yet a power from him the other wrench.
But on their border both the brothers act,
And fiercely fight to keep their line intact.
More loud and deaf'ning grows the general roar
As mountain streams of lava downwards pour.
Dark heavy masses upwards furious fly,
Hoarse as artillery thundering to the sky.
On all around throws down a lurid light,
Illuminates the ship throughout the night,
Till breaking dawn shuts Apee out of sight.
By Banta steer, and at a steady rate,
We coast Comoda, through the Sapia strait.
Eternal sunshine seems to dwell around
The islands green, by Neptune's waters bound.
The heat subdued, by gentle breezes fanned,
Which pass the strait, and steal along the land,
And bear the scents of sweet umbrageous vales
Around the ship and press her bleaching sails.
A charming scene; the passing landscape grand
As to a panorama moves the land,

The green-clad islet and the sunlit peak,
With varied tints from indentations deep,
Conspire to please the mind, and cheat the seas
Of all their trials, and monotonies.
Then onward out in open water stood,
And sighted soon the isle of Sandalwood;
Ran down its coast before a gentle wind,
Then left the scented island far behind.
Towards Timor a pleasant passage make,
And sight the land and run through Rotti's strait.
Light winds and calms prevail along the shore
Where spread the mango groves of low Timor.
We hug the coast, attract the natives' eye,
Who for the ship their paddles quickly ply,
As arrows swift across the waters glide
Their light canoes, and gain the vessel's side.
To barter fruit; the different kinds are few,
And quick are dealt with by the hungry crew:
Hard bargains drive until they have no more,
When off they fly to gain their native shore.
    Away again, the marshy land we flee,
And stand across the Arafura sea.
And dangerous reefs pass close upon our flank,
As we skirt shallows, known as Sahul-Bank.
    With flying lead the treacherous passage feel,
And grope the bottom 'neath the vessel's keel:
Which, shallowing fast, and breezes falling light,
We loose the anchor and ride out the night;
Away from land, and naught can be discovered,
Save open ocean by the reefs discoloured.
    At daybreak weigh and ply the guiding lead,
As great Australia bears direct ahead.
A steady wind soon brings the land in sight,
With Cape Van Dieman bearing on the right.

Reach Melville Island, run the coast along,
And cast our anchor at Port Essington.

PORT ESSINGTON.

Low land we note, a spacious harbour trace,
And from the ship appears a pleasant place.
Upon a wharf projecting from the shore
Effect a landing, and the place explore.
  A post of men upon our vision falls,
Bound to the soil because their duty calls.
In mercy's cause was first the post conceived,
For passing ships which through the strait proceed,
From east Australia going west about
To India's shores, by much the nearest route.
  But dangers hidden in the passage lay,
And Scylla there disputes the right of way;
A net of reefs throughout the strait she spreads,
To catch the mariner in her unseen webs.
  Though Neptune spares and, generous, gives their lives,
The fatal land the offered boon denies.
Along the coasts the savage prowls the shore,
To slay the victim and his corse devour.
There's no escape, 'tis death obdurate waits,
To catch the mariner wrecked in Torres Straits.
  But though the post in spirit well conceived,
By it more victims fall than are relieved,
So uninviting here to cast their lot,
That colonists most careful shun the spot.
  So insalubrious all the country round,
From noxious gas exhaling from the ground,

Port Essington.

That beasts by instinct fly the baneful plain,
And naught but savage tribes of men remain.
  Of these some are induced to work for rum,
Or with tobacco paid, away they run
To seek their food of nature; prowl the shore,
And gather shellfish till there is no more;
And eat themselves away till time shall fly,
And grow more fish, their greatest luxury.
  The lowest type of human kind are these,
Who seek no shelter save the bushy trees;
On natural roots, and fish, and berries live,
Or creatures wild a passing chance might give.
  Of man himself, admit they sometimes eat,
Indulging rarely in so great a treat;
And epicures, when driven to the test,
Will all agree that black man is the best.
  No thought have these to plant or sow for bread,
Or fell a tree to raise the sheltering shed,
Crude wooden spears the only things they form,
And naught but frightful scars their bodies 'dorn.
  And oft is seen a naked female black
With all her house and household on her back.
Some larger tree had shed its bark, and made
A covering for herself and new-born babe.
  Upon the heated ground, or sandy shore,
They lay themselves, and draw this covering o'er.
All others bare and unprotected lie,
With naught above them but the starry sky.
  They sleep and roll and wallow on the strand,
From head to foot are covered with the sand;
Make for the sea are curious objects seen,
Wade in for fish and wash their bodies clean.
  And here with friends I wander round the place,
Some pioneering civilization trace:

Frail dwellings find of European construction,
But not a hut of native wood's production.

Public gardens all the troop supply,
Where tropic fruits grow most luxuriously,
With spreaded leaves the plantain shades its root,
And luscious mango bears its yellow fruit.

Perfume oppressive sheds its fragrance round,
From ripened fruit that, falling, strews the ground.
Black sandy loam makes up the heated soil,
And spoils prolific compensate the toil.

But oh! the sand flies, how they chafe and bite!
Mosquitoes too in new blood much delight.
Upon our flesh white swelling lumps they raise,
As in our ears they pour their song of praise.
The garden quit, and still the conqueror sings,
Can man be vanquished by such tiny things?

We choose a spot upon a rising mound,
Where sylvan branches cast their shade around:
Then make a blaze, and rest secure awhile,
As, native like, we sit around the pile.

Beneath its smoke we lie protected hid,
Puff a cheroot, and sweet defiance bid,
Lulled by its fumes inspiring thoughts arise
All worldly care before its influence flies.
— And in this mood again I inward dream,
The vanity of conquering man the theme.
His vaunted height before mosquitoes flees,
And proves again his power is in degrees.

Born in a sphere, encompassed at his birth,
E'en insects point him out his place on earth.
Beyond the truth he soars, and upward springs,
To be defeated there by meaner things.

Though some will say he's kindred to the ape,
Acknowledges no higher form or shape,

Of all creation, Nature's last perfection,
Not e'en surpassed by his imagination.
  Unto his use all else is rightly given,
Lord of the earth, aspiring unto heaven,
All Nature's made for him, and him alone,
He carves an ideal future of his own.
Presumes the high designs of heaven declare,
Claims as his right its own peculiar care.
O'er creatures all, assumes the imperial crown,
And moulds his gods in likeness of his own.
  Can rear the column, raise the temple high,
Another Babel soaring to the sky.
Within his grasp with Hope he upward flies,
And Heaven attains the instant that he dies !
  Then 'wake again, to wander through the lanes
Of small green trees, that cover all the plains.
Drop on a knot of natives.   Drawing near,
We find them practising to cast the spear,
Their only weapon, which with force they throw,
The only piece of workmanship they know.

  No hills to mount to greet the cooling breeze ;
No soft pure air that gentle zephyr breathes ;
No fresh green vales, of which the mind can dream,
And in its fancy hear the purling stream.
  But fancy all ; for here the soil is dry,
Not e'en a pool on which to rest the eye ;
Though oft the heavens a sudden deluge pour
Which sweeps the country round from shore to shore.
  Lightnings tremendous, thunders' crashing sound,
Vertical columns strike into the ground,
And rive the trees, and hurtling far beneath
The covering earth, the bolt is buried deep.
  A deluge pours, urged by the gustful wind,

Soon leaves no trace upon the land behind.
Into the soil of loam it quick descends,
Sustains the root on which the tree depends,
Moistens the ground, with humid vapours rife,
And deleterious acts on every life.

A tale of woe the sons of Britain plead,
And pray that from the place they may be freed,
With joy they hear it is with this intent
The ship has called to take the remanent.

Of what was once a band of hardy men,
Accustomed to a state of discipline ;
To live or die let Nature take her way
'Tis duty calls them here, and here they stay.

Whose badge of honour is the spacious globe,
In every clime has fame her grace bestowed
For deeds heroic, where'er duties call,
By which they steadfast stand, or dying fall.

Exiled for years, with joy they catch the word,
Prepare at once, embark all things aboard,
Each strives to save his household goods and stock,
His pigs, and poultry, and his fleecy flock.
To serve at sea, when fresh provisions fail,
A consequence of too prolonged a sail.

In turn they seize a boat, and make a trip
And safely take them all on board the ship.
With thoughts of home their hearts are in their work,
As to an ark the tight clean ship convert.
A pen for beasts, whose incongruent roar,
Awakes the deep and echoes to the shore.

Soft muse, assist me ! though the boon I ask,
To thy pure strain an uncongenial task,
How shall I twist thy numbers to deride
The horrid sounds I'd have thee to describe ?

Or how compare the harshly grating notes,
Of fifty kids and half as many goats ;
A hundred ewes all baaing for their lambs,
And these shrill answering, bleating for their dams.
Guttural swine, with low phlegmatic gruntings,
And the keen pipings of a hundred sucklings ;
A score of kine in turn are bellowing strong,
And chanticleer proclaiming loud and long.
   A crowd of Frenchmen cavilling in debate,
Pathetic Irish at a friendly wake,
Or rogues in office loud for justice crying,
When some home-truths around their heads are flying.
A thousand maniacs raving at the moon,
Could not have raised the din to such a tune.
   No, none of these are like unto the sound
Which 'wakes the ship, and grates on all around ;
We can't compare it, and must let it rest ;
Our bliss in ignorance will stand confessed.

All things of value in the ship are pressed,
And to consuming flames consigned the rest.
A yawl for use within the harbour lay,
Not worth the care to man and take away.
   A form of survey hold, unfit they find,
At once condemn her to be left behind.
A shell beneath her keel is placed with care,
Which sends her up in fragments through the air.
   The natives gaze on all, and take delight
In fell destruction's hot and speedy might.
No care have these to save a single thing,
But to the flames more piles of fuel fling.
   The cosy house, and sheltering shed they shun,
Naught else appreciate but snuff and rum ;
Down to the boats to see the sailors go,

All naked are—but this they do not know—
Young girls and boys in various groups arranged,
And none but white men think the matter strange.

Whilst these about the shore are careless straying,
The adult natives from it all are staying,
And hold aloof, from close connexion flee,
And prowl the bush as beasts, and keep as free.

Their caste they keep ; as soon as drawn its breath,
The Creole babe is quickly put to death.
As a birth unnatural seem to them to lie,
And so as monsters doom them all to die.

Few days await, the adverse wind to veer,
And for the nearest route would eastward steer,
Though seldom danger could our course debar,
The Torres Straits are all too dangerous far.

CANTO IV.

PORT ESSINGTON TO NEW BRITAIN.

THE anchor trip, we shun the rocky ground
To pass Papua, this a long way round.
With all on board unfurl and stretch the sails,
And pray the wind may blow in steadying gales :
To gain the port incumbrances discharge,
And set the passengers on shore at large.

    With fresh'ning wind we steer to north about,
Pass by the right, and sight the Timor Laut :
For Banda run, and reach its pleasing bay,
By islands formed which all around it lay ;
Are fresh and green, and towering to the skies,
Fringed round with blossoms mirrored in the tides :

    As studded gems arise from depths profound,
And shed a fragrance through the air around.
One of the group shoots up a tapering cone,
Stands from the rest apart, sublime, alone.

    About its base the azure waters spread,
Whilst clouds of smoke are issuing at its head ;
Calm and serene around the ocean swells,
And tranquil peace o'er all the scene prevails.

    At Neira land away on shore I stray,
And from a neat-built pier I take my way ;
A cosy house appears, the Governor's home.
Around and through whose garden we may roam.

Then up the rise the pebbled streetway led,
And tufts of grass are growing where I tread;
So little used no traffic can be heard,
And all seems quiet, lonely, undisturbed.

At intervals Goonong is casting down
Dark flakes of ashes, covering all the town.
Ungenial clouds in arid showers flow,
Forbidding plants of any kind to grow.

Stout trees alone upon the land are found
Whose roots, long-stretching, enter deep the ground,
And line the shores with blossoms clustering white,
Reflected by the ocean's waters bright.

The lofty hills with foliage covered green,
But which, alas! do not pour down the stream,
To bless the Dutchmen, Chinese, and Malays,
On its refreshing limpid winding ways.

Though nutmegs have, to all the earth supply,
Upon the outer world they must rely;
For food and raiment not within their range,
For these the planter must his spice exchange.

Bright in appearance are the islands seen,
Though fair without, all desolate within.

No moistened spot whereon to grow his krout,
How could a Dutchman settle here about?
For who so fond as he of swamp and dyke,
Though trade and beauty both attract alike?

And what were paradise without its fruit:
Its life-sustaining, esculent plant and root,
Its sunlit hills, its shaded grots and dells,
Its running streams, and moistened grassy vales;
Its soaring birds, beasts browsing in the glen,
To join as one to bless the first of men?

A friend at hand reflecting on the place,

A prudish vanity affects to trace ;
In contact brought, and closer to the view
Comparing all, its outward beauty to
A haughty dame, in costly rich costume,
The latest wonder of the artful loom,
With studied taste she each device prepares,
The borrowed charms of Venus's girdle wears.
What beauteous rolls of locks are clustering there,
The spoil of some fair maiden's ravished hair,
Without what grace, what mystery beneath
And whence, alas ! those doubtful shining teeth ?
    Those folds of cambric, and that pointed lace
The mind bewilders, to its wonders trace.
With practised step she proudly sweeps along,
In mien majestic o'er the verdant lawn.
    For her must be reserved the trapper's toils,
The ermine's coat and sable's downy spoils,
Its shell the tortoise, and the mine its gold,
The miner's vanquished hopes which can't be told.
The bird its plumes, the Arctic seal its skin,
And man his all, if he essays to win,
To bribe such charms must yield the heavy fine
Mistaking plumage for the form Divine.
    When thus compared the joy is passing small,
For there exists a converse to it all.
When stripped of these !—there may remain, 'tis true—
A charming creature still, or still a shrew
Of fifty summers, rigid, blank, and cold,
Whose pleasures are to triumph and to scold.
A very terror, one of Nature's freaks,
As bare and barren as these sterile streets.
    ' What strange comparison !' I quick reply,
With indignation starting to my eye ;
' You are too harsh, my cynic friend, I fear,

Some sad experience methinks you bear,
If not too mean such venom to employ,
Against the prize yourself may not enjoy.

　' What else has man to look for in this life,
Beyond a faithful, loving, charming wife?
Beside this boon all else with doubt is fraught,
And in comparison is brought to naught.

　' Bad some may be, and light and trifling more,
But he who loves them not indeed is poor.
Was not God praised when Eve to Adam given,
The greatest gift of all bestowed by heaven ?'

　Then on we lead, my friend a fort espies,
Beneath surrounding trees it hidden lies :
And as neglected as the roads we pass,
(Quite overgrown and green with stunted grass ;
Placed it would seem to suit the Dutchman's taste,
For who for such a place would powder waste,
Or fight for beauty nowadays alone,
When neither would the risk of life atone?

　We stay to view the lovely scene around,
From our position on the rising ground ;
Enraptured feel at such a glorious scene,
The hills bedecked with blossoms pure and green ;
The mirrored trees beneath the water vying,
As on transparent blue our ship is lying.

　Then back again, the black road winding down,
To find the Dutchman settled in the town
Is smoking still ; enjoys his mid-day naps,
Drowns all his cares in lager-beer and schnapps :
At ease appears to pass away his life
At home, contented with his frugal wife.

　She, neat and prim, domestic cares surround,
And children clean about the floor abound ;
A pi may pour its ashes through the night,

At morn she sweeps the flags and keeps them white ;
From such a stock of thrift and besom these,
No wonder Tromp aspired to sweep the seas !

The day is spent ; again we reach the boat,
And find ourselves on board the ship afloat ;
Prepare to start, and load the parting gun,
Salute the governor with full twenty-one.
Between each gun a rocket high ascends,
And bright blue-light, from each yard-arm depends ;
To finish off, a large bouquet is thrown,
The spoils of insalubrious Essington.
Next morn, as bright Aurora gilds the way,
Our anchor weighed, and on our course we lay.
A zephyr stealing fills the laggard sails,
And, gathering strength, the nimble ship propels.
She urges on, the sparkling waters glow,
Leaving the islands sinking far below ;
Behind the banks of sea, and mists of night,
They're seen no more, and drop quite out of sight.
But barely lost, when now the looming land
Again breaks on us with its rocky strand ;
New Guinea touch, despatch the boats ashore,
The rugged coast aad highlands to explore :
Where crested birds of paradise are found,
Though savage tribes of men possess the ground.
The boats return, and plenty crowns their toils
With numerous trophies of the rifle's spoils ;
What crested heads, what wond'rous tails are there,
Setaceous feathers woven fine as hair !
What tinted pinions, crimson coloured breasts,
Laid now for ever in eternal rest ;
All in a heap their charms dishevelled lie,
Besmeared with streams of ruddy sanguine's dye !

Strange in variety, and stranger still in name,
Which none but ornithologists explain,
Though Paradise may please the vulgar mind,
The learned, to enigmatic lore inclined,
Apodes name them, with Emu Ptilorus,
Meneura, Lyra, Scythrops, and Cerropois.
And others strange more curious still they call,
Most difficult it is to name them all ;
Nor will they rhyme, however much one tries,
Nor, diving deep, can find where reason lies.

The weather bad, and rains and mists prevail,
Our stay is shortened, and we onward sail ;
The wind is strong, and short the distance sped
Ere islands green are standing right ahead.
We thread the way through shallows, rocks, and deeps,
O'er silent beds whereon the zoophyte sleeps ;
The groping lead at times no bottom feels.
Then suddenly it springs beneath the keel
Almost to touch ; we through and o'er them slip,
And Kessing Island reach and moor the ship.
In varied beauty all the islands are ;
Volcanic signs in almost all appear ;
So long it is their fires have ceased to fall,
That virgin forest trees adorn them all.
Here in the bay, composed of rocky ground,
Where reefs of coral form the harbour round,
The town is placed ; and Holland's sons are there,
Still spreading through the islands everywhere ;
Thrive in a swamp, or at earth's utmost bounds,
Whilst freedom pure their lone existence crowns.
The place is poor, we nothing can obtain
To refresh our abstinence across the main :
But spend a day, again unfurl the sails,

And spread them out to catch the softest gales.
    Still by the reefs we steal, and grope the way,
To pass Pitt's passage though our course essay.
Studded its length with islands, rocks and shoals,
The lead alone the dangerous way controls ;
And as the sun withdraws his radiant light,
We cast our anchor to ride out the night.

    Day after day we work the way along,
Night after night we let our anchor down ;
Oft-times we send the boat to explore the reef,
To cull the novelties from out the deep.

    Mollusca strange, and varied in their form,
Anemones the ocean's bed adorn.
With teaming life the submarine abounds,
Building its castles on the rocky grounds.

    Then east away we greet the rising sun,
Between Batanta and Waggeou run ;
Obstructions many through the passage lay,
And shallows still impede the direct way.

    Close by Papua sail the coast along,
The winds in fitful gusts are blowing strong ;
The reefs too near ; the sea begins to rise,
And our good ship to mount and dip her side.

    The furious squalls, though but few moments last,
The sails in ribbons tear from off the mast ;
And hurl the ship careening to the tide,
Whilst green seas boil, and rush into her side.

    As though great Æolus, full of mischief bent,
Some inexperienced demi-god had sent
To work his will, and blow a general blast
With bloated bags so many days to last.

    Who in his bungling had the work begun,
The thongs had severed, careless, one by one,

At intervals he lets a bag full fly,
And in a cloud it spreads across the sky ;
 So insignificant appears in show,
Yet in an instant lays the good ship low ;
So sudden comes, so quick again it flees,
And leaves behind it just a gentle breeze.

 Tempted again, again our sheets display
Of canvas white, are leading on the way
When, suddenly, a burst the ship careens
And sends her over toppling on her beams.

 Pressed by its weight, her yards dip in the tide,
And waters rush, and fill the leeward side :
She struggles hard between the wind and waves,
And gradually rights, and every danger braves.

 In one of these more serious sudden caught
Between the reefs, with greatest danger fraught,
Fast by the shoals we think to easy slip,
When thumps tremendous feel throughout the ship.

 Still on she bounds, with lighter grating shocks,
And shakes her sides, and cheats the hostile rocks,
And safely swims, into deep water goes,
And parts the seas, and spurns the treacherous foes :
Tight solid oak ! we praise her perfect frame,
She proudly drives majestic o'er the main !

 Thus are we tried for days, not knowing when
The hasty squalls shall catch the ship again.
Unbending sails engaging all the crew,
Repairing these, and setting others new :
Till from the land we draw towards the sea,
And flying terrors once more let us free.
Indignant Neptune rolls along the main,
And drives the squalls into their caves again.

  Then steer away, and on we gaily swoop

Between the islands of the Admiralty group ;
Light airs and calms and gentle winds prevail,
By night we anchor, and by day we sail.

The laggard ship lolls idly on the tide,
Canoes of naked men hang to her side ;
At first great care and doubt they seem to show
Towards the ship, until her purpose know ;
So many years since one had passed in sight,
That old men only ever knew the like.

We launch a boat, despatch her to the land,
To see what dwellings occupy the strand,
But natives fierce come gathering to the shore,
Forbid our landing to their homes explore.

Hostile in mien, they poise the ponderous spear,
Urged on by rapine or by needless fear,
Wait but the signal from their chief to throw,
With loud menace to strike the pending blow :

Pause then the crew, as their intention saw,
The better part in prudence to withdraw ;
Dumb motions try to be allowed to land,
The natives all in fierce defiance stand ;
The boats retire, indignant let them go,
The Lion scorns to fight with such a foe.

Next morn the natives paddle from the shore
Around the ship, on every side they pour ;
Most keep aloof, to reconnoitre run,
Nor can they be induced to nearer come.

Yet there was one, undaunted, closer pressed
In his own estimation highly blessed,
A chief who leads, no idle fear alarms
And seems to govern by the force of arms ;
And hands and legs for these he calls to use
His arguments to force as he may choose.

Above the rest, in high distinction shows

For ornament—a gimlet through his nose ;
His long drawn loops from ears enormous hang,
And well-strung limbs proclaim the lusty man.

Erect, around the ship his paddle plies,
But will not be induced to mount her sides,
In doubt he seems our movements to descry,
Our guns look strange to his unpractised eye ;
Or if he shall his naked warriors rise
To seize the ship, an undisputed prize.

His better judgment bids him to beware,
A nest of hornets may be lying there ;
Too great the risk, tho' little can he know
The awful power that from her sides may flow.

That gimlet whence ! or where our power to trace ?
What freak of fortune gave it such a place ?
Some poor mechanic must have served before,
Bartered, or stolen, parted evermore.

Emblem of wealth, the mystic jewel wears,
Exempts the chief from slavish servile cares,
The precious relic prized and cherished more,
Than shining splendour of the Koh-i-noor !

And few are those whose business 'tis to sell
Cocoas, and cocoanuts, and tortoiseshell.
By ancient means conduct their puny trade,
And deal in all things by exchanges made.

Suspicion haunts them, nothing will they trust,
The article be handed to them must
With which to trade ; to judge it on the spot
They all consult, and turn the offered lot :
A calculation keen o'er which they dwell,
'Twixt iron hoops and bits of tortoiseshell.

And small the portion their first offer make,
But double quickly if no less we'll take,
For worn gold lace, as well as trifles puny,

Anything will pass, save ready money ;
   Trinkets, shining buttons, old meat cans.
Glass, broken pieces, bottles, pots and pans,
Nails of iron prized with special care,
But solid cash can find no value there.

   Throughout the day, around the ship abide,
But fear forbids them all to mount her side,
Are towed for leagues, 'til all the sales are made,
And bartered off is all their stock in trade.

   Then on towards the east again we lay,
And leave the islands settling far away.
A few days' sail we make the land once more,
And coast along New Britain's pleasing shore,

   St. George's Channel bringing next in view,
By which we steer, to run the passage through.
Again canoes are springing from the shore,
Hang by to trade away their scanty store.

   Tall swarthy men, as nude as nature formed,
By her soft airs and genial sunshine warmed,
They paddle round and active seem : but none
Will board the ship, though much induced to come :
No reason known is, why they all should pause,
Some vile kidnapping might explain the cause.

   We cruise the coast, in search of water sailing,
And much amusement find in native trading.
For 'change a shell or fancy bird appears,
Unwieldy clubs, or ponderous barbèd spears ;
Not so much valued as the produce new
Of the land's abundance, to the hungry crew.

   Of these their wants providing day by day
Most scanty are, however much they pay.
Through length of voyage, water short on board,
A portion small allotted each afford.
Provisions have which merely life sustain

For luxuries unknown are to the main.
   Close with the shore, exploring every day,
For water seeking send the boats away,
No points of land laid down the ports to mark,
Or ill defined upon the ancient chart.
   A jutting spur and calms our progress stop,
As in a cove we let our anchor drop,
So oft erroneous every headland trace,
That supposition only names the place.
   No sooner moored than from within the bay,
A large canoe is paddling on the way
Towards the ship, across the heaving tides,
In which a native stands erect and guides.
   And fearless seems as close along he lays,
As if inured to all the seaman's ways,
The light of confidence had on him broke,
And shows itself at every pliant stroke.
   He sweeps around, and doubles to the tide,
Nor stays to ask, but mounts the vessel's side,
Turns to the deck, his tongue the silence breaks,
Surprising to our ears, he English speaks;
Explains that whaling ships for water seeking,
And hence of English he had learned the speaking.
   'Now if,' says he, 'my service you command
And 'tis in need of water pure you stand
I'll lead the way to where the flowing rills,
Bright, clear and sweet are bursting from the hills;
A genial place, where beasts and birds abound,
And trees for ever green spring from the ground.'

   His proffer take, decide to-morrow's dawn
Shall find us coursing o'er great Neptune's lawn,
To where the Naiads dwell, the promised port
Of gurgling streams, and teeming woodland sport.

But now, well armed, we send the boats to shore.
A landing force--if need be—to explore,
The port of Hunter ; pulling for the strand,
To learn what people occupy the land.

And unopposed we disembark the men,
Meet no obstruction to our prying ken.
Mud huts we find wherein the natives dwell,
And in profusion note the oysters' shell.

Worked in to fashion the small hollow cairn,
Around the place, in square, a low wall formed,
And naked children occupy the space,
Plump in their shape, and smooth each tawny face :

Play on the ground, and lively seem to view,
With dancing eyes, the unknown strangers who
From standpoint high look down with seeming scorn,
Which neither elevates nor does them harm.

From these we turn, a survey then begin,
To note the hut, and take a glance within.
From off the ground rude benches there arise,
Of leaves well dried the family couch comprise ;

Inside the place, sufficient space allowed
To sleep them all : or if a passing cloud
Its waters pours, and moistens all the plain,
They burrow safe protected from the rain.

This its sole use, for like the birds of air
No other cause will ever find them there :
And Sol perpetual always seems to shine
Soft, pure and radiant in this favoured clime.

And here the natives all most friendly are,
Tremendous fellows with huge heads of hair ;
With Britain's sons some close alliance claim,
Though not in race yet in their country's name.

Then with a friend I wander far away,
And from a hill observe a lovely bay.

And trace the cove ; some large canoes perceive,
A cosy house is nestling 'neath the trees :
    We reach the place, and to our great surprise,
A house of fair proportions greets our eyes,
Some marks of Europe's civilization : clear
That one of England's sons had settled here.

    For now we find some lusty children grown,
Half caste in colour, English speaking, own
Their sire's return ere this expected had,
To welcome us was sure he would be glad :
    In such a place ! here at Earth's utmost bound !
Ah ! where may not an Englishman be found?
Or Scotchman? who, 'tis said, will find a home
In any country through except his own.
    We found him settled in Brazilian hills,
In Africa he trades and delves and tills,
In Flowery Land, takes a Celestial bride,
Who though an outcast, proves a faithful guide.
    With pirates then, the eastern islands through,
In native dress we found him at Sooloo ;
In every clime, and corner of the earth,
Britannia's progeny can find a berth.
    We look about, and wander by the cove,
Up through by-paths, and in the woods we rove,
When suddenly, some heavy footfalls hear,
A very Crusoe seemed he drawing near.
    ' Hail, thou ! my countryman,' he loudly shouts,
' And what good fortune drove you hereabouts,
I watched you closely, as from sea ye drew ;
Sent my lieutenant round to ask if you
Fresh water sought, to take his usual post,
And point it out upon the Irish coast.'
    Beneath a tree, outside his porch we sat

In conversation long; we smoke and chat,
His history told, in which he proved to be,
An ardent stoic in philosophy.

  ' Do tell us, friend,' I said, ' why you prefer
To quit your native land, and settle here.
Your mien and language have conclusive proved,
Society in higher grade had moved.'

  ' It may seem strange,' he said, ' but life to me
Not worth preserving save that it be free :
For this I work, desert my native land,
And with these people take my final stand.

  ' Whose laws are simple, easily understood,
By those who seek their own and others' good ;
Whose wants are few, and luxuries unknown,
Benignant nature gives as seeds are sown :
For fish the sea, for fowl we hunt the land,
And till sufficient for our health's demand.

  ' Religion pure, from it we have no fear,
For Nature's laws are all we study here.
For this I shun the crowded hall and mart,
Where form and custom hold their baneful court,
Vie with each other in the selfish boast,
Of who shall grasp, and who retain the most.

  ' We have no coin, and long may we withstand
The evil root, and keep it from the land.
Shall not seduce us with its glittering lure
To evil actions, and to thoughts impure.

  ' Here I may say I rule,—for what is power,
Save that entrusted to us as a dower ?
We must accept the boon as Nature sends ;
And dedicate it to her own high ends ;

  ' In prominence, or wheresoe'er its seen,
Superior knowledge always rules supreme,
For good or ill, ourselves may not define,

The secret's hid in Nature's great design,
And all is settled in a right divine.

'Years past,' said he, 'as now advanced by you,
In worldly parlance I was "well to do,"
But found no footing in the sphere I stood,
And took no pains to make that footing good.

'My sire a merchant, owning many keels :
His only child an ardent wish reveals
For bold adventures ; fretting to be free,
Naught could engage me but to go to sea.

'I importuned him when a splendid ship
Was fitting out, in her to take a trip ;
Though long had he this wish of mine resented,
Withstood it still till he at length consented ;
And so, with bounding heart, and sails unfurled,
I sought the ocean to explore the world.

'And southward steer, and at Madeira stay,
Sargossa Sea, and Rio on the way,
Then eastward ho ! a boisterous passage make,
Towards Australia, and through Bass's Strait;
Around the coast, and at Port Jackson call,
Discharge our cargo, and refit withal.

'Then off again towards the north we stand,
With gentle winds we course along the land,
Gaily go onward o'er the rippling sea,
'Til "Torres Strait" is hailed upon the lee.

'New Guinea then brake fairly to the view,
As nearer still the flying vessel drew,
The breeze was fair, and broad appeared the deep :
We think we know a passage through the reef.
For through it much the nearer way is found,
For craft from hence for southern China bound ;
The chart consulted, traced with true precision,

The nearer way had choice in the decision.
  'Oh, false resolve! what demon dogs thy steps!
What councils wise, and nicely weighed precepts,
What generous hopes, what secret joys appraised,
What patient toil, and what great fabrics raised,
What thrones thought firm, and nations safe withal,—
In one soft breath hurled to destruction all!
  ' The word went forth—That we would try the strait!
Broad, intricate, beset with dangers great;
Precautions take to send a boat ahead
To feel the passage with the sounding-lead.
  ' What boots it care, precaution what avail,
When Error steers, and Fate fills out the sail,
And draws the line across the destined spot,
And cuts the cord upon a pointed rock!
And leaves us there to struggle but in vain,
Betwixt the mighty sea and savage main.
Man-eating tribes that prowl the coast thereof,
And numerous other ills we know not of.
  ' There all was lost; held by the hidden snare,
What high resolves and blighted hopes lay there!
With riven planks the waters inward sped,
Half filled the ship, which settled by the head.
  ' The boats are manned, with full provision stowed,
As from the wreck towards the shore we rowed,
With ammunition and what arms we had,
A mournful train, forlorn of hope and sad;
And found a cove wherein to safely land,
And laid our boats and stores upon the strand.

  'Alas! how futile all desires to plan,
When adverse fate derides the hopeful man.
His purpose high in adamantine binds,
And future projects casteth to the winds:

Marks out another road, another scheme,
Beyond his power to think, his mind to dream.
For oh ! the tides of fortune still oppose,
Tumultuous sounds from out the bush arose,
Ominous voices, breaking close at hand,
Are heard in savage joy along the strand.
In numbers great the natives line the beach
And plunder everything within their reach ;
In taking all we have they do persist,
And threaten savagely if we resist.

 ' Our crew enraged, from out their hands they tear
The pillaged goods, and could no more forbear
To guard the stock they had so careful stored,
Struck at a black, and knocked him overboard :
This signal made, they in a general rush
Despoil the boats, and all our hopes do crush.
The fight grew fierce, the blacks assault our men
Who in return assault the blacks again ;
These use their clubs, their spears in showers descend,
Whilst those with broken oars themselves defend.

 ' I launched a boat—the smallest,—pulled away,
Convenient at a distance off I lay,
My rifle plied, and down at every round,
The foremost black would give a yell and bound :
Still raged the fight, and battled well our crew,
"Till every man the natives ruthless slew,
Then drew away, from off the sandy beach,
To where my rifle would no longer reach.

 ' I seek the ship, and fly the fatal shore :
All lonely left, in sadness to deplore
That I was spared from out the luckless crew,
More trials to bear, more woes to undergo.

 ' Ah ! what a fearful day was that to me !
Alone upon the wreck, far out at sea,

Blue sky above, the ocean blue around,
And savage men withal possess the ground.
  'In wandering mind I felt myself beside :
Wistful, I gazed into the gentle tide,
More gentle far than these, the savage race,
Their awful customs, and their grim grimace.
Among such men,—if rescued—dumb must feel,
High heaven alone to whom I may appeal,
And meekly bear the torture, pain and death ;—
My brain so reeled I had no reason left.

  'All day my pensive thoughts could find no rest :
The fate of all the crew I too well guessed.
Vacant I gazed as night was drawing near,
Bright from the ocean's bed the moon rose clear.
  'Ah, what a contrast ! were I free in thought
What pleasures would the smiling orb have brought,
But horrid phantoms all my senses cloyed,
The glorious moon could not light up the void.
  'Lonely I watched the waning night to close,
As Sol in greatness from the ocean rose :
No wink of sleep, still gazing on the sea,
Stark staring mad I seemed myself to be.
  'Or if to fly, where ever could I go ?
'Twas better far to sink at once below :
Eternal sleep will close my eyelids fast
In one brief moment all my troubles past.
  'Then from all thoughts of reverie I wake,
As splashing sounds of paddles on me break,
And, turning round, I careless seem to greet
The vile canoes my eye-balls listless meet.
  'A power compelled, I could no more control,
The yawning waters fascinate my soul,
I mount the rail, and take the dreadful leap,

Unconscious screamed, and sank into the deep
'I knew no more, the world was lost to me,
As fairly dead as anything could be ;
'Till sometime after, on a bed of leaves
I wake, to find myself among the thieves.

'But now all dread had flown, I thought no more
Of vile atrocities that day on shore ;
Seemed so reduced, and very little prized
The life thus saved, or if I lived. or died.

'Returning thoughts began to 'wake anon,
And speculate upon my doom to come.
It could not be their rough attentions poured,
Merely to wreak their vengeance when restored.

'I scanned the hut. looked round about the place,
And thought I saw some kindness in each face.
A stalwart black just entering at the door
Pointed to something lying on the floor.

'Upon my arm I raised, and looking round,
Beside my bed, on leaves, my rifle found,
With all the ammunition I possessed,
Together with my clothes, and large sea chest.

'The rifle took, he stroked it up and down,
As though some living wonder had been found,
And sniffed it over. muzzle, breech and stock,
And hugged it close, and tried the shining lock.

'Then put it to his ear, then to his eye.
And points the piece, as if to fire it try :
With greatest care restores it to its place,
As I had shown him, in its polished case ;
Its prowess,—even here,—had gone before,
He guards it well, the treasure covers o'er,

'And bids me sleep, and heaped again the leaves,
And propped my head, to give me greater ease.

I felt relieved, and rightly now surmised
My life was saved as by my rifle prized.
   ' My chest they knew because an ample stock,
Of ammunition like to that without,
Found in the boat, where I had made it felt,
In retribution prompt and swiftly dealt.
   ' For days I could not quit my leafy bed ;
And when at length was by attendant led
Out round the place, and just as soon as dared,
Began to think of how the crew had fared.
   ' Succeeded fast to make them understand,
To tell me where the boats lay on the strand ;
The chief the first to catch my wish, and tries
To explain they were among their enemies.
   ' And pointed to the place along the coast,
But dared not go there, though so fierce in boast,
That they would fight, annihilate, destroy,
And eat them after, with the greatest joy.
   ' For years I lived here, often strained my eyes
To where the seas, projected, touch the skies :
No sail perceive to which my life I'd trust
And feel the immunity upon me thrust.
   ' Oft launch my boat, and out to seaward stand,
At times almost to lose the sight of land ;
Returning home, for days would rest again,
Then turn to hunt and seek the bounding game ;
   ' But dreading lest my power in powder waste,
And on a level with these men be placed,
Contented rest with arrow, spear and trap,
The birds of plume and other game to track.

   ' Thus pass my time, with exercises tire,
Then with the natives sit about the fire,
Invent a tambour with discordant sound,

And move their souls to dance and caper round.
 'When twilight set, it was their great delight
To assemble round me 'til the fall of night,
To hear the many things that I could teach,
Which, otherwise, were far beyond their reach.
And every day surprised them more and more,
They ne'er had known canoes to sail before,
And scarce would venture 'til I showed them plain,
They might with safety sail the glittering main.
 'We prowled the coast in search of pastures new,
And round towards New Britain gradual drew :
I searched the land, and wandered far and wide,
My guardian chief attendant at my side :
And round about here, found the natives were
More docile, kind, painstaking with their hair,
With folds of tappa-cloth about the waist,
Which show at least they have some kind of taste.
 'I waited long, and sailed the coast around,
Resolved if once a passing sail I found,
Unceremoniously to quit the shore,
And seek the stranger, and return no more.
With patience still, I calmly led the chief,
Lulled all suspicion, fostered the belief,
By subtle means, to gratify their ways,
That I would stay the length of all my days.
 'And fifteen years had passed before I saw,
A sailing craft across the ocean draw :
I was afloat and stood towards the sail,
And dropped athwart, and loudly 'gan to hail.
 'They heard my call, and hove the vessel to,
And o'er her side quick peered the curious crew,
Down on the craft I trimmed my sail and hied,
Hung to her hull and mounted up her side.
 'The captain stared, and viewed me with surprise :

A half-clad white man stood before his eyes :
Himself was Dutch, a little English spoke :
With mutual gaze we thus the silence broke.
  ‘ In effort strong, I cried. “ I’m English, sir !”
“ Mein Got den ! vat for you doin’ here !”
Was his reply: “ In te name of all vot’s goot,
Vare for you come here, vit de nigger broot ?”

  ‘ I soon explained what cast me them among,
With much distress revived my mother tongue :
To one of English ten of native spoke,
And found my language altogether broke.
With greater ease began then to relate,
How I was left abandoned to my fate.
The chief would not consent that I should leave.
But hoped he may my great distress relieve,
And take me on, assist me in my view,
To the nearest port that he was going to.
  ‘ We sailed away, and very soon I found,
The Dutchman was for South Australia bound.
Port Jackson hail, we run between the Heads,
And on to Sydney town the craft proceeds.
  ‘ On shore I went, to agents quick repaired,
And told my story how the ship had fared,
About the wreck, the thieving natives who
Had stripped the boats, and murdered all the crew,
Except myself, who by a tribe was spared,
With whom for fifteen years their life I’d shared.
  ‘ The agent then—a kind and humane man—
Declares at once he will do all he can.
Exclaims, “ Poor man ! direct I’ll set about ;
The truth of what you say, I cannot doubt :
And I will write to see how matters stand.
Meantime, about us here keep close at hand ;

Take this," he cries, " your present wants supply,
If more you need at once to me apply."
He gave me coin, and told me when I could,
Return it back—as well he knew I would.

' Alas ! what visions fill the human brain,
What stores of bliss, desiring hopes maintain !
Could it but live on hope, what joyous days
Would crown the race in its confiding ways !
But fate more stern cuts from the mortal's grasp
The dangling cup he fain would seize and clasp.
' And long I waited anxiously to hear,
For fateful news instinctively I fear,—
My parents' age, myself for ever lost,—
Their only hope—might well their lives have cost.
' An adverse star had passed across my life,
And left it to vicissitudes and strife ;
The link once broke, and oh ! what miseries flow,
And where 'twill end, ah ! who shall say or know.
A father's care, and all that wealth commands,
Cut off at once by fate's unsparing hands.

' At length an answer came across the sea,
Quite full of woe which gave a shock to me.
My parents both had died from grief and care,
Unknown my fate, or if I lived or where ;
And more the missive then went to relate,
A relative of wealth held the estate,
Prepared to fight, by every means retain
'Gainst any source, or right or wrong the claim.
Had sworn me dead, and as the next of kin
Declared the heir was, and, admitted in,
Had fortified the post, and edged it round,
With bribes and politics defends the ground.

'I'm not surprised, my agent here remarks,
Impromptu some experience imparts.
Says he : "However right, yet to my eyes
Possession is nine-tenths, the other lies
Within the purse, and family connections,
To guarantee thee in thy expectations.

' " If thou hast none, it is thy great misfortune,
They smooth the way, the hardest heart will soften :
With these e'en truth itself will lie secure,
Without them, friend, much intrigue may ye fear.
For some believe in truth, but more in money;
Some the infallibility of Judge and Jury;
And some in law, although they often see
Its learned interpreters so widely disagree.

' " And some on politics with faith rely,
And some on force, and all the world defy,
And some for even justice vainly call,
But force is found the safest guide by all.

' " Where all's confused, where lies the plainest proof?
Where all the attributes of simple truth,
Grope through the maze to find where justice lay,
To find that force blocks up the rightful way.

' " Therefore, my friend, if peace you seek to find
To rest contented, undisturbed in mind,
You'll shun the trial, try to conquer here,
And push your fortune in some other sphere."

'Struck dumb by such a blow, in heaven's sight,
The tide of fortune overwhelmed me quite ;
I counsel sought, the might of gold I saw,
I asked for "justice," and was offered "law"!

'And, to my gaze, therein the spectres rise,
With silver tongues, and armed with polished lies.
See him protected by the golden shields,

12

How dexterously the wordy weapon wields :
See with what skill he throws the venomed dart,
In high perfection of the sophist's art :
In what disdain he holds all honour's laws.
Seeks and obtains the sycophants' applause.
Who at his beck, the ready hireling crew,
Breathe forth their fawning preconcerted cue.

'None knows as he who by experience taught,
Who through the earth the fight for truth has fought,
A keen observer of the world in strife.
In Nature's lap has dangled with his life,
That she's progressive, never can restore
The severed links as they were known before.
Leaves us to mourn, retracing to our cost,
To find the missing ties were better lost.

' I shuddering think to find myself enrolled
Against the tactics of unscrupulous gold.
Against the phalanxes of legal lore.
For he that hath to strip the suppliant poor.

' I'll off again, where peace and plenty dwell,
And fly the influence of the gilded spell ;
From all such terrors I had much to fear,
So back I turned anon and settled here.

'Reflecting on myself, the life I led.
Or why live on, or were I better dead ?
'Tis but a life, whatever may befall,
And yet that life is reckoned with withal.

' Or wherefore given, in the power to give ?
Or if fulfilled, then why allowed to live ?
For purpose saved, whate'er that purpose be.
I must pursue, though all unknown to me.

''Tis Nature's doom ! and I admit it quite.
Nature gives force, and force makes all things right .

'Tis but her way, there can be no denial,
And for the triumph this is but the trial ;
  ' For out of wrong doth every right proceed,
And out of right shall every wrong succeed ;
But not perfection, that's to all denied :
Errors alone our erring footsteps guide,
Wide is error, broad as East from West,
A point perfection on which naught can rest.

  ' A plan I cherished with a firm resolve,
Civilized lands to quit, for good and all :
I sailed from Sydney Town to find a home,
Where I might settle, never more to roam.
  'These islands, found, seemed suited to my taste,
And peopled by a docile pleasing race,
Happy appeared, and I determined, too,
To be as happy, and some good to do.
Had I my right, in England made my stay,
Indulged in pride, and spent my life away,
With indolence, and wanton pleasure run
A targe for keener wits to prey upon :
A useless life, to benefit the knaves,
For fools will squander as the wise man saves.
  ' All is human, there's a force behind,
Engendering every thought to every mind :
All are its tools, yield blind submission to,
Unseen, but felt in everything we do,
That animates us to our high belief,
And prompts the action of the meanest thief.
  ' I studied long and practised what I thought,
Unlearned the many things I had been taught ;
At length succeeded, closed the mental strife,
And would not now attempt another life.

' And now, my friend, if such a home should charm,
A life of freedom pure your bosom warm,
If no engagements tie your constant mind,
Amongst us may a pleasing welcome find.

' Here come and live, in genial ease retire,
With exercise as Nature's claims require ;
Where all is free, the pleasant wide domain,
The rolling hills, the undulating plain.

' The forests green, that with the mountains rise,
The dew of heaven collecting as it flies,
Life's sustentation,—all unknown a dearth—
Spontaneous springs abundant from the earth,
No aid we need from stimulating wealth,
To bring us plenty, comfort, ease, and health.

' No matrimonial quarrels vex the state,
Free love unfettered shoots his arrows straight,
As birds of air, they couple as they list,
No thoughts but love intrude their minds to twist.
Sickness unknown, no dire disease invades
The healthful body, or the mind enslaves.
Evils destroying none may know the taste,
No foolish luxuries can find a place ;
Live isolated, do a little trade,
Each benefited in the exchanges made.
No dens of vice or reeking slums to face,
No politicians clamouring for place,
No agitations or convulsive throes,
Internal enemies or foreign foes.

' Knowledge enough to all their wants provide,
They hunt, they play, and care for naught beside;
Nor seek they more for anything beyond
Their island home, by ocean guarded round.

' All are alike, nor rich, nor poor are known,
All reap in plenty what they may have sown :

No mad ambition haunts the peaceful mind,
In Nature's bounty all that's needed find.'

'My friend,' I said, 'in such a heaven to stay
I fear I'm not prepared without delay;
Myself to such a transformation bind,
Requires reflection of the gravest kind.
'No! no! too well I know a favoured strand
Where, heaven permitting, I shall one day land.
Though pleased I would resign the treacherous main,
My fate impels me not to here remain.
'To abide with thee at present cannot dare,
To pass a life entirely free from care;
Peace may be yours, as now becomes your due,
But I am young and different far from you.
'Though such a life may fair to many seem,
With me, my friend, must ever be a dream.
For there are many things that bar the way
Against the consummation of my stay;
Against it duty, honour, friendship, stand,
To force me homeward to my native land.
'Priv'leged I am, with naught at all to lose,
The world before, the fairest spot to choose,
And come what may in life's revolving chain,
A change with me must be a change of gain.'
'But here,' says he, 'we've neither loss nor gain,
Calm and oblivious roll our days the same:
'Tis loss and gain that set the world asunder,
In other words, a ready means of plunder.
'The vulgar call it so, the gentle try
To express the same and not the word apply;
Therefore with those 'tis policy, civilization,
Advancement, power, trade, income, speculation:
All these repressive are, to other's cost,
For where there's money made there's labour lost.'

Then to the court a lively maiden sprang,
Her joyous voice with prattling English rang,
As to his knee she bounded with a skip,
'Oh ! father dear, we went to see the ship.
Down by the reef I strolled, and Zella found,
We launched the small canoe and paddled round :
We saw the guns, the masts, and all the crew,
All dressed in white, and all are white men too.

'Eyed us askance.'   Her arms around him flung
Confidingly, about his neck she hung,
And softly whispered as she nearer drew,
'Are all your countrymen so good as you.'

Our friend, amused, assists her to disperse
Her faults in English, as she should converse,
His face illumed with joy, as in accord
She frames the sentence, or drops in the word.

His open features broad and fine, display
A man of thought, and kindness every way ;
His measured tone, his free and witty mirth,
At once proclaim him one of gentle birth
And education, though so wild let run,
Furrowed with care, and bronzed by tropic's sun ;
In prominence the mind's fertility,
Stamped with the die of rough gentility.

Spell-bound I listened, charmed with great surprise,
And as I gaze my thoughts conflicting rise,
All English speak, and peering as I stood
Could trace the signs of native lusty blood.

In Europe's fashion partly clad with taste,
And part with native cloth below the waist,
Display at once the limbs of graceful form,
And give to each an Oriental charm.

'And now,' says he, 'at thy disposal stand,

Our humble home, and products of the land ;
We know no difference here, all as one flock,
And all alike are as one common stock.

    ' Nature's children, fearless, frank and free,
We sport, we play, work for ourselves, and we
Let Nature rule, subservient at her side,
Walk in her paths, observe her as our guide ;
Go where she points, and seek the silent way
Why all must yield to her unerring sway.

    ' By few indeed are seen her true precepts,
And who can fathom her extremest depths?
From systems vast to minute atoms small,
Pervading all things, perfect, all in all.

    ' Destroying, forming, novelties to give,
The weakest crumble, and the fittest live ;
Sublime and whole, and, rightly understood,
Evolving ever universal good.

    ' As to her creatures, all that's needed known,
So in their actions her control is shown ;
Nay, not a thought but her behest inspires,
So not an act but her decree requires.

    ' Her triumphs great we praise, and fear her rod :
We say 'tis Nature, and you say 'tis God ;
Equal with you we claim the law divine,
And Truth alone will stand the test of time.'

    With this he pressed us still again to stay,
But answering thus, we rose and broke away :
    ' No ! no ! my friend, you plead to us in vain,
For we must go where higher natures reign,
Where, more developed, fiercer wields the strife,
Where all must fight for it who value life.

    ' Go where the flag of promise had its birth,
And spread its influence throughout the earth,

To friendly commerce held the proffered hand,
And sent its argosies to every land.
   ' Where art and arms in combination toil,
Defy all comers to invade their soil,
Excepting those with good intent declare,
They come their trials and their wealth to share,
Obey their laws, and take their destined place,
Among the workers of a generous race.

   ' Go where the hives this busy throng engage,
Where centred lie the wonders of the age ;
The hissing steam, the blasting furnace roars,
Ejecting flame, and pouring glowing ores ;
Where spinning-wheels continuous buzz around,
And rollers crush, and ponderous hammers pound.
Where mighty engines test their awful strength,
And bulky ingots yield their breadth to length.
   ' Where grimy workers sweat to hold the pace.
With all things moving in the timèd race.
Each in his sphere their labours well discharge.
Work for themselves and all mankind at large.
   ' Go where the young, who o'er their studies pore,
Imbibe the thoughts of ages gone before,
Stored up in tomes, receptacles of gains,
The shallow loses, and the wise retains.
   ' Whilst those, to lower labours must incline.
As shadowed forth within the law divine.
The wiser soar, and circling higher, find
A broader scope to view and judge mankind.
   ' Go where the race, with inspirations fraught,
Though seas divide, are flashing thought to thought ;
Where Nature's holds are yielding to their might,
Her secrets searched and many brought to light.
   ' The Earth is delved to where her forces lay.

Found in the gloom, and dragged to light of day,
Their powers controll'd, directed to fulfil
The many needs of its all-conquering will ;
The race extant—excepting in the name—
Republics, Empires, Kingdoms, still the same.
    ' Severe the work its station to withstand,
Where Nature drives and holds a tight'ning hand,
With social leagues, and high monopolies bind.
Wheels within wheels, the unsuspecting grind,
    ' As onward ever is her course controlled,
Her votaries dazzling with her thongs of gold,
Flames through the whole with shining silver rein,
Her car of Juggernaut she drives amain :
Fanatics crushing, 'neath her golden wheel,
Who worship not her as the true ideal.
    ' With promise great, that those who win the prize,
Shall through the world to high dominion rise ;
That prize the greatest in her power to give,
The race the fittest shall survive and live.
Nor live in vain ! this gift by Nature given,
Must lead mankind the nearest way to heaven.'
    We bade adieu ; and hurried to the strand,
As sable night was shadowing the land :
On board to dream of castaways, their trials,
Of native islanders, and sunny isles.

    Next morning when the dawn of day appears,
Our swarthy guide across the channel steers,
Direct on for the opposing shore he stands,
And points the way with both extended hands.
    New Ireland make, whose rugged coasts seen nigh,
Ere any opening in the land espy :
And as it's found the gentle breezes fail,
Declining more to fill the wanton sail.

Ship idly lies, and in the narrow strait
We launch our boats, to further progress make ;
But ere 'tis done towards the shore she falls
And rubs her sides against its rocky walls ;
  So deep the pass unrippled by the breeze,
The yards, outstretching, tangle in the trees ;
And from the woods the friendly natives spring
About the trees, and to the rigging cling.
  And board the ship, and seem in much delight
With everything, so novel to their sight ;
Appear at once by far a better race,
With rich brown skins, and finer fashioned face.
  A garment twisted round about the loins
A grotesque ornamental fashion joins,
A huge head-dress, with frizzled hair dyed brown,
Or whitened, as a pantomimic clown ;
Or one side black, the other ochred red,
Devices various to adorn the head.

  The boats lay off, the ship draws from the trees,
And from the rocks the sylvan embrace frees,
And slowly glides on through the narrow strait,
Into a deep, calm, open, charming lake.
  The Cyclops had, in ages long gone past,
Their furnace here, and blew a blazing blast ;
The waste of lava rough had scooped a gorge,
The refuse of the boiling, roaring forge ;
The work had finished, and the fire withdrawn,
The whole subsiding in the cooling down,
Into the cleft great Neptune poured his flood,
In occupation where the crater stood.
  Old Time lays on, and mellowing all the soil,
Obliterates the scoria of the toil ;
In art divine Sylvanus paints the hills,
With bright green tints the space of woodland fills.

And here I love alone to stray away,—
Strange taste, my comrades oftentimes would say,—
Across the hills, towards some point of land,
From which I may a prospect full command.

Am often found within the deep ravine,
By waters rushing, or the purling stream ;
And hours spend about some lonely spot,
The peak's high summit, or the Naiad's grot.

And much I feel enraptured with the place
As through the woods a high point gain to trace,
The many charms such fairy spots obtain,
And in an ecstasy I thus exclaim :—

' Earth's cares and trammels disengage my mind !
And let it soar, in unison to find
That inspiration which the subject needs,
Which buoys the hopeful, and the poet feeds.

' Awake, my soul ! all minor things avaunt,
Leave me to sing of Nature's lovely haunt ;
That paradise which all so long have sought
Is hidden here by the same hand that wrought,
Where Phœbus gilds the scene with glittering ray,
And god of ocean greets the god of day.

' The limit where the imagination dwells,
On sylphs and nymphs, and fairy beings' spells,
Where chaste Diana bounding from the woods,
Awaits to bathe her limbs in Neptune's floods ;
Or, fleet of foot, the flying virgin train,
Pursued by Satyrs, or in chase of game.'

Here feathered tribes in plumage gay abound
Without a fear, and flitting closely round ;
Now soaring high, below their shadows throw,
And in the deep a pure reflection show ;

Which now lies calm, deprived of all its force,
The ship no anchor needs to stay the course ;

No tide to drift her to the wastes of sea,
No winds to force her to the shores a-lee.
  Surrounding hills upon her cast their shade,
As in her place appears by Nature laid :
Around her thrown a soft and silent charm,
Suspended lies on Neptune's azure arm ;
The elements deprived of all their power,
And Nature sleeps, in this her charming bower.

  A single man walks by the silver tide,
His gentle Eve is sauntering by his side,
A bond of love hangs nestling at her breast,
Its parents' blessing, in its parents blessed :
In detail Nature working out the plan,
Another Abel growing into man.

  And time now flies, more quickly than before
Sweet days are passed, betwixt the ship and shore.
New Ireland, whose beauties hours beguile,
Outvies in grandeur far the Emerald Isle.
  As picturesque its green-clad rocky coast,
And, but for salt, Killarney's lakes might boast :
Port Carteret in memory lingers clear,
And dwells for life within the mind to cheer.
  A wondrous depth of water here is found,
And long the pull to get from off the ground
The anchor which, by slow degrees we trip,
And have it up securely to the ship ;
And spread our sails, run through the channel free,
And once again are bounding o'er the sea.

NEW IRELAND TO SYDNEY.

Run south direct, and in our easy flight,
The Solomon group soon falls within the sight ;
Down by the isle of Satisfaction steer,
And that of Eddystone go passing near.

Right through them all, perceiving, close ahead
Across the bow, a shoal of Grampus sped,
In boiling foam a steady course preserves,
With fountains spouting high in graceful curves.

They occupy a wondrous space around,
As on they urge with heavy plunging sound,
Tremendous fish majestic swim the seas,
And naught disturbs them in their seeming ease.

As all feel wearied by the irksome route,
Are pleased to find such game at which to shoot,
An enemy assume, in numbers strong
Surround the ship, and in their midst among.

Sharp rolls the drum, to quarters calls the crew,
The foe is breaking sudden to the view,
The quiet ship is roused to active life,
And rises ready to commence the strife.

Quick all around the cannons loudly roar,
As from her sides the fiery torrents pour ;
In hot discharge, a quick succession keep,
And solid bolts are hurled against the fleet.

To trim the sails the sailors active bound,
To break his line and close the foe around,
Manœuvring a champion ship to rake,
To throw a broadside and his timbers shake.

With practice sharp our forces strong employ,
Our duty is, to sink, to burn, destroy,

In fierce assault.   Withal our thunders fail
To make much havoc with the numerous sail.
    A field day's sport, leviathan the game,
Coursing and bounding o'er the azure plain,
Such as the grisly god great Neptune breeds,
And wide domain of Oceanus feeds.
    Some, bounding high, leap straight into the air ;
Some rush along, their curving bodies bare ;
Some dive direct, huge tails are seen to rise,
One leaves the school, and fast and furious flies.
    Then off they turn, and spout a cloud of spray,
And roll along, and puff and steam away ;
Amongst the shallows spread themselves around,
And find their safety on the treacherous ground.
    Some lag behind, and give themselves to die,
Turn their white bellies to the attesting sky,
We haul the wind, forego the hostile chase,
And leave them there to live or die in peace.
    From off the shoal Jack trims his sails in haste.
Quixotic warfare is not to his taste,
And points his yards, and sneering ' Let them go.'
He inward groans to meet a sterner foe.

    Stand south away, down by New Holland sped,
Sight Hervey Bay, and pass the Indian Head,
When loud again infuriate Neptune raves,
And the brave crew as stern his anger braves.
    So furious flies the sudden whistling blast,
That every sail burst fluttering from the mast,
And eager ocean raging for its prey,
High leaps aboard, impatient of delay.
    The ship drives on before the raging storm,
A floating waif across the ocean borne,
Until the crew a new strong sail display,

Between the masts, upon the straining stay ;
  With this she dares, and turns to face the gale,
And bravely fights it with the assisting sail :
Too close the reefs with black'ning night at hand,
Before the morn our wreck may strew the strand.

  And all the crew a sense of duty feel,
With readiness attend the high appeal,
Without a sail to urge the watery way,
Save that alone that's dragging at the stay.

  And ere the morn breaks through the low'ring sky,
To 'scape the rocks are active all to try,
With new sails set, contending with the waves
Whilst Æolus roars, and fierce and fiercer raves.

  With mighty gusts he presses on the more,
Towards the rocks that line the beaten shore,
Tack on and tack, and hugging close the wind.
Approaching now, now leave the rocks behind.

  So close they work, so quick the yards fly round,
That at each tack they still were gaining ground,
And try the ship up to her utmost strain.
Which nobly acts : as yet all seems in vain,
For now another sail is rent in twain.

  Undaunted still, the tempest driving hard.
With steady grip the sailors man the yard :
Feet, hands, and teeth to lashing ropes they cling,
Lest to the waves the blasts their bodies fling.

  Not far away they know the threatening shore,
Their voices drown'd are in the general roar ;
They heed it not, determined to prevail,
Hang to the yard, unbend the riven sail,
Succeed they must, for in its very face
Another flaunts, and set is in its place.

  But ere 'tis done much weather ground is lost,
We think we are within the breakers tossed,

But fortune smiles, their bravery rewards :
The men descending quickly from the yards,
Haul to the gale, the trembling ship careens,
And to the deep points down her slanting beams.

The huge high waves she breaks upon her prow
And sends them over in continuous flow,
The boiling surf is close upon her lee,
She forward draws, and points her head to sea.

And off she drives, and leaves the foaming coast,
As through the haze it gradually is lost.
For four long days we battled with the blast,
The fifth it lulled and blew its blatant last ;
But left us bare, small spars and cordage broke,
And all our sails in shreds at one fell stroke.
Some spare ones find, and these at once they bend,
And all engage ; the rest, to patch and mend ;
And one by one upon the yards they hale,
Until again we speed with full spread sail.

Down by the coast of east Australia led,
And catch the land again as seen ahead,
The wall-like cliffs along its length arise,
And shut Port Jackson from our longing eyes.

Stand for the coast, and long no inlet traced,
But Botany Bay upon the left is placed,
Where Cook on landing first the Port espied,
And traced the lake-like harbour far inside.

Close in we steer, and find the crooked course
Through which, with baffling winds, our way we force :
On either side its sandstone cliffs arise,
And deep blue water calm between them lies.

The estuary past, a sense of wonder grew,
The spacious lake broke sudden to our view,
With islands dotted, dropped in here and there,

And ocean's azure plains lie everywhere.

Upon the left here runs the sandstone wall,
Which long had stood there at great Nature's call.
Her bulwarks massive, picturesque and grand,
To bind within their limits sea and land.

Far in the north the green-clad hills extend,
With many a shaded grove and graceful bend :
The islands shut the harbour's width from sight,
As far away it stretches on the right.

And on we sail along the southern beach,
Until the famous town of Sydney reach,
Where Britain's sons their genial tastes retain,
In varied beauty of that fine domain ;
Where mansions rise, and health and wealth abound,
Where nature spreads her teaming bounties round,
The land with beasts, the sea alive with fish,
And every comfort that mankind could wish.

A state congenial have we found at last,
As in Farm Cove with joy our anchor cast,
Where fresh green lawns are sloping to the shore,
By which we lay our wearied ship and moor.

CANTO V.

SYDNEY.

An English home ! what joy within we feel,
As happy thoughts upon our senses steal ;
Where sounds of busy life and active men
Are heard once more, to be enjoyed again.

Most spacious wharves, by convict labour raised
For which the mother country should be praised,--
Weeds of ill growth cast from the purer font,
Their ways of evil turned to good account,
That loyal sons, who from her side had strayed,
By these may find a home already made.

The convicts freed, and penitent by toil,
Hang to the place, and love the genial soil ;
Sent from their country for their mutual good,
Now bless the act that gave them ample food.

Each happy lives, and in domestic life,
Proud of his offspring and his frugal wife ;
Where love conjointly all past care atones,
And blest contentment rests upon their homes.

Unnoticed here, the place with these abound,
And good and bad are still amongst them found ;
Of that which brought them here no trouble find,
But freely speak of it with open mind.

By discipline subdued, and ample time,
They learn that fairness better pays than crime.

With plenty crowned, and 'neath a mild control,
Most generous hearts we find throughout the whole.

All English still such genial kindness show,
We know not who they are or want to know
Beyond the few, and caste is known no more.
Some may be rich, but none are very poor ;
Some force their way at cost of other's fall
But honest men are here most prized of all !

Some are on whom the stamp of nature found.
As savage beasts still prowl the country round.
Extremes of human kind, in these we trace
The enemies of all the human race.

Untamed by laws, which guide the common stock,
All feeling pure the vile bush-rangers shock,
Whose depredations, wild and cowardly fame,
Will hunt them down, and soon efface the name,

But here all order reigns, and men resign
Their thoughts to peace, in every new design,
With splendid roads, and open busy streets,
Cosy villas, neat secluded seats.

The well-built town, as England is the same,
And all its pleasures here revived again;
The graceful dance ; the sprightly drama lends
Its inspiration to its numerous friends,   .
And Shakespeare glows at earth's extremest ends.

And friends I traced who, some few years before,
By an appointment left old England's shore,
Were settled here, upon Goat Island found,
Full up the harbour guarded well around.

Where magazines of high explosives are,
Of which my friends the guardian keepers were,
Where Paramatta rolls his tides, retained
Within an estuary of beauty famed.

With some of these enjoy the peaceful shore,
So late from savage lands we prize the more.
Gay days we spend, invigorate our lives
With country tours, and pleasant rides and drives.
    And now resolve a visit to the Bay,
And plan a picnic, there to spend a day ;
Vehicles hire, and with a plenteous store,
The boon of pleasure seek again once more.
    And England's offshoots join us in the route,
And fairer seem as here transplanted out,
No thought have these the stock from whence they came,
England to them an island o'er the main.
    In it their dreams some mystic grandeur find,
Which nations sways, with millions of mankind,
Whose sovereign Queen a spell around them throws,
Whose fame unsullied as a halo glows.
Whose name in childhood all were taught to lisp,
And in whose prestige find a secret bliss,
Some close connection with the monarch feel
And show their sympathy with the grand ideal.
    And then we are off, and quit the town to gain
A level, broad, and wide extending plain
Of drifting sand, that's glaring to the sight,
And bleaching pure, and fine and dazzling white.
    As where the gale of sullen Boreas brings
The charged snow-cloud upon its ladened wings.
Then lulls its force, and throws profusely round
The feathering flakes, and covers all the ground,
The leafless bushes, struggling through the flow
Of barren sands, resembling new-fallen snow.
Down axle-deep the labouring horses strain
To drag us through the fine soft sandy plain.
    Beneath the load their well-tried strength gives way,
When from the car, impatient of delay,

The friends leap out, the fair ones still remain
To urge the steeds and guide the slack'ning rein.

Pure artless girls, such natural smiles they bring,
And on the way their voices sweetly ring,
Fine healthful maidens, active, full of life,
Aspiring each to be the future wife ;
Of erring man her destined part to take,
To love, and be beloved, and propagate.

Knee-deep we pass across the sandy plain,
Boots, shoes and clothing filling with the grain
Of fine quicksand, that pierces every break,
And flies as snow at every step we take.

Arrived at length, we scramble up the hill
Which Cook had mounted, every sense to fill
With joy to see an inland lake, and view
The site whereon the future city grew.
His active thoughts at once a colony form
The nucleus of a nation yet unborn.

A lonely inn close by the bay-side stands—
An oasis amidst a waste of sands,—
Put up the steeds, and by the fair ones led,
Unpack the stores, prepare to make a spread.
From hampers large the viands are withdrawn,
And placed on snow-white cloths upon the lawn.

Veal-pies, blanc-manges, chicken, and a round
Of splendid beef, at just a penny a pound,
Supply so vast, no higher price is claimed
Or ever thought of, asked for or obtained.

With hunger keen, enjoy the fatted calf,
For which 'tis said John Bull a weakness hath,
And do our best to clear the varied hoard,
Whilst wit and humour sparkle round the sward.

And, hunger quelled, we on the grass recline,

And toast the ladies in a generous wine,
Contented, all awakened spirits flow.
We rise in knots, towards the sea-side go,
And bend our way, the well-known spot explore,
Where Cook on landing set his foot on shore.
Along the beach we find the sand stone block,
Less durable than fame there stands the rock,
On which—to mark the place a copper plate
Declares the great discoverer's name and date,
When first this son of Britain pressed the strand,
With leaps of joy upon the new found land.

And long I gazed, as here before me lies,
The plate that brings the mariner to my eyes,
In fancy shows his boat upon the shore,
His sailors wandering to the land explore.

His ship far out, all snug and calmly lay
On the bright waters of the shallowing bay;
Upon a sand hill high alone he stands,
A telescope held firmly in his hands:
Is gazing on the country far and wide,
Towards the port extending round inside.

Then with his men again is wand'ring round,
Where flowering shrubs in gay variety found,
So pleased with these as o'er their wilds they stray
He names the place appropriate Botany Bay.

A name in after-times of disrepute.
Though of the error here may none dispute,
In childhood's dreams how oft it caused a dread,
And restless thoughts to crowd around the bed;
In awe the guileless held its direful fame.
And evil ones felt terror in the name.

Yet in reality how changed the land,
What would not childhood give for such a strand?
The bright warm sea, the fish that swarm the shore,

The plants and shrubs that strew the bayous o'er,
All sparkling gay beneath Sol's radiant beams,
The very ideal of our youthful dreams.
    Why this fair Earth should be so much deplored,
Or life's great glories studiously ignored,
Terrestrial joys suppressed, how can we tell,
Save unwise motives at the bottom dwell?
Naught is so black as augurers do paint,
And naught so vile as childhood's mind to taint.

    Then, starting off, again descend the mound,
Break off in pairs, and stroll the beach around :
Amongst the heather bells we frisk and play,
And rapid flies the joyous time away.
    Romantic scenes that tend to tie with love
The souls of men, and send their thoughts above,
And round about, where Cupid springs his darts
To pierce the wayward warm and softened hearts.
    Close by our side the charming damsels pressed
In summer toilets, gay but neatly dressed :
Plain leghorn hats to shade their shoulders round,
And light costumes that gently sweep the ground ;
Who of themselves can render good account
With sparkling humour straight from Nature's fount.

    No sirens these ! although their voices, soft
As music sweet, allure the wanderer oft,
And lead him on through flowering meads to roam,
Regardless of the care that pines at home.
    Severe the trial, though warmed by virtue's fire,
'Twixt human laws and nature's soft desire,
'Twixt love and honour, duty, fear, and shame,
Rebuke of conscience, loss of generous name ;
All these combine to cheat our natural love,

Descended as it is from realms above.

As round we stroll from off the pleasing shore,
Bright glens of heather passing o'er and o'er,
Emotions swell with undisguised art,
The destined hour must come when we must part,

As lingering on through flowering bushes gay,
Love in soft accents pleads the sweet delay,
And whispers lightly, 'Stay thy wayward course
Nor rudely tear thyself with fretful force.

'Why so much haste to prove thyself unkind?
Is the raging main more pleasing to thy mind?
Where tossed by billows, catch the fitful sleep
Through night's dark tempests and the rolling deep.

'Or pressed by gales adverse, where rocks arise,
And roaring waters bounding to the skies,
Threat loud and harsh to burst thy ship in twain,
Its fragments scattering o'er the beach and main;
Can these all be preferred through life to live,
To all the blessings meads and I can give?

'Such gifts as Nature gives shall all be thine,
Extended plains, which none shall say are mine,
Where birds and beasts rejoice in Nature's plan,
And all exulting save ungrateful man.

'Abundance full shall welcome here thy stay,
The spectre want for ever chased away;
Gaze on these beauteous shores, and softly dream
How many times you may enjoy the scene.

'The soft bright heath shall spring beneath thy feet,
Flowers spontaneous, pure, thy presence greet,
Why should'st thou go? forgetting these and me,
To waste thy youth upon the dreary sea,
Forego the scheme, and with one joyous kiss
Chase all thy cares away to realms of bliss.'

Here I confess the point of Cupid's dart,
And fain would tell the promptings of my heart :
Great doubts arise, I feel the secret pangs,
My pilgrimage upon the balance hangs.

But, like Ulysses, bound severely fast,
Lashed by the tyrant Custom to the mast,
Whose thongs unyielding, wrestle as I may,
And stronger binds me as I would away.

And love may plead, and nature spread her charms,
He still obtrudes, and shouts his false alarms,
Makes fair ones quail beneath his thousand rods,
And fear the demon more than all the gods.

And time is short, and dangerous too the stay,
The living blossoms pleading still delay,
But back we turn companions to regain,
Despondent each that e'er we meet again,
In such communion of the heart and soul,
That seizes both almost beyond control.

Rejoin our friends, a light repast we take,
And haste away, a quick return to make
Towards the town, as day is on the wane,
No light to guide us o'er the barren plain.

With horses fresh we fly as fleeting wind,
For home we hail, and leave the Bay behind;
And there arrived, we yet the union keep,
No thoughts intrude of rest or needful sleep.

Assembled gay to lead the mazy dance,
And sprightly music all its charms enhance,
Knits souls in harmony with pure delight,
And swiftly sweeps away the joyous night.

And daylight dawns, and though with ill accord,
Stern duty calls aloud to haste aboard ;
Abrupt farewell we take, and doubt if more
Our eyes shall rest again on friends ashore.

Then off to ship we put, and drowsy feel,
Hastily down towards our cabins steal,
But short respite of sleep we catch before
The chains are rattling to the ship unmoor.
    And off we move, and catch the breeze again,
Run through the cliffs, and out upon the main,
Steer south direct, and quickly bring to view
Tasmanian heights, and close towards them drew;
Make Stormy Bay, and run the coast-line down
And let our anchor drop at Hobart Town.

HOBART TOWN.

A splendid roadstead, roomy, open, clear,
High lands surrounding, with an atmosphere
To brace the nerves : —though Sol shines brightly round
The adjacent heights with glittering snows are crowned.
    Salubrious clime, and Nature formed the place
A garden suited to the human race,
Outside the tropics, clear in ocean stands,
Whose gales refreshing purify the lands,
Of small extent —as swiftly o'er them ride,
Scattering noxious gases far and wide.
Unlike the great Australia left behind
Where fitful hot and cold there blows the wind,
Where Sol burns bright, accumulates his strength,
Which by the gale is borne throughout the length
Of all the land ; and in its fiery force
Parches and dries up all within its course.
So that the heat of scorching baleful sands,
Sheds its dire influence o'er the genial lands,

And as a blight it spreads on all around,
Blistering the leaves, and splitting all the ground.
   But here the air is pure, and green the trees,
As Sol's bright rays are tempered by the breeze,
Which scales the snow-clad hills, and gently sweeps
Down o'er the lowlands to it's native deeps.
Where charged with gases, mix with Neptune's gales,
Who urges war, and with it never fails,
With Jove's assisting bolts, to raise alarms,
And clear it off amidst their thundering storms,
As from on high the rains and lightnings pour,
And all are shriven in the general roar.
   Here from the centre of this pleasing land,
Where lakes and fountains pure upon it stand,
Down o'er the rocks are sent life-giving streams,
And through the vales where springing foliage teams,
The snow-capped heights, above and all around,
Supply the fonts to fertilize the ground ;
So Sol's pure shafts, with intermittent rains,
Call into life and feed the leafy plains.
   Close off the town—well built—we quiet ride,
Where Derwent rolls along its silver tide,
Into an estuary grand and broad and gay,
Towards the sea and out at Stormy Bay.
   Scenery bold, with mountains, hills and dells,
Broad fertile plains where flow the gurgling rills
To moisten all the land, its herds to raise,
And, grateful all, proclaim their thanks in praise.
   A land so fair as this the direful bane
Of Crime's ill-gotten sons, here yet remain
The convict once ; contented seems to thrive,
Busy in life, an active trade to drive.
   The harbour's shores, not long since bare, display
A row of wharves, by which his shipping lay;

Those wharves and stores raised by his convict hands.
Now serve his cause to trade with other lands.
By thrift and skill and honest labour grown,
Rich in the product of the seed he's sown,
Upon a footing with his neighbours round,
Where open hearts and hands are always found.

No more alarmed, to guarded language keep,
Proclaims his mind to all in open street,
One of a group opes out his honest heart,
And thinks that honesty's the better part ;
His rising voice essays to show the proofs,
And convict lips let fall some striking truths.
Says he, ' We all can either till or deal,
In such a home there is no need to steal,
With honesty a thriving trade may drive,
With energy may all do well and thrive.'

Another joins, ' We've listened to your lay,
And honesty best policy you say,
What honesty—from policy—you call,
To me, my friend's, no honesty at all ;
If by that stream of honesty you walk,
Then let us have a little honest talk.
' And would not you, my honest friend, in dealing
To turn a thousand, do a little stealing ;
Quick steal a march upon another slow,
Cut with sharp practice in, and let him go ?
Hot-beds of crime we know for ever dwell,
But where to fix the evil, who shall tell ?
Where vices end and virtues are, so fine,
No judge on earth could yet detect the line.
And vice will conquer whan the stronger grown,
Nor deigns it fit to live in slums alone,
Where law can touch it with its shriving hand,

And choose the few from out the sweltering band.
These few condemned the chains of slavery wear—
The many pass who should their durance share—
Legion their name, from every class they draw,
By skill alone defying every law.
As numbers drive close by the legal ledge,
And desperate fight upon its treacherous edge,
Where hot and sharp is held the doubtful strife,
And deeds performed, ah, e'en to very life !

  ' And some will rise from it in fortune's flow,
And some will sink into their chains below.
For what is right ! where these ambiguous laws,
With right and wrong can make a common cause ?
What man so gifted as to judge it free,
When learned men agree to disagree ?

  ' In groves of plenty, or in lands of dearth,
All still will scramble for the things of earth ;
All is stern war, and he the stronger hits,
Who strikes in boldly with superior wits.
By polished form, or dexterous to persuade,
By force of circumstances, deeply laid
By suasive tongue, deceptive used to gain,
And waxeth rich, with neither toil nor pain :
However glozed, or by what name they go,
All cheats they are, and why not call them so ?

  ' Or who in tests of virtue are so tried,
As to soar above a well-directed bribe,
Who so magnanimous, benignly rash ?
Declined may honours be but not the cash.'

  ' All may be right,' another quick replies ;
' Our ignorance is where the error lies :
Abuses multiply as science rids,
Whilst custom claims what natural law forbids.

  ' And those who have the power will use it still,

To promote designs, and consummate their will ;
A man may steal, but he must steal in form,
To all the meshes of the law disarm.
Must know the weakness of his brother man,
Then steal he will because he knows he can.
   ' Then what is vice, or where to draw the line,
When left to human judgment to define,
Where all impelled by hopes and fears and hates
And where the love of gain predominates ?'

Among such people here my business led,
I could but lend an ear to what they said,
And thus replied : ' I think you may be right,
That civilization through is but a fight,
   ' Where vice and virtue both together roll,
And both contagious running through the whole,
By arts seductive impregnate the mind,
And lustful joy will propagate its kind.
   ' Vice and virtue ever will contend,
And gold the stronger either will defend,
Acknowledged vice the worst when searched aright,
Which swells unchecked, degrading all alike.
   ' All is not chance, but Nature's partial love
Still sends her favourite sons far up above,
To rule supreme, as she may still dictate,
Inspiring love, or long remembered hate.
   ' But here you have a Paradise !' I cried ;
' The irony of fate exemplified ;
Eden itself could claim no fairer birth,
The loveliest spot of all this lovely earth.
   ' Why should you grovel then in search of gain,
When there before you lies the extended plain ;
Health-giving bourns, enjoy them as you can
And conquer Nature try instead of man ?'

But Eden's lost! the golden apple thrown
And discord reigns, and breaks up many a home,
For California! mania holds the rage,
Distorts their minds, and all their thoughts engage.

Australia now her maiden nugget shows,
An exodus towards its birthplace flows,
For this bare myth prosperity is sold
And many starve in maddening search for gold.

Yet so it is with all the human race,
Forsakes the substance to a phantom chase:
'Tis Nature's scourge, affecting all alike,
Turning her sunshine into gloomy night.

Unscathed how few who shall her secret know,
Of how to rest contented here below,
Yet there's no want, no high desire of man,
But Nature in her bosom holds the plan,
Resource as boundless in her secret haunts,
As fields of grain are to the sparrow's wants.

Close to the shore, and by the town we lay,
And mutual visits drive the time away.
By one invited to inspect the town,
To see his home, and all the country round.
Free settler he, who here has made a home,
Is quite contented never more to roam.

In harmony a secret friendship feel,
He asks us in to join the midday meal.
'Board luck,' says he, 'and simple too the fare,
Accept the terms and welcome quite you are.'

No words conventional which asks to go
As compliment—and seeks the answer 'No;'
We take his invitation, join to dine,
Which pleases better far than to decline;

And seat ourselves around the table spread,
Where Father Matthew had some converts made :
Wholesome viands the frugal board adorn
All stimulating liquids held in scorn ;
Each lusty son and daughter takes a place,
And all composed the elder gives the grace.

Submissive all, and willing to obey,
They show their love to him in every way,
From avocations each are just released
To find the welcomed strangers highly pleased.

An interest in old England all display,
Would like to see it much, but not to stay ;
Know liberty too well to fly from this.
And love the mother country where she is.

The meal complete, the boys to business go,
Method and care in everything they show,
Our friend proposes then to take a ride,
And kindly says he will the means provide.

'I'll mount myself,' says he ; 'proceed with you,
The girls will join us with their saddles too ;
We'll spend the day whatever else betide,
And will be off for a long country ride.'

Well mounted all, at once we quit the town,
Along the road laid out to Launceston :
A splendid way, through cultivated lands,
My friend explains, — well built by convict hands.

Hill, mountain, vale, diversify the scene,
Irregular, broken, mantled o'er with green
Of Nature's painting ; a genial sun full glows
Upon the peaks all crowned with glittering snows.

Mid-winter now, and yet the days are warm,
The nights are chilly as the early morn ;
The trees are fresh which in the valleys dwell,
The melting snows from heights the rivulets swell ;

By which we dash, along the solid road—
As fine a way as horses ever trod—
Free minded girls, the pair enjoy the ride,
And urge their steeds close by the strangers' side.
  Artless and gay, and full of life and fun,
Try to outstrip us in a friendly run,
And bounding off, the anxious sire exclaims.
' Be careful, girls, nor loosely hold the reins.'
  Abjures the younger one, and kindly begs,
' Your horse you know is treacherous on his legs,—
Watch well his gait, sit firmly in the seat,
Keep up his head, and make him lift his feet.'
She heeds him well, most joyously attends,
To obey his counsel, and to amuse his friends.
  And on we course along the lonely road,
Turn down a cross, espy a neat abode,
A homestead farm, by trees embowered around,
Far isolated from the roadside found.

We near the spot where sullen silence flies,
And homely sounds of lowing herds arise ;
A braying ass sends forth his grating strain.
And chanticleer awakes the wide domain.
  Arrived, my friend directs us here to stop,
Alight, go in and on its inmates drop,
An old acquaintance known, essays to tell,
Who long had settled in this place to dwell ;
By patient toil and thrift were well to do,
Had made a home, and independence too.
  The elder dead, his widow here remains,
Two lusty sons still cultivate the plains,
Increase their stock, extend their farm and show.
What may be done by prudence here below.
  We quick dismount, and in a moment more

A comely dame came bustling to the door ;
To greet her friends, with joy her aspect teams,
And happy welcome from her features beams.
　The lusty dame in pure Hibernian sings,
'Right welcome are ye sure, whate'er ye brings,
How are yees now? what stroke of fortune sends
Thee by this way, together with thy friends?
　'Come, darlings, come, and rest yourselves begin ;
My own two lads will soon be coming in
From off the moor, they should be now in sight,
Pleased will they be to find yees here to-night.
　'And right good boys they are, and seldom roam
Beyond their fields, and this our humble home.
Since my poor man has gone they've dried my tears,
And proved a solace to my sorrowing years.'
　Then in we go, and seated all around,
Plain rustic furniture inside was found ;
Chairs rough in pattern, table white of pine,
Home made it was, off which the household dine.
　Upon the hearth bright embers, where the cakes
Of wheaten meal the heated griddle bakes.
These for the boys, when they from farming steal,
To rest their limbs, and join the evening meal.
　The anxious dame, solicitous to know
How all friends are, who living down below
Beside the sea ; so seldom goes she down
To visit those at far off Hobart Town.

　Our friend replies, 'Our present business here,
To sup with you, and taste whatever cheer
There may be had, or kindly fortune sends,
To stay the cravings of ourselves and friends.
So long a ride has sent us all, I fear,
But hungry mortals down upon you here.

' Of friends anon ; but first our need appease,
Of these we'll speak when we feel more at ease.
Come get a pair of poulets underway,
Myself will aid you to prevent delay.

' More meal,' he cries, ' and I will quickly make,
And on the griddle heap the wheaten cake.'
Turns to his friends colonial fare to praise,
Impress our minds, and all our envy raise.

' Pure wholesome food,' says he, ' as ever sought,
And beats your fine wheat flour all to naught,
Withal 'tis pure, raised by most willing hands
From off the cleared and cultivated lands.
Untaxed, unshackled, free as nature gives,
And happy he who thus contented lives.'

And here the dame is shouting loud for Dan,
The stable boy, and general serving-man,
Who from the transport sent new life to breathe,
To serve her here upon his ticket-o'-leave.
Of good repute, and as he truly says,
So happy never was in all his days.

And thus engaged we leave the friendly pair.
In concert the impromptu meal prepare,
And scour the fields, and mount the neighbouring hills,
Whose landscape fine our admiration fills.

And on we stroll, and quickly bring to view
A pair of stalwart lads, who nearer drew,
Clad in coarse cloths are winding through the dale,
Up from the plain that joins the shady vale.

Behind them roll three helps, who joyous seem,
Whistling and shouting to the double team,
On whose broad backs they mount and sideways sit,
In bantering parlance use their rough-hewn wit.

Hibernian all, whose strong rich Irish brogue,
At intervals from each to other flowed,

As passing by from these such compliments fall,
'How are yees, girls? am glad to see yees all.'
These greet with smiles the happy jovial train,
And prize the recognition of the swain.

Still more attention pay the sturdy pair,
The rising blush proclaims their gentle care,
As mantling sparks rise in each damsel's face,
They forward bound to meet the soft embrace.

If dreams we had these soar before our eyes,
Our small attentions into nothing flies;
Quite unprepared for such a scene to trace,
A little envy may have found a place.
But quickly gone, for soon it is perceived,
The girls and boys are all in all agreed.
For Cupid long had laid his snares and caught
The happy pairs, absorbing every thought;
And holds secure that naught where he decides,
Shall lovers part, or break the sacred ties.

Then round I turn about to view the scene,
Though lovers' freaks the most engrossing theme:
With but poor grace I bring my mind to bear,
And thus reflect on Cupid and the fair.

'What power,' said I, 'the gentle rebel wields
To him mankind its soul and body yields;
He victor springs where this disputes the right,
And by the ears he leads it on to fight,

'And holds the scales by him to rise or fall,
By sweet decrees he rules and governs all,
Supremely reigns and soars above the plan
Of all the schemes devised by erring man;

'The mightiest monarch on his suffrance stands,
The right divine is held in both his hands,
And force may league in compact power conjoined

More strong his love than human force combined.
Factions may link, unmindful of control,
But short their date, for he pervades the whole
Eternal reigns, and must be found at last,
To purge their acts, and all their hopes to blast ;
With power divine he swoops to overwhelm,
And lends his mighty aid to sway the realm.'

Then back again we stroll to join the group,
Along byways we wander with the *troupe*,
Where all are friends, from artifices freed,
No introductive ceremonials need.
Thy friends are mine, no thought from whence or where,
And no such talk as who or what they are.
Suffice to know are here, our language speak,
And welcome are they to our board and meat.
And off we pair, and file down through the brush,
And by ravines, with many a leap and rush,
Across the fields, and back again we roam
And gain the precincts of the country home.
With day's decline we stroll about the farm,
And seek the piggeries, cow-houses, barn ;
On diverse chat we course the place around,
Till night's dark mists obscure the moistened ground.
Then turn again, and seek the friendly roof,
To put the strangers' kindness to the proof,
And seated round the board enjoy the boon,
As burning logs light up the cosy room.
Our friend begins, as promised, then to speak
Of all acquaintance. old and strong and weak,
Their varied ailments—light of these he made—
Of speculations, and success in trade.
'We are growing fast,' he cries, 'in every way,
Free colonists are landing every day,

We'll welcome these, and all who have a mind
To be industrious a home shall find.

 ' And some there are who, from defect of brain,
Or fashion's laws, unable to restrain
Weak hearts withal denying Nature's claim,
Would rather die than lose their honest name ;
Beneath a garb of decent outward show,
The dreadful pangs of griping hunger know.
Around them plenty lies within their grasp,
They seize —at first successful—not the last
Reviled, debased, they seek another sphere
And find a paradise by coming here.

 ' These, too. are welcome and shall find solace,
Where poverty alone is their disgrace.
To us unknown their foolish pride unbend,
Industrious are, and good assistance lend ;
Pursue a course, too anxious not to stray
Where false society ever points the way.

 ' Unwise men stray, and hunt the earth for gold,
Leaving their homes for next to nothing sold,
Their wives in poverty, themselves undone,
Precipitating that they fain would shun.

 ' The world is large magnanimous and free,
With one stern, just, immutable decree,
That all shall toil her bounteous gifts to spread,
And daily work to gain their daily bread.

 ' And health shall follow, guaranteed by this,
With health's reward of happiness and bliss ;
There's naught beyond it, try how much we will,
By cunning, study, and unbounded skill,
The man who lives, fulfilling Nature's call,
Is on an equal with the best of all.

 ' And men there are, confirmed to evil fame,
So lost withal they don't deserve the name,

Hobart Town.

As beasts of prey they lurk within their lairs,
And spring upon their victims unawares.
  'Cowards at best, who nightly prowl the road,
To catch the industrious wayfarer abroad,
Pounce on the unprotected to engage,
And rob the labourer, of his weekly wage.
  ''Tis not long since, here in the open day,
When all the lads were at their work away,
One of these villains steals upon the farm,
Affrights the dame, alone, with great alarm :
With pistol primed he runs the homestead through,
And rifles everything within his view.
  'Since then she keeps at home poor honest Dan,
Who prides himself a match for any man,
And swears by all if e'er they come again
Their forfeit lives shall rest alone with him.'
  'True,' says the elder son, 'depend he will
The next intruder give a wholesome fill,
That rifle which you sent to him so kind,
He prizes much, and always keeps it primed.
  'And holds his eye in practice at a mark,
And keeps it near at hand for instant work,
He'll try his prowess on the next to maim
And deal them justice with a steady aim.'

  The night advancing and a lonely road,
We all prepare to stir again abroad ;
Are bid good speed by all the houshold, who
Throw their kind blessings in a last adieu ;
And loving hearts are severed for a time,
The time when each shall call each other mine.
  Bright heavens above, a splendid way before,
And cantering on we cross the silent moor,
And pass between the hills, whose sombre shade

Obscures the road, along the sheltered glade.
    Known to our steeds, which make the welkin sound,
With beating hoofs upon the solid ground,
Till through the gloom is seen the flickering light
Of habitations, breaking on the sight;
We greet the beacons of the peopled town,
Right glad to find ourselves again at home.
    On board we go, next day the sails are bent,
And fresh'ning winds their fleeting forces sent,
But ere the port we quit, a grand review,
And battles mimic exercise the crew.
    Manœuvring, some active hours are spent,
Sailing in line around the clear Derwent,
Abreast the town, and all the canvas furled,
A sharp bombardment at the place is hurled.
    Boats called away, equipped for ready fight,
All fully manned, proceed in hostile might
Towards the town, approach with care the strand,
The garrison defends its native land.
    Then from the ship the heavy broadsides pour
To clear the foes in force along the shore,
These with sharp volleys ply the invading crews,
Nor readily permit the landing choose,
Until convinced that their resistance strong,
From the iron hail that sweeps the shore along,
Could not be well maintained; and in command
They slow retire; the boats push for the land,
Effect a hold, and gallantly succeed,
To embark their fighting men with greatest speed,
And press their pieces, mounted to the front,
Dislodge the foe, and in the battle's brunt,
To play their part, and at the distant ranks
To hurl destruction on their van and flanks.
Then on they press, the garrison retreats,

Dogged and sullen through the spacious streets,
And, closely pressed until they reach the square,
And make a stand and firm resistance there.

Whereat the battle rages in its might,
And all the town is startled with affright,
From side to side on each their volleys pour,
Loud culminating in a general roar.

Nor those will yield, nor these their ship will seek,
The tug of war is hot, where Greek meets Greek,
Until our men their ammunition spent
Back to the beach in slow retreat are sent,

And gain their boats ; as each respective runs,
Covered beneath the ship's protecting guns ;
A parting volley give on either side
The finale echoing o'er the silent tide.

At distance safe the garrison appears,
Then hail each other with tremendous cheers ;
Ours reach the ship, and spread their sails again,
Bounding from friends away towards the main.

And north-east steer, and fresh'ning breezes blow,
In gusts at times the labouring ship lays low,
And on she drives responsive to the gales,
'Till land again the seaman gladly hails,

NORFOLK ISLAND.

An island high shoots boldly from the sea,
And Norfolk named, one of a group of three,
A garden where the great Pacific Ocean
Lashes its cliffs in one perpetual motion.

And occupied by criminals alone,
The worst of all transported find a home,

Alas ! no peace, for restless as the waves,
Their liberty is all each madly craves.
  A pleasant land, but here no inlet find,
To shield the ship from rolling waves and wind ;
We stand in close, and send a boat away
To effect a landing in the open bay.
And off and on await impatient near
The boat's return, whose safety much we fear :
A larger send, by which we quickly learn,
The first was bruised, impeding her return.
But both at length towards midnight's approach
From ship were seen upon the waters float ;
Arriving safe, we spread our sails and flee.
The boisterous coast, and stand again to sea.

  And o'er the Ocean's wide domain we lay.
Light gales propitious urge us on the way ;
Bright sunny days, and nights transparent clear.
The studded heavens alight with stars appear.
  Night after night I lonely pace the deck.
Or with a friend in concert oft reflect
Upon the skies, and Nature's boundless space,
With orbs and atoms in the ethereal race.
  Says he, ' Yon star, that with us seems to fly,
Across the ether of the bright blue sky,
'Tis fixed we say, and yet withal instead
Millions of miles must move still unperceived :
Beyond our own, round which we move : so far
That Sol to it, is but a twinkling star ;
And all his moons, with their soft borrowed light,
If eyes like these are there were lost to sight.
  'Those central suns, which smaller orbs control,
A system each, and radiate the whole :
Their influence felt where'er they strike the eye,

Exalt the man and lift him to the sky ;
As orb round orb, system round system roll,
Show him a wonder in the stupendous whole ;
That he an atom hidden in the earth,
Perceives them all intuitive from his birth.
With mind expanded, dares to use their light,
To guide him o'er the seas by day and night :
To calculate on every turn they take,
Enquire their substance, density and weight ;
In such a field he finds himself so small,
And yet as great a wonder as them all.'
   ' True,' I rejoined, ' and speculations say,
That greater wonders still existing lay,
In other worlds might higher forms exist,
That life is not confined alone to this.
As suns superior govern smaller orbs,
So man o'er his inferiors are the lords ;
As far beneath him these ; then who shall tell
What beings live, and who as far excel
Him, as he they ?   As the central sun our own
Must be surpassed by other suns unknown.'

   Thus while we gaze and pass the time away,
Our ship is urging on the southern way,
A few days more again the land we make,
Stand on direct and through the famed Cook's Strait.

NEW ZEALAND.

New Zealand's isles, imposing bold and green,
Whose mountain tops with glittering snows are seen,
Although the sun benignly shines by day,
And warms the lowlands with his beaming ray.

Upon the right New Munster lofty stands,
Diversified by vales and broken lands;
Opposing these New Ulster on the left,
Between the two, a spacious way is cleft :
Filled in with ocean's waters deep and blue,
By which we steer, and run the opening through.

But sailing on, we tarry by the way,
And at the port of Nicholson we stay,
Close by the town of Wellington we stop,
And furl our sails, and let our anchor drop.

Fine open cove, and crescent-shaped the shore,
By which I lonely stroll to make a tour,
And take advantage of the splendid weather,
To note the races settled here together.

The day is when their great imperial Queen
In anniversary the day had seen ;
Whose virtues shine, and all the nations weld,
Whose name by these religiously is held
As something 'twixt the spirit high above
Sustained in glory by her people's love—
And their own chiefs, whose lustre fades away
In this great light, as night recedes from day.

And to her fame high holiday is kept,
The day apart to games and feastings set.
Great Fashion too hath spread her lengthy arms,
And robes of silk the Maori lady 'dorns.

Who don the veil to hide the sallow face
But ill bestowed upon the tattoed race,
Who on the green with viands spread around,
Turn their gay clothes, and squat upon the ground.

Their ungloved fingers to their mouths convey
The dainty morsels which before them lay ;
Those less refined, in greater numbers strong,
About the beach in knots assembled long,

In native pride, disdaining innovations,
Follow the bent of their own inclinations.

  Around a fire, engaged in friendly chat,
About their shoulders loosely thrown a mat
Of plaited flax, inherent here in growth,
Some art display, and covering sexes both.

  The place is young, the English few appear.
The missionary seems the leader here :
The pioneer the wildest tribes to tame,
Imperious sways in civilization's name.

  And charmed they listen to the Christian's call
And bid farewell to freedom, health and all,
Their hunting-grounds no longer open stand
Are closed and fenced to cultivate the land.

  And find themselves but supplicants to kings,
Who from afar great civilization brings :
Submitting spacious groves to confiscation,
Procuring holy writ in compensation :
Prepare them for the unknown world to come,
Which much they need—the race's mission done
Awaits but time, with civilization's aid,
To rank their nation with the mighty dead.

  Short time is spent, again we spread our sails,
The harbour cleared, we meet with gustful gales :
As from a spout, are rushing through the strait,
And drive us back behind the land to wait,
Until the blast had spent its force, and then,
We onward steer around the land again.

  And Auckland make, a few days here we stay,
Good harbour room for any ships to lay.
The land is high, and as an isthmus stands,
Connects the island's more extensive lands.

  The town is sparse, irregular, and long,

And factory stacks are rising there among ;
There's naught about it picturesque or grand,
Nor much improved by civilization's hand.

    And as the wintry winds ungenial blow,
And driving rains and drizzling mists aflow,
The new-made roads and streets in mire appear,
Deserted, cold, and are at times most drear.

    Although the fitful sun breaks through the clouds,
Makes it more cheerful, and with life enshrouds,
We cannot roam to look for lonely dells,
The purling streams are turned to muddy rills.

    The eve more pleasant, where the gay saloon,
To its inhabitants a grateful boon,
Where softest music dulness drives away,
And makes the night more joyous than the day.

    The adult Maori is most useful found
For labouring work, to cut and clear the ground,
To man the craft that 'round the sea-coast ply,
To trade with all the isles themselves apply.

    Short time is spent, again we put to sea,
Coasting along the shore upon the lee,
Pass Cape Van Dieman, and the Northern Cape,
The three King's Islands leaving in the wake.

    Then south about, for Bay of Islands steer,
And for the land again are standing near.
Run in the Bay, with pretty islands crowned,
A softer atmosphere is thrown around.

    We find the relics of a village burned
By Maori raiders, who had on it turned,
And drove the white men from their houses new,
Pursued and many killed who from it flew.

    But they must pay for it, in life and lands,
Do but assist the pioneering hands,

Who came to teach them civilization's ways,
And to what use to put their spacious bays.
   Mistrustful each of other are they here.
The races kept aloof by mutual fear.
One thinks he's won, that thought his mind elates,
The other knows that retribution waits.
   We do a trade, some splendid cattle buy,
Grass in abundance to them food supply,
And wait not for the hostiles to engage,
For on the land they must exhaust their rage ;
The ship is freed as favouring breezes rise,
With spreaded sails across the ocean flies.
   And well we know, as round the isles we steal,
Old England lies direct beneath the keel ;
How similar upon the earth they stand,
Climatic influence, and breadth of land :
   Though June is here, with biting wintry blasts,
And hail and sleet at times are driving past,
Old England there, that lies beneath our feet,
Enjoys her days in calm mid-summer's heat.
   So north we steer, as furious gales arise
And Æolus blows from out the southern skies ;
And every day the air is warmer felt
As near we draw towards the Torrid belt.
   The sky is clear, the wind and waves are free,
The long high billows of the great South Sea,
Are steady rising, press the sails with force,
And drive the ship upon her destined course.
   As a fleet steed, when wolves by hunger pressed
Hang on his flanks, forbid a moment's rest,
Their sharp pursuit the noble creature feels,
And spurns them from him with his flying heels,
In terror urged, and scared by pale affright,
Swift o'er the barren wastes pursues his flight,

And sniffs the air, and shoots across the plain,
With head erect the sheltering wood to gain,
Mane flaunting high, he cuts the flying wind.
And leaves the ravening creatures far behind—
So with the waves, they roar and foam around.
Fain would engulf us at a single bound,
And hoarsely rave, and threaten to devour,
Hang to the ship, and show their awful power :
But swift she runs, and mocks the billows high,
Ploughs through the surge, and makes the waters fly.

From depths profound upon the aqueous globe,
Leviathans of Neptune make abode,
In couples play, and dive beneath the keel,
Rise at the side, a length of back reveal,
Shoot far ahead upon the bounding tide,
Await the ship, and linger at her side :
In feathering spray they spout their fountains high,
To again outstrip us in the race they try.
We watch them long, as something to attract
Our minds, from off the waste and trackless track.
And on we sail, and run a distance through,
The Friendly Islands drawing nearer to.
And Tonga Island quick is brought to sight,
Basking beneath, and in a sea of light,
Whose natives kind, a friendly pleasing shore,
Great Cook bore witness many years before ;
Where graceful palms and cocoa-nut trees tall,
A tropic aspect give the islands all.

Tonga Tabu.

Close by we stand, and bring our vessel to
The cosy village of Tonga Tabu :
Make for the shore, again imprint the sand,
Where natives gather thronging to the strand ;
Tall, stately men, some seven feet high and more,
And Tappa cloths about their loins they wore :
Their sleeky skins, of rich-brown colour found,
Their limbs are perfect and their bodies sound.
 The women tall and robust, with a face
As Amazons, appear a warlike race,
Or such as should produce the men of arms.
To shake the world with mighty war's alarms :
To assert great Nature's law that they shall win,
Who, by her aid, in primitive life begin
To first provide a fine proportioned frame,
Accompanied by a noble healthy brain,
Which needs but cultivation to define,
The soul and body of the man divine.
 And all seemed pleased to have in sight once more,
So large an English ship, close by their shore.
Their history, composed from mouth to mouth,
The name of Cook is known to them throughout.
 Beside the village, on a rising mound,
With gentle slope, above the level ground,
A snug built house, raised high upon it stands,
O'erlooks the place, and all adjoining lands.
Appears well-built of wood of varying kind,
And something English too about it find ;
With jalousies are all the windows shaped,
The frames of which by Tappas fine are draped ;
Devoid of glass the airy structure shows,

To suit the atmosphere that round it glows ;
And sloping down, to shade it from the sun
On every side the light verandas run.
High large-crowned trees surround the neat retreat,
With every comfort seems the whole replete ;
Fine feathery palms, that throw a deepening gloom,
An orange tree made white with joyous bloom,
On all around it casts an odorous scent,
Soft, sweet and pure, to all the senses went.

I stood and gazed, and as I gazed I saw,
A person staid in years towards me draw,
Whose hair was white, decided English face,
And unkempt locks that might a recluse grace.
Down o'er his breast a length of gray hair flowed,
His limbs in folds of Tappa cloth enrobed.
His gait is light, as o'er the sands he springs,
And in a rough salute a welcome flings.

With him I wander all the village round,
Where bread-fruit trees are springing from the ground ;
Among the cairns, of varying form and size,
He points the one wherein the chief resides.
And round about it runs the light stockade,
Firm in the earth its upright stakes are laid,
By lattice-work the interspaces closed,
Diagonally laid, and neatly all composed.

About we walk, through rows of splendid trees
Of fine bread-fruit, which spreads its shady leaves :
My guide explains its vast and varied use,
For food its fruit, for other claims its juice ;
Its fibrous bark to make the coarser cloth,
And for canoes its useful timber's sought.
Then back we stroll and to his house again
He bids me welcome, and to enter in.

To rest and listen feel myself inclined,
And rough equipment in the room I find.
But neatly draped, for as he tells me true
His hands had built it all and furnished too,
'Twas for their chief, he said, the place designed,
But he was doubtful and the gift declined.
    Then introduced me to his native wife,
A lusty dame passed into middle life ;
In native fashion robed, and hair trimmed neat,
A dark brunette, with sandals to her feet ;
Countenance full, and features well defined,
Such as bespeak an intellectual mind.
    'I came,' he said, 'resolved to work alone,
In pleasure reap as I in care had sown ;
Our chief's high confidence trust to retain,
Contented live, and shall my time remain.
Both King and Judge, in him with truth combined,
Alone to conscience is his will resigned ;
Justice and mercy equal right asserts,
And all receive their true and just deserts.
    'Where truth prevails 'tis simple all to guide,
And natural laws for all things will provide,
Their lack of worldly knowledge makes, 'tis true,
Their desires simple, and their wants but few ;
To balance well and not exceed the bound,
Is the highest art amongst these people found.
But missionaries have, of Gaul's extraction,
Been avaricious in their bold exaction ;
Inventing faults, and instigating more,
With Jesuit influence unknown before ;
On their confessions are imposing fines,
Equally as on their manufactured crimes.
    'And now, my friend, I wish you to believe,
No need have I to anyone deceive.

Before you stands not what to you appears,
A convict who has served his seven years.'

Struck with surprise, I sprang from off the couch,
Stood up erect, with open eyes and mouth.
'Impossible !' I cried : ' that such as you
Could know the vile disgrace alluded to !'
'Oh no,' says he, ' 'tis no disgrace to me,
Though convict, honest in reality ;
As pious missions are by frauds supported,
So honest men at times will get transported.
' I will not vex you with the tedious trial,
Injustice done me there is no denial ;
Places given, falsehoods introduced,
With wills and codicils and deeds produced.
Of all the jargon to confuse designed
To rack the brain and mystify the mind,
'Gainst which the heart rebels, and ease recedes,
Commend me to a pile of musty deeds.
False cards were played, by these the suit was won,
The knaves succeeded, and myself undone ;
Denied by all, still, as a simple fact,
I here protest against a shameless act.
' But saved I am, from all such dangers free,
The solid globe now lies 'twixt it and me ;
And right or wrong, I live to bless the day
That such an act had cast me here away.
' My friend,' he says, ' now tell me, if you can,
What written law is just 'twixt man and man,
The man accomplished keen the acts defines.
And works the law to further his designs.
' An honest man to follow nature must,
'Twixt man and man know only what is just,
Therefore, when at the bar brought to the test,
He's sure to win who knows the law the best.'

I think it strange, with diffidence receive,
And for my country's sake could scarce believe,
Incredulous felt, but could not all refrain,
In deepest thoughts, to feel and thus exclaim :
　' Oh for the Judge ! the great discerning mind,
Whose virtues place him o'er all human kind,
Who at a glance the inmost soul might scan,
And drag to light the false and honest man !
Whose vision clear admits no spurious flaw,
He sees the truth, and swift asserts the law,
No fawning lies could him the least affect ;
Whose God is truth, in which his soul is set.
　' Yet such a Judge as this I wish to trace,
Must be a slave to serve the human race ;
Must stand alone, admitting no one near,
For such a Judge could find no compeer here.
　' Presumption all, so by the many prized,
That he on earth would still be but despised,
No sympathy could such a champion find
Reward must lie in his celestial mind.'
　' You're right,' he joined, ' and to him something near
Is he who governs this our island here ;
But avarice I dread is drawing nigh
Soon to prevent that promised destiny.
　' Now here I live, and second in the reign,
My only care the confidence to gain
The subjects of my prince, and guide aright
Their minds and actions in the truest light ;
　' Their traits are good, and somehow take a pride
That equal all, in all things should divide,
And know enough their just rights to defend
As all are trained to this particular end.'
　' Here hold, my friend,' I said ; ' just kindly say,
Are you not better quartered far than they,

Have you no luxury to those denied,
Superior nothing, or amount supplied ;
Nothing that may their rivalry inspire,
Awake their jealousy or mind's desire ?'
     'Oh no,' says he, 'indeed we are beyond
The petty wants to which your hints belonged ;
True once I thought as you, but now I find
A truer nature lives in human kind.
     'I built this house, 'twas for the king designed,
And wrongly thought 'twould please his noble mind,
He free assistance gave to raise the pile,
From naught but curiosity the while ;—
     'And, finished off, I asked him to accept,
Nor could I think he would the gift reject,
But quick at once he made me understand,
'Twas against his wish, and custom of the land ;
     ' " Keep it," he said, " you seem to like it well,
And do not mind beneath its roof to dwell,
I never will in such a structure go
And far prefer my wigwam down below."

     'Since then we live here, if I really thought
The better structure any malice wrought,
Down it should come, and not a stick remain,
To be the cause of further strife again.
     'All are alike, and show they have no care,
Nor envy us our castle in the air ;
And hint a high wind soon may rush around,
And send us flying levelled with the ground.
     'No ! no ! my friend, here love and truth controls,
There's scarce a spark of envy in their souls ;
If traced at all, 'tis only seen to lie
In motives pure, in which they strive to vie.
     'By laws —unknown in general to mankind,—

We seek for sympathy alone to bind.
Such laws, so rare, on very few bestowed,
To rule impartial, and to be beloved ;
To truly rule, the ruler not exempt
From mutual bonds that make the whole content.'

' Adieu !' I cried, ' we may no longer stand,
On speculations vain about the land,
We have long diverged ; now let us to our task
Or why in very truth we may be asked,
Where is the service here ? or what the plea
For law and lawyers on the briny sea ?
Or what have Neptune's sons to do but roam,
Their vast domain within their floating home.

' No lawyers need, no watchful night-police,
In harmony agree to keep the peace.
With hearts elate they bound across the sea,
From all voracious duns and bailiffs free.

' Such cares as these fall as the fleeting wind,
Which fills their sails, and leaves their debts behind ;
Know naught of law, nor does it trouble more,
Until again they touch the fatal shore ;
Where by the sirens and the crimps are met,
Who take all fish that come within their net.

' No road they find so clear to give them peace,
As the ocean wide where all their troubles cease ;
One at the helm, solicitous to their call,
Who knows his men and kindly judges all ;

' To him they look, no complications dread,
Braving all dangers by his bidding led,
To where he lists : he shall be right because,
His acts and deeds are in his country's cause.'

With anchor weighed and stretching sails we soon,
The Friendly Islands leave lost in the gloom

Of coming night, as eastwards on we steer,
Till islands more are seen approaching near.

    As emeralds laid upon the vast expanse,
Cook's archipelago the scene enhance,
Through which we run, Society's Islands find,
As calm succeeds the soft and lessening wind.

    And still we lay as on a glassy lake,
And naught whatever does the silence break,
Till from afar upon the ocean wide,
A shoal of whales approaches to our side.

    In sport and play about the ship maintain,
Furrowing and surging through the silvery main ;
In sprayey foam their fountains spouting high,
Catching the hues from off the light blue sky.

    Then off they go, we follow in their wake,
As light soft airs again the stillness break ;
And note Tahiti, breaking on the sight
As evening falls, and closes with the night.

    A glorious morn, as dawn breaks in the east,
Before her votaries Nature spreads a feast,
As like a gem, upon the ocean lies,
Embossed in hills the Alpine peaks arise.

    Fine lofty lands, whose mountains towering high
Lost in the clouds, are pointing to the sky ;
With chasms deep, umbrageous vales abound,
Fringes of spray the glittering reefs surround.

    The waters clear, proximity reveal
The coral rocks, fast passing 'neath the keel ;
The passage cleared, and snug at anchor are,
Within the realm of Island Queen Pomare.

    And here we found, as sailing east had run,
In early meeting with the rising sun,
Had gained a day with Otaheitian time,
Which westward reckoned had along the line.

Therefore we seek again the restoration,
To set us right with western calculation.
Two days, of equal day, and date observe
An unison with nations to preserve.

OTAHEITA.

As Cook had told, some eighty years before,
A race here lived who some resemblance bore,
To those of old whose innocence had shown,
That deities exist, in realms unknown,
Who on occasion, various forms assume
From out the sea, or from the shining moon.
In sympathy enwrapt the mariner tells,
In social concord live among themselves ;
Prolific Nature her abundance brings
Spontaneous from the earth the bread-tree springs.
No nipping frosts forbidding fruits to grow,
No blighting blasts are ever known to blow,
Where all seemed happy, innocent and free,
As Neptune guards them in a boundless sea.
What then more natural to their wondering eyes,
A troop of white men coming from the skies,
Beyond the sea, the vault of heaven alone,
From whence they came, from their celestial home,
In such an Ark—as they may well define —
Could but be built by art and hands divine,
In whose capacious womb, the wonder bore
Rich fruits, and animals unknown before.
Should give them all their primitiveness possessed,
And in exchange to feel that they were blessed,

A loving welcome show, or to adore
The godlike strangers, on their native shore ;
   And still more deep, as when these men began
With glittering instruments the skies to scan,
Could tell when through the vault an orb would run,
Across the surface of their bright day sun ;
Again must take it as a heavenly sign,
Of their connection with the things divine.
   Prepared to sail, and promised to renew
The short acquaintance, and to sea withdrew,
They know not where, or whither they had gone
To realms unknown, supposed to be their home.
   But Cook returned, more wonders still he brought,
Society with all his men was sought
With confidence, a strong affection grew,
And fiercer love infected all the crew.
   Though bars were formed, and stricter barriers raised,
For which the gallant sailor should be praised, —
The wrench was great when he had left the shore,
Never again in life to see them more ;
Still in their minds, a vision oft appeared,
And Cook in name was as a god revered.
   The *Bounty* came, and all the latent heat
Again burst forth the voyagers to greet,
More latitude for Eros to display
His force and skill, ere these could get away ;
   His bonds grew strong, and loving hearts were knit
In close communion with the shore and ship ;
An ardour glows the dormant flame to kindle,
An honour thought is with the gods to mingle.
   Unseen the traitor holds them in his power,
At this their joyous and most fatal hour ;
Against his wiles the gods will not defend,
Such lust unchecked must in disaster end.

Disputes arose, and urged by Eros's cause,
Vile deeds performed against all human laws,
Once set in force, and who its course can stay?
Where lustful nature points the destined way.

Man called for vengeance, 'twas to him denied
By other hands the vengeance was applied,—
Away from ties the amorous gods beguile,
To serve in penance on far Pitcairn's Isle!

We land, and stroll about the cosy town,
Through orange groves, by Britain's sons laid down,
Round where the Frenchmen drive their various trades,
In hogs and poultry, fish and new-laid eggs.
Abundance have of vegetation's crop,
And fruits unrivalled lie about and rot.
Then back again, emerge in open square,
Where native females congregated are;
Sturdy brunettes, descendants of that race
Whom Cook had known and met with face to face.
All stand around, most curious to see
Religious service in festivity,
Church militant, which condescends withal
Their presents to receive however small;
Not long since known, exchanging for produce,
The invidious dollar finds its ready use,
In condonation of some new transgression,
With equal service for a strange omission.
In contributions or attendant sales,
Throughout is found a paucity of males.
Then off we start, for 'Venus Point' we lay,
And reach the spot towards the fall of day,
Where Cook had trod our imaginations trace,
And speculate as to the very place,
Had pitched his tents, and anxious that the day

May be propitious, clouds all chased away,
In science's cause a length of way had come,
To note the planets' course across the sun.

    Upon the scroll of fame his name enrolled,
The great discoverer in the southern world ;
Renowned alike for seamanship and skill,
Unbounded resource, and undaunted will.

    But Cook is gone ! yet Venus still is there
In prominence, as pure, divinely fair,
Goes shining on, and will for evermore,
When love, and fame, and race have gone before.

    As in the west recede the evening stars,
The planet Venus tracks the course of Mars ;
The bright red sphere sinks in the twilight's gloom,
The brighter radiance lingers by the moon ;

    From an eclipse, behind the orb descending,
A brilliant rare, the crescent moon depending,
Together move, declining from on high,
Their soft effulgence lighting up the sky.

    Next morn at noon a rowing galley's seen,
Bearing within the Otaheitian Queen
Towards the ship, and gains the vessel's side,
As the booming guns are rolling o'er the tide.

    The Queen looks well, a gentle smile we trace
Upon her well defined and light brown face.
With English all a friendly bond conceives,
And from our chief an ardent grip receives.

    She takes his arm, around the ship they stroll,
In converse deep pours forth her anxious soul,
With tears deplores, in ireful condemnation,
The act that gave the Gallic domination.

    Implores him to beseech her sister queen,
Who in her gracious wisdom might esteem,

Them worthy still her high consideration,
And lend her aid against the usurpation.
    Her men had fled, within the mountains saved,
Born to freedom, could not be enslaved ;
Of her protection, and of these bereft,
None but the aged and the women left,
To save them from the vile impending curse,
Of French politeness, and of something worse.
    For while we held the place all had been well,
That naught but sorrow since had them befell,
And importuned him,—as their lot deplored—
That all her older friends may be restored.
    She pleads in vain ! it is the fate of all,
The strong shall flourish and the weak shall fall
Progression's tides are all resistless flowing,
Then why dwell on the manner of the going,—
Impelled, impelling, civilization's cause,
By war and peace fulfilling natural laws.
    So now desist and set aside the theme,
Receive the guests accompanying the Queen,
Some ladies fair, and trained Tahitians brown,
And gentle French, the *élite* of the town.
    The band begins, the pairs are quickly found,
In graceful curves the stately waltz goes round,
The measured step, the soft and thrilling strain,
The mazy dance exhilarates the brain.
    The Queen is not a paragon of fashion,
For fifes and drums is said to have a passion,
Amused she sits and looks upon the scene,
Brought to an end,—in deference to the Queen.
The band withdraws, the drums and fifes appear,
Are more congenial to the royal ear,
She seems delighted with the rolling sound;
And holds the drummers marching round and round.

Until the time the entertainment ending,
And to their boats the assembled guests descending ;
The Queen the last, again affected grew,
With great vehemence, in the last adieu !

The guns are thundering a hoarse good-bye,
And rockets o'er the town are soaring high,
As night advancing draws its sable veil,
To Otaheitians bid a long farewell.

OTAHEITA TO VALPARAISO.

Then off we sail, with light and baffling air,
Across the silver sea that looks most fair,
On for the high bold peaks of Eimeo lay,
And at Port Talou spend a pleasant day.

Deep in the mount and calm the frigate lies,
Surrounding hills high pointing to the skies ;
And jagged rocks in piles the landscape fill,
As to some ancient ruined citadel.

We seek for shells, and some the rifle ply,
With hook and line our skill at fishing try ;
Some range the woods, and mount among the crags,
And specimens obtain with well-filled bags.

For fish the boats with nets are sent around,
With great abundance all the coasts abound,
Return well ladened with the finny spoils,
To refresh the crew and compensate their toils.

Upon the hills we cast a longing look,
As out we draw from this romantic nook,
Around whose base the surf in sparkles seethes,
Scarce wind enough to keep us from the reefs.

As from the east light airs and calms ensue,
So long the islands round are kept in view,
The ship lies idle, and reluctant seems
To quit the site of these enchanting scenes.

We linger long among the islands bright,
Fair Otaheite bearing on the right,
Small swift canoes flit past in general use,
And double-decked ones bearing earth's produce.

But go we must, our course lies in the east,
And naught in nature is allowed to rest—
The breeze grows strong, and round to westward veers,
As on her course direct the vessel steers,

And bounding leaves the islands far behind,
Holds south about a brisker wind to find,
Which plies its force to lash the ocean round,
And sends us flying o'er the liquid bound.

Waves follow high and try to o'er us break,
She spurns them all, and leaves them in the wake,
Careering on, by wings of canvas pressed,
Mounts the sea-horse, and rides upon its crest.
The liquid steed bears high its stately head,
As free as wind across the ocean sped,
In graceful curves it flaunts its glittering mane,
In pace majestic drives across the main.

On its broad back it bears with ease the ship,
Her prow, her stern and sides alternate dip
Into the hollows, and becalmed a lee,
Below the billow in a vale of sea.
Raised on its brow, and then the rattling blast
Tears at the sheets, and bends the pliant mast,
Before its force she's borne and rapid glides,
'Till all is checked and gradually subsides.

We near Pitcairn's, upon the north 'tis brought,

Where *Bounty's* mutineers asylum sought,
Whose progeny upon it long lay hid,
Communion with the world for years forbid.

  We think to make the place, the winds adverse,
Some hundred leagues away from off the course,
Eastwards we steer, and pass the island by
For south America's west coast we ply.

  Then by the wind we run a length of sea,
Full fresh and fair, the good ship sailing free ;
Stand on direct until the land is found,
For Valparaiso track the shore around ;

  And find the break the highlands run between,
The town itself is nestling close within,
Our way is checked, and further progress stopped,
With sails clewed up, and bower anchor dropped.

CANTO VI.

VALPARAISO.

THE harbour 'closed by hills on every side,
Save where the open bay lets in the tide,
Scarce room enough for any town to rest,
Two level streets is all it does possess.

And houses cling upon the slopes around,
Roads but afforded by the broken ground,
The harbour clear—as from the hillsides steep—
From all impediment, roomy is and deep.

The air is fresh, salubrious the clime,
Occasional rains, more frequently 'tis fine,
Sol's tempered rays shoot from the spring-time sky,
As breezes sweep down from the mountains high.

Some time we rest, and range the hills among,
Refreshments needing from a voyage long,
Which in abundance can be here obtained;
Our health restored, and vigorous strength regained.

Chilians are free, impatient of control,
Urbane and gallant as the *Hispanhol;*
From whom derive their geniality,
Their suave mien, and hospitality.

Shipping is numerous in the sheltering bay,
With California to and from they lay,
Broad cast, developing the diggers' toils,
Trading and revelling in golden spoils.

16

The town's *en fête*—full dressed—the ships are gay,
Banners floating o'er the whole display,
A joyous scene, exciting festive thought
To cheerfulness, the holidays have brought.
　Dose-ocho day, September the eighteenth,
The guns are roaring from the shore and fleet,
In anniversary they loud proclaim
Their independence of the crown of Spain.
　People alert, all business suspended,
To three whole days the revelries extended ;
Three times each day are booming as in action,
The belching guns from battery, ship and bastion.
　We quit the town, and make for the *Piancha*,
Where tents are pitched for rollicking and dancing,
In open air, above the sun-lit sea,
Where all are holding high festivity.
　Where flageolet and lively gay guitar,
With grotesque antics in performance are ;
Sambo-quaka, with its swerves and vaults,
The light *fandango*, and the thrilling waltz.
　In silver trappings *cabelleiros* dash,
In satin shorts, and silken cords and sash ;
Full liberty of action all pourtray,
Abandoned to the frolics of the day.
　As round they ride are by the fair ones met,
The lively dancing girl, and pert *grisette ;*
Dismount, persuaded by the softest words,
And make their spurs to rattle on the boards.
Though some decorum mark their conduct through,
More boisterous became as evening grew,
One quarrels fierce, a jeering crowd creates,
As in his cups from fun degenerates.
　Then on we pass, and from the plateau down,
Where bright illuminations mark the town,

Where all saloons are gay with brilliant light,
Keep up the revels well into the night.

Then off to sea we put at duty's call,
Where stern routine again enfronts us all ;
To keep all clean, the exercise of arms
In mimic action, and midnight's alarms.
And north we sail, and make again the land,
As for Coquimbo harbour on we stand,
A few days spend ; I wander to the shore,
The strand around and gentle hills explore.
     And here again an Englishman I found,
Engaged in operations underground,
Who all about him spreads an ample store
Of smelting pots, and heaps of copper ore ;
     By plodding on, and an undaunted will,
A body healthy, and a natural skill,
Had wealth amassed, the time was now at hand,
When he again would seek his native land.
     Then off we are, a pleasant breeze prevailing,
From out the south as we to north are sailing,
For Callao, a week is barely flown,
When in its port we let our anchor down.

CALLAO.

We look about, at once begin to trace
The mouldering ruins of the great earthquake,
Whose solid walls had stood the test of time,
Though in the sea they partly now recline.
     An island close, Fernandez is its name,
Which from the quake into existence came ;

A fisherman, 'tis said, was fishing by,
Was carried upward on it safe and high,—
Fernandez named—escaping quite unhurt,
As the island 'rose from out the heaving earth,
To tell the story—as a dreadful dream—
The one eye-witness of the awful scene.

And here the pelican his practice plies,
As from on high into the sea he dives,
Quick to return, a fish across his bill,
He gollops down his spacious crop to fill.
Then off again, majestic sweeps around,
By slow degrees high in the air he's found,
With sudden check he halts ; himself uprights,
Claps his huge wings and downward straight he strikes.

Dogs are numerous, killed they often are,
Their bodies cast to vultures of the air,
The turkey-buzzard used to clear the street
Of all refuse, of scraps of bread and meat.

Four leagues away, is water running down.
The limpid stream, supplying all the town,
Is all they have, for here the rainfall's found
To stand at zero all the cycle round.

The Andes chain attracts the liquid store,
Adown whose sides the streamlets constant pour,
And heavy dews at night, default of rain,
Fall shrouding down and cover all the plain.

We plan a trip : The once-famed Queen of Cities,
Renowned alike for ancient pride and riches,
Whose tribunals with tyrannies had raged,
Whose streets were once with solid silver paved.

City of kings ! whose boast it was to find,
Priestcraft and force and gold in one combined ;
All righteousness in everything defying,

Presuming to a civilization trying.
A spurious kind, a higher wave had rolled,
And in its reflux swept away its gold
Down to its ships, the wastes of waters o'er,
Had left fair Lima with its grandeur poor.

We mount a 'bus the city far to gain,
That plies between, across the sandy plain,
Soon to yield up to swift advancement's team,
On iron rails and whisked along by steam.

We labour on upon the rut-worn road,
The horses sweating 'neath the heavy load,
The scourgings hot, and irritating reins,
The surge and toss the diligence sustains.

A cross is seen, to show the spot whereon
The tidal-wave had rushed a ship along,
Had left it there a monument to tell,
Of what had then to Callao befell.

Anon through Lima's ponderous gates we roll,
Where grandeur once enlivened up the whole,
Which now we find, as to our expectation,
The vaunted city in dilapidation.
Its glories gone since Spanish rulers reigned,
Themselves in pride, and palaces maintained,
A scourge to all who came beneath their yoke,
A scourge that burned and all their powers broke.

And as we roll the ruined gateway through,
And pass along a splendid avenue
Of leafy trees, then lo ! before our eyes,
The ancient city of Pizarro lies !

We urge the way into a spacious square,
Where famous buildings congregated are,
Cathedral grand, with broad and lofty tower,
Appears neglected from the loss of power.
The streets are clean, and well laid out with shops,

On either hand, with Europe's varied stocks ;
Make a fair show, but such their prices high,
That none but wealthy persons dare to buy.
People are few, none but the trading-class,
Who from their shops along the footways pass,
A mixèd race, from Spanish dons descended,
Left to themselves—a prey—quite undefended.
Ladies are seen about, who pass the street
In black and white ; are mostly dressed and neat,
One eye alone allowed to see the light,
From vulgar gaze the face is hidden quite.

We pass along, to the cathedral go,
Its lofty portal entering in below ;
The light subdued within the sacred pile
Where candles burn on altar, nave and aisle.
Ladies devout to saints are kneeling down,
And priests with broad-brimmed hats and shaven crown,
And saints demure, in varied postures are
In supplication, or prostrate in prayer.

Rich tapestries ! a wonder to behold
Of length and breadth, made stiff with threads of gold,
From roof to floor, in gorgeous folds are hung,
By silver cords and golden tassels slung.

A glittering mass is the high altar raised,
Of gold and silver crucifixes blaze,
With tier on tier elaborate reredos shine
With ornaments and gifts of Byzantine.
With silver columns, candelabra gold,
Rich caskets chased, some costly treasures hold,
A sight to strike a terror to the soul,
As Christ and crucifix surmount the whole.

We quit the place, and stroll around the square,
The Palace of the Inquisition there,
Where acts of violence once disgraced the age,

And fire and sword atoned the zealot's rage.
  The turkey-buzzard on the flat roofs high,
As ornamental coigns against the sky,
Are sacred held in superstition's lights,
Some way connected with religious rites.
  Was he not then the vulture of the air,
When fumes of heretics assailed him there,
Watching serene the acts and deeds of man,
Where these had finished and his own began ?
Trees evergreen, approving Nature smiles,
The living waters spout—though man reviles,—
Tyrants are gone, and all their victims slain,
The vultures there—the sacred birds—remain.
  Ominous appear, obey their fateful call,
Will pick his bones again should he but fall
Back to that ebb where wild ambitions reign,
And savage acts—of ravening brains—obtain.

  The ' Golden Ball ' invites us to its fare,
Where trading people congregated are,
Part restaurant, but mostly a hotel,
Within whose walls we find a place to dwell.
  Refreshed we rest, again we wander down,
And find the streets are busier through the town,
Bazaars well stocked in open air are laid,
But ladies scarce with whom to do a trade.
  Vast public buildings, palaces in squares,
In every street the church its structure rears,
Whose tracery and mouldering plinths display,
Their fallen greatness and the swift decay.
  And as we stroll, the notes of music hear,
Borne soft and sweet upon the evening air ;
Led by its strains towards the barrack-yard,
And there invited inward by the guard.

Whose *Capitan* urbane with smiles we meet,
Who tries his best to broken English speak,
Advancing firm, holds forth the proffered hand,
In motions graceful makes us understand,
That we are welcome, wander where we list,
No Englishman could be denied in this;
Since war for independence had began,
The name of Cochrane was a talisman.
But music's voice a general language plies,
Appeals to all to love and fraternize,
  'God save the Queen,' in sympathetic strain,
And loud we join the anthem in refrain.

  To 'Golden Ball' return, the eve prolong
With softer music, and the joyous song,
Where, wearied out, we sleep till morning's light
Had chased away the heavy dews of night.

  When on the road again roll to the shore,
And to the ship, and feel a pleasure more,
For having seen the City—long the boast—
The Queen of all upon the Western coast.
We put to sea, fresh cooling winds prevail,
As for the north towards the line we sail ;
Blue sky by day, the moon so clear at night,
That read we do by its soft rays of light.

  As nearer on to the equator drew,
The lighter still the less'ning breezes grew,
A sparkling sea, beneath a glittering sun,
As for the land of Mexico we run.

  A calm ensues, the winds are hushed to sleep,
The helpless ship lies lolling on the deep ;
Heaves to the swell which ever way she's cast,
And beats her wings against the straining mast.

  Most strange it seems, a waif upon the main,
Lost to the world until a breeze again

Shall lash the leaden mass to active life,
And speed us gaily on amidst the strife.

We watch it close, barometer to fall,
Deplore the calm, an incubus on all,
Impatient grow, and scan around the sea,
For anything to chase monotony.

At length a ripple glitters far away,
On which our anxious eyes and glasses lay,
Extending wide as shoals of fish appear,
In numbers vast are porpoise drawing near.

They roll along, surround on every side,
And plunge and blow, awake the silent tide,
Play by the ship, outstrip each other try,
And curve and twist, and throw their bodies high.

The sport is great, the rifle's whizzing ball
Must needs to strike them wheresoe'er it fall,
And makes them leap, in consternation drive
Among the whole, to shoot above or dive.

They tarry long, then roll themselves away,
And leave us there for yet some time to lay ;
Our isolation keenly felt, that we
Must stay behind upon an inert sea.

Light puffs succeed, contrary winds we hail,
As better far so we may onward sail,
And stretch away ; then in again we stand,
And Cape St. Lucas sight, the nearest land.

At north the gulf of California lying,
With Tres Marias on the right espying,
Pedra Island high, a bare white rock,
On which the sea-birds rest and breed and flock.

A mark conspicuous, to mariners guide,
With Pedra Blanca near the land inside,
Which with the river's bank outstretched and horned,
The harbour snug of low San Blas is formed.

SAN BLAS.

We anchor there, and scan the coast along,
And at San Blas with Mexicans among,
We spend some time upon its sandy shore,
Where sand-flies bite and irritate, make sore,
Assisted by mosquitoes' subtle darts,
Which swell the flesh with poisoned burning smarts,
No peace will give, or night or day no rest,
And naught can save us from the tiny pests.

Houses look strange, each as a mud-built cube,
Of but one room, with door and window crude,
Except for quaintness, nothing to invite
The curiosity, or please the sight.

A race most mixed, from Spanish boasted blood,
Through Negro, Red-man, Creoles far removed;
Unenterprising, sloth beyond control,
Though priests inform them that they have a soul.

Here at this place with torrid heat oppressed,
And all around with Nature's gifts are blessed,
Beasts in the uplands wild and teeming run,
With every clime that holds beneath the sun

There in the mine is found abundant store,
Where slaves alone and criminals get the ore
For other's use,—as these degenerate lie,
The sport of every fraud and keener eye.

Upon the Santiago boats are sent
On sporting tour; but most on duty bent,
Collecting treasure of our merchants' own,
For safe transporting to their firms at home.

On their return, towards the north we ran,
And stay a day at Boca Tecapan,
A river large, whose oozy banks abound
With fish and fowl of every kind around.

Again the boats are sent towards the shore,
The river's banks and lagoons to explore ;
We watch them close as from the ship afar,
Perceive the foam upon the river's bar.

The first is seen, safe on the roller rides,
The larger swerves, and on her broadside drives,
In spite of all their efforts with the oar,
Is topsy-turvy turned, rolls o'er and o'er.

And bottom up is onward seen to float,
The men are rescued by the smaller boat,
Save one who in her still suspect to lie,
From whence if not delivered soon must die.

They land her crew, then tow her to the shore,
And on the river's bank they turn her o'er,
And find their man, all but exhausted quite,
With but sufficient time to save his life.

Upon the stream the sportsmen hie away,
With rifle ball an active part to play,
Where alligators either swim, or run
Along its banks, or bask against the sun.

The hunter then must use his subtle arts,
To pierce the creature in unarmoured parts,
For oftentimes the ball will strike it fair,
And from its shell go whizzing through the air.

The boats return, are ladened with the spoils,
With heaps of game that recompense their toils ;
Of parts alone, as severed at the neck,
The alligators' heads bestrew the deck.

MAZATLAN.

The anchor weigh, towards the north we veer,
The river Mazatlan are drawing near,
And landing there, and looking round the place,
Some marks of higher civilization trace.
    The people friendly, indolent and gay,
Invite you to their homes, where you may stay
Long as you please, partake their frugal fare,
Unbend your pride, and find a welcome there.
    Their clime is soft, to light guitar they sing,
No care whatever what the morn may bring.
The Mexican has glut of silver ore,
And California's mines their treasures pour.
    But he to earn unmindful of it all,
Does not exert himself at Nature's call,
He cannot starve, for she does all provide,
Nor will he work if he should live or die.
    With jealous eye away his wealth to give,
And tariffs high are made prohibitive ;
Yet he must trade, and trading even more,
Must pay for it in gold or silver ore.
    The English here in active commerce found,
Do all the business of the imports round ;
Are now invited to a ball on board,
And care they take to bring their separate hoard
In gold and silver and platina rare,
Consigned in safety to their country's care.

    Again we note the subtlety of Jack,
A hidden foe, alert, is on his track,
Must circumvent by force or stratagem,
To do his duty to his countrymen.

No wooden horse his pensive thoughts employ—
Such as that one that forced the gates of Troy,—
Such clumsy means is not his calculation,
And far beneath his well-known reputation.

    The river's bank he chose to build a booth,
Dimensions ample and its flooring smooth,
Adorned with bunting gay, and spires of gilt,
And paints his sign, 'The House that Jack has built.'
To all his friends affords a welcome hearty
To join in his projected picnic party.

    They take his hint, into his booth they pour
Their weighty hampers, with their varied store,
Whose surface bears the flasks of generous wine.
Beneath, the spoilings of the silver mine.

    Towards the spot are all their footsteps bent,
And tumble all their treasure in his tent,
Rough pieces are, the partly cast ingot,
And heavy lumps from out the smelting-pot,
And cases small, the gold in grain is packed
And nuggets large, in coarser cloths are wrapped.

    And all are busy entertaining guests,
The banquet board is reeking with repasts,
The loving cup is freely passed about,
Midst toasts of health and happy joyous shout.

    Jack glorifies, by strategy has won,
Business and pleasure both combined in one,
Evading all detection active plies,
Across the river's bar where rollers rise.

    And all the day is making easy trip,
With treasure ladened from the shore to ship,
Once in his boat, upon the waters free,
And he will fight for it if needs must be.

    The banquet o'er, again the stirring strain
Of music sweet enlivens all the train,

Dances commence, the sets begin to move,
Of all arrangements everyone approve.

Ladies are few, but these endurance show,
Into the dance a lively vigour throw,
Until at night, when frittering fast away,
Confessing all a charming happy day.

Then clear away, dismantling the booth,
The anchor weigh and off to sea we move
A pilot take, and breezes soft prevail
And up the gulf of California sail.

A lovely trip, landscapes, on either hand,
Low rolling hills reach to the higher land,
Which broken lies, with shadowy deep ravines,
Presenting change, with fresh and varied scenes.

The sea is smooth, the soft blue sky is clear,
The land is green, enchanting hills appear,
The balmy air is scented by the trees,
And borne towards us on the evening breeze.

The sun by day the sea with sparkles fills,
Now in the west with crimson tints the hills;
And as it sets the moon is rising bright,
Changing the day, unnoticed, into night;

Few days are spent upon this inland bay,
As slowly on we pass the pleasing way,
When on the right the port of Guaymas find,
And from its banks is seen the town behind.

GUAYMAS.

Close by the shore we let our anchor down,
And business sends us quickly to the town,

The pilot with us, who good English speaks,
Though Spanish blood within his pulses beats.

Has all the pride and independence of
The ancient race, that in this country sought
The rich Golconda, sparing none that may
The secret hold of where the treasures lay.

But kind is he, and generous to a fault,
Pleased to converse correct, and English talk,
Escorts us round the place, and shows us all,
Teatro grande and the small town hall.

The country trace ; from off the parched-up ground
Rise barren hills, and far away are found
High granite peaks, grotesque the mountains rise,
With broken tracts and chasms down their sides.

The people all make welcome, flock and court,
Are pleased to have so fine a ship in port,
Ask all particulars of our friend and guide,
What crew we carry, and how long abide.

And as we talk, the town hall standing near,
Practice peculiar is enacted here ;
Out of its porch come rushing to the street
The magistrates, and rabble at their feet.

And a delinquent in their midst is found,
Rushed to a building post, securely bound,
A rough official, strip of long cowhide,
With its sharp edges to a handle tied.

He plies it oft, the poor mulatto swerves,
Unknown to us how much of it deserves,
We pity him whatever it may be,
Another sign of low degeneracy.

And quit our friend, who makes us promise more,
Some other time when we may come to shore
To visit him,—points out his house,—would like
An evening with us, with himself and wife.

More bullion find, in heaps of silver pure,
With golden grain, and nuggets held in store ;
And time is spent to get it safe on board,
Secure below to stow the precious hoard.

Here less restrictive, free the people are,
We mix with them in pleasures everywhere ;
Parties on board the gaieties enhance,
On shore at balls invited to the dance.

The band is lent, at the *Teatro* play,
Which fills the house as long as here we stay,
With passes free they all the crew invite,
And open entertainments day and night.

At post-meridian ! on a Sabbath day,
By streams of Mexicans are led away,
Towards the ring where bulls are in full roar,
To join in combat with the *Matador*.

And as we urge the dusty road along,
Fair girls, creoles, and negresses among,
The latter in fine muslins light and gay,
Their coloured legs and naked feet display.

With great *Señores, Señoras, Señoritas,*
Negro servants, children *Bonitas,*
In colours gay, but most of them in white,
All gathering on to see the great bull-fight.

At which arrived, and thousands crowd the *circo,*
Upon rough seats in tiers above the earth ;
Of vast dimensions is the circle round,
And great the area of the central ground.

And mounted well the *Picador's* are,
In coloured satins and in rest a spear,
Are marching round in gorgeous full array,
Await the opening of the pending fray.

The bellowing bull, impatient to take flight,

Behind the bars is goaded to the fight ;
And these removed he makes a rush in chase,
To find the flag red blazing in his face.
Which disconcerts him ; for a horse he drives,
The *Picadore* as quick his spear applies,
Which brings him up ; an assistant at his side,
A fiery weapon fixes in his hide.
It cracks and tears, emits a stinging blaze,
Excites the bull up to an awful rage ;
And rushing on, with fearful bounds and jumps,
Throws off a lance and gores a horse at once.
   The *cabellero*, nimble in retreat,
Springs from his back, and gains the lower seat ;
The horse is down, and plaudit loud begins,
With clapping hands and ' Bravo, toro !' rings.
   The bull draws off, with head erect stalks round,
The hapless nag is dragged from off the ground ;
Applauses cease, the fight resumes again,
And crackers numerous madden high his brain ;
And ribbons gay are prodded in his skin,
And large rosettes, with pointed sharp steel pin,
A *chulo* smart a ready touch applies,
And fair hands clap, and shouts of ' Bravo !' rise.
   One as an ape, in tough bull-hide protected,
Between his horns and on his neck projected,
He clasps his arms,—the bull may toss in vain,
Is carried round and does his hold retain ;
The angry beast is well-nigh done to death,
With eye-balls fierce he pauses long for breath,
'Til urged by pikes, and crackers at his tail,
He makes a lunge the nearest to assail.
   The *Matador* then comes upon the scene,
As a *Hidalgo* grand in dress and mien ;
Leisurely stalks, and with a glittering blade.

Toledo's own, tough, tempered, truly made,
In his right hand; his left holds forth a flag,
The bull enraged makes at the phantom rag,
Beneath whose folds presents his ample breast,
The *Matador* prepares to give him rest.
Plays yet awhile, then throwing high his hand,
Points up and flourishes his bright steel brand,
Up to the hilt into his breast it drives,
The bull is paralyzed and drops and dies.
The horses hitched, away the carcase bring.
Another rampant, loosed into the ring,
With little change performances the same,
"Til half a dozen bulls had thus been slain.

We quit the *circo*, and then returning back,
Perceive the pilot hastening on our track;
Invites us to—with him—the evening spend,
And on towards his home our footsteps tend:
To find his dame, and grown-up daughters two,
A little girl, and sparkling *machachu*;
A spacious room, in which the family dine,
Receive their company and take their wine.
Coffee partake, and cigarettes we smoke,
As well as may be chat and laugh and joke;
Talk of the day's amusements full and long,
Till *Padre* prompts the girls to sing a song.
Guitars they seek, and strum their fingers o'er,
Some Spanish ditty forth their voices pour,
Though coy at first their natural spirits flow,
At music's touch these still more ardent glow.
Some dominoes play, and some would dance a reel,
And some to sing an inclination feel,
And some at draughts will pass away the time,
Our friend the pilot gives us 'Auld Lang Syne.'

The *Madre* kind, solicitous doth prove,
Her eye upon her danghters' every move,
Though much familiar gallantries abound,
No liberties of any kind are found.

Girls joyous are, whose dulcet voices ring,
As, in our honour, ' Home, sweet Home ' they sing
In purest accent, and in cadence sweet,
Though not another word of English speak;
We think it strange to listen to the song,
The awakening strain we had not heard so long,
And praise the grace, and soft pathetic air,
As rendered by the Spanish ladies fair ;
Whose winning ways, and cheerful artless smile,
The fleeting hours of evening beguile.
The symphony—with joy—appropriate hail
As from this point for ' Home, sweet Home ' we sail.
And bid Adieu, in memory to retain
Their gentle kindness, and our ship regain.

GUAYMAS TO VALPARAISO.

Next morn we sail, the people line the strand.
Adieux are waved with high extended hand,
Close in with shore the band a farewell play,
As by we move and slowly glide away.
And gathering speed, across the waters far
We hear the echoing still of loud huzza,
Till in the distance every sound is lost
As back we sail beside the silent coast.

And reach the line, where wearying calms ensue.
Bonitas large the flying-fish pursue :

Listless we watch them in their watery chase,
As calms persistent hold with warm embrace ;
Then let us free, as passing breezes rise,
With spreaded sails across the sea we glide ;
When veering south, and blowing in full force,
We haul to wind across its adverse course.

Sail after sail is lessened as it proves,
A gale in progress swift and swifter moves,
And hurls with force, the ship is backward borne,
Till heaving to she battles with the storm ;
Stay-sail alone, is driving at the main,
Her gained position fighting to retain ;
The drift is dense, and howling tempests rave,
And petrels sweep and run along the wave.

Four days we wrestled with the raging main,
The fifth it lulled and set us free again,
To spread our sails, pursue the watery way,
For Valparaiso on our course we lay.
Make for the port, and on arriving found,
A recent quake had shaken all the ground ;
Houses were rent, and others levelled down,
Some people killed, and terror filled the town.

And ships were rushed, and tremors felt beneath
As boiling waters bubbled, hissed and seethed ;
Some anchors lost, were swallowed in the gape
And high commotion of the great earthquake.

All busy are, receiving stores in haste,
Refitting ship, preparing for the Cape.
To brave that sea that Anson braved before,
Whose fleet it scattered and its tempests tore.

VALPARAISO TO STRAITS OF MAGELLAN.

Homewards away ! though hardships still await,
Ere we can clear the dreaded wintry Cape ;
Where tempests rise from out the ice-bound pole,
And seas unchecked as hills of ocean roll.

A favouring breeze and out to sea we sail,
Which gathering high is rising to a gale ;
All canvas set, we plough the watery plain,
Towards the south careering o'er the main.

But fickle Æolus proves again unkind,
And in our teeth as rapid drives the wind,
Throws all aback, to save the ship we toil,
As the meeting surges burst around and boil ;
Close reefed one sail is left upon the mast,
To stay the ship against the furious blast ;
Tremendous seas bound high and o'er us break,
Assault her hull, and make her timbers shake ;
The sea is wild, the setting sun is low,
Throws on the whole a lurid crimson glow.
The seamew screams, and hovers in delight,
A threat'ning aspect of the coming night.

But it subsides, the morn appearing clear,
All sail is set, towards the land draw near ;
Deciding on Magellan's strait to try,
The wind propitious, and its entrance nigh.

The route is short ; to this advantage reap,
Must pass the dangers of the silent deep,
The storm, the rocks, the close resounding shore,
That many a craft as good had braved before ;
At peril braved ! to sink or swim the stake,
To emerge with joy, or to repent too late ;
To cheat the wintry Horn its icy dues,
Or in the attempt to sink, to die, to lose.

For here great Æolus holds his blustering reign,
And Scylla treacherous, hid beneath the main,
From waters deep her silent monsters lay,
Ready to catch the unwary on his way,
Secure the prize, and howling Indra roars,
Provokes the waves, and lines the adjacent shores,
With bleaching ribs, the plank torn from the deck,
And spars that tell the story of the wreck.

The wind is fair, in force, our course we shape
Direct for land, and make towards the strait.
High rugged cliffs on either side arise,
And huge seas roll between, and wash their sides :
At intervals the long majestic wave,
Drives slowly on the mountains high to lave,
With force direct runs up the rocky side,
And cascades spout with each receding tide ;
From fissures great, and every open cleft,
The foaming waters burst and rushed and leapt,
Exhausted scarce, as the returning sea
Flowed up the height, in grand conspicuity.
The coast is black, the high granitic peak,
Looks frowning down upon the restless deep,
Though gales subside, and may exhausted cease,
Great Ocean's rollers never cede the peace ;
Rush at their base, they solid gloaming stand,
To check the inroads made upon the land ;
In form majestic, high in air they loom,
Shadowing the strait with a Tartarean gloom.
And dwarfs the ship amidst so vast a scene,
As on she drives, and heaves and rolls between,
Close by her side the surges rush the steep,
Assault the crags, and into caverns leap
With thundering roar, they strike at every flow,
And drag them piecemeal to their depths below.

The snow-capped heights look lowering bleak and raw,
Frown on the waves which at their bases gnaw,
And bid defiance—though the time must come
When even these—their destined tenure run—
Must conquered lie subdued, succumb, and steep,
Their forms annihilate beneath the deep,
    As all submit to Nature's subjugation.
Ah! what is there in all her vast creation,
Has not a power superior to it all,
That checks, controls, and consummates its fall,
Fulfils its end, and in itself imbued
With dissolution, and alike subdued,
All to survive in everlasting change,
Impelled, impelling through her wondrous range?

    We pass all by, and rolling through the strait.
For Mercy Harbour on our course we make,
And search it out, a desolate place to find,
With wild surroundings and a wintry wind.
    Next morn at dawn, we onward stretch away,
And reach a calmer spot named Fortescue Bay :
Two merchant craft that had been sorely pressed,
For months had lain here with their crews distressed :
All anchors gone, with masts laid by the board,
A doleful tale of that which had occurred,
Were all but through the strait, to westward bound,
When one of them, the foremost,—took the ground.
    With generous thought the other had delayed,
To render all he could of friendly aid ;
Whilst so engaged the winds came rushing round,
And drove them both from off the treacherous ground ;
But stayed not there, the raging sea awoke,
Their anchors dragging and their cables broke,
And drove them back upon the flying blasts,

Up through the strait and tore away their masts.
Along the black Terra del Fuego coast
The waves had swept them, and their hulls had tossed,
Quite uncontrolled by willing hands and minds,
Full at the mercy of the raging winds ;
Against the walls of rock had dashed their sides,
And hurled them off again upon the tides,
'Till driven here, with all their topsides rent.
The furious winds had ceased, their forces spent.
    We succour them, give all we can afford,
Of spars on which again to raise the yard,
Stores for sea use, for which in need they stand,
As game they had by hunting through the land ;
And leave them there to fit as best they may,
Their masts and sails, and try to get away,
Never again, as both of them declare,
From east to west the boisterous strait to dare.

    Then on we urge, and through the narrow way.
And at Port Famine make a shorter stay,
Where bends the strait, the land appears more fair,
Where penal settlements of Chilians are,
And pleasant range of scene, with rolling plain.
Though misadventure gave it such a name.
    Terra del Fuego looming in the south,
Whose craters long had burned themselves quite out ;
Whose rugged coasts can no attractions show,
But black and bleak it scowls on all below.
    The Land of Fire, that once had seethed and rolled
With lava hot, but now left in the cold,
With icy capes, and barren blasted rocks,
Exposed to withering storms and ocean's shocks.
    The Patagonian side more interest claims,
With rolling mounds, and wide extending plains,

Where herds of wild guanaco rove at will,
And numerous beasts through meads and groves and hill.
   No Patagonians in the Straits are found,
From the land of ice on to the northward bound
Long having crossed,—we are behind their time-
Migrated all, gone to the warmer clime :
As birds of air with freedom take to flight.
Ere wintry blasts and frosts begin to bite.
To run with Sol, to share his brighter ray,
As on he draws and points the genial way.
   The strait is broad as we to eastward steer,
Upon the north the Sandy Point draws near ;
A colony of Chilians on it lies,
And from a fort the Chilian colour flies.
We give salute, expecting a return,
But all is still, no ammunition burn ;
And landing there, excuse we have to hear,
Their guns were ready, but no powder near.
   Then sail away, the northern coast in view.
Larido next, Elizabeth Island too,
Run for the main, along the land we lay.
And let our anchor down in Gregory Bay.
The sea is calm. and while we here remain.
The boats are sent the land to hunt for game.
The sleek guanaco haunt the plain in herds,
With beasts of prey and some enormous birds.
Throw off their scouts the strangers to engage,
And keep without the deadly rifle's range.
So clear the land, and level all around,
No cover for the sportsman can be found ;
But bones of all lie bleaching in the sun,
Of those that have their quick'ning courses run.
Their range of plain and distance are too great,
To afford a chance the bounding game to take.

Then off again, the eastern end we make,
And anchor well inside of Virgin Cape;
Await the wind and adverse tide to turn,
To sail away again at early morn.

STRAITS OF MAGELLAN TO RIO DE JANEIRO.

We judge us clear, ourselves congratulate,
Have cut the Horn and passed the dreaded strait.
But Neptune plans, and Æolus lends his aid,
To test our skill, and know of what we're made.

For ere the morn broke through the eastern sky,
The winds had risen and the waves ran high,
The land obscured, and threat'ning on our lee ;
We get our anchor and put off to sea.
Too near the point, most dangerously we stand,
As great seas bound, come rolling to the land,
As in their hollows low the ground we feel,
The rocky bottom grazes on the keel.
Although the winds are rising to a gale,
We dare not tack, or touch the straining sail,
The noble ship drives fiercely through the wave,
To leave the coast, and all her life to save.
Struck with suspense the crew in silence stand,
And grasp the rail and gaze upon the land,
Most anxious feel amidst the moaning dirge,
Look wistfully upon the driving surge.
An awful moment ere our safety solved,
Or in one common lot to be involved.
The point is passed ! and great relief we find,
The good ship bounds and leaves the rocks behind.

Safe through the strait, more free we breathe awhile,
When the god of ocean holds a further trial.
Great Sol is set, dark clouds obscure the skies,
Sudden and sharp the cyclone takes its rise ;
The fore sheet loosed the blast takes full control,
And swiftly into ribbons sends the whole ;
Annuls its force, the gallant ship relieves,
And rights her safely through the yawning seas.

    Sail after sail in quick succession fly,
In Gordian knots their lashing strips they tie ;
Straight from the yard they wrestle to be free,
Quit the tall masts and with the tempest flee ;
With force immense the driving hurricane raves,
No sail assisting to combat the waves,
As screaming through the rigging cut the blasts,
And threat from out the ship to tear the masts.

    Lashed to his post the hardy seaman stands,
To watch the ship, though helpless are his hands :
Secures himself lest to the sea he's borne,
And feels impotent through the raging storm.

A CYCLONE.

    The ship drives on the furies to engage,
Brooks no control, and battles with their rage ;
They press her hard, annihilate would fain,
She fights them all, and hurls them back again ;
Crushed by their weight her oaken timbers creak,
Her straining seams let in the wanton leak ;
True to the test she meets the awful strain,
Together holds and dares the mighty main.

The whirlwind circling to the centre fast,
Contends aloft, and rushes down the mast,
To vortex drives, where dire commotion reigns,
And in its midst the helpless ship detains.
Devouring seas anticipate the wreck,
Huge liquid columns thunder to the deck,
Tremendous waves bound high and hiss and slip,
Burst up aloft and cover all the ship :
Full at her sides they rush with fearful shock,
She stands them all, rebuts them like a rock ;
In wild array she mocks their rage and moan,
And fights the night out with the fierce cyclone.

The battle over, and the morning's sun
Reveals the wreckage and the havoc done ;
Spars hanging loose, and sails their shreds display,
Boats broken, bruised, and some were washed away ;
Ports driven in, hammock nettings smashed,
Stern windows broken, and all skylights crashed :
Large shot were jerked from out their racks and rolled,
About the decks hurled flying uncontrolled.
In conflict still the heaving swells arise,
Each bursting point of liquid upward flies,
Across it all a gentle breeze upsprings,
And fills with force again our fluttering wings.
And one by one upon the yards are bent,
A bran-new sail, or one that had been rent,
Quick now repaired, repairing more and more,
As Neptune's trials drew upon our store.
La Plata pass upon the eastern main,
As for Brazils we shape our course again ;
With Raza light and Sugar Loaf our guides,
To Rio harbour, where the good ship lies.

RIO DE JANEIRO TO ENGLAND.

Since from this port we last had anchor weighed,
The circle round the Earth completely made :
As eastwards on our course continuous plied,
Now from the western hemisphere arrived.
Refresh the crew, and get our stores complete,
And off again to sea we swift retreat ;
And hasten on, for England is the cry,
All pray the rising winds may gather high,
And send us swiftly through the hills of foam,
To bless our eyes again with scenes of home.

The Line re-crossed, 'tis warm, a charming night.
The stars are clear, cast down a brilliant light,
The heat is tempered by a gentle breeze.
Barometer has fallen some degrees.
We heed it not, no timely warning take,
As naught appears a change to indicate ;
Are sailing on observing usual care,
The weather settled and the night most fair,—

When like a bolt the sudden wind-cloud burst,
And hurls the ship abeam with fearful force,
An officer alert and quick of eye,
Springs to the lee and lets the main sheet fly.
Half buried lies the ship beneath the main,
The squall flies past, she rights herself again
By slow degrees ; as from her sides outpour
The weight of waters that had held her o'er.

The ocean seethes, with flashing sparkles round,
Its boiling hisses are the only sound.
About, an incandescent radiance white,
But slightly tinged with red, the air is bright ;
Electric currents 'round the ship are cast,
Spread at the yards, go rushing up the masts,

At every point St. Elmo's lights are seen,
Are shining brightly with a silver sheen ;
And form a cross, a glory to behold,
That strikes with awe the timid and the bold ;
The Celt devout has crossed himself and prayed,
And muttering softly says—' The ship is saved !'

Then on we press, across the North-East Trade,
Close hauled, but free, the northern course is made,
On to that zone, where western winds prevail,
And Boreas aids us with a north-west gale.
And veering west we ride upon the waves,
The flying ship the ruffled waters cleaves,
Goes bounding on as though her native land
Held some attraction in its fostering hand.

Roll on, good ship, and furrow through the sea,
For straining eyes are gazing long for thee ;
And yearning hearts for thy arrival wait
With open arms to clasp thy living freight !
England, my home ! again thy white cliffs bright,
And verdant downs, relieve my longing sight ;
What memories rise, in contact touched once more.
With all the objects of thy sunlit shore.
England, my nurse ! and foster-mother true !
Who sends her sons the earth to ramble through.
Its trials dare, that naught beneath the sun
May come to them they may not overcome.
England, my Hope ! who shall thy tale relate ?
What gifted mind that task shall undertake,
What brain shall compass round thy glorious name
And in full justice hand thee down to Fame ?

Elliot Stock, Paternoster Row. London.

www.ingramcontent.com/pod-product-compliance
Lightning Source LLC
Chambersburg PA
CBHW060608030726
47498CB00005B/1596